JUDE

JUDE

Kate Morgenroth

Simon Pulse
New York London Toronto Sydney

SIMON PULSE
An imprint of Simon & Schuster Children's Publishing Division
1230 Avenue of the Americas, New York, NY 10020
Copyright © 2004 by Kate Morgenroth
All rights reserved, including the right of reproduction
in whole or in part in any form.
SIMON PULSE and colophon are registered trademarks of
Simon & Schuster, Inc.
Also available in Simon & Schuster Books for Young Readers
Designed by Mark Siegel
The text of this book was set in Garamond.
Manufactured in the United States of America
First Simon Pulse edition April 2006
10 9 8 7 6 5 4 3
The Library of Congress has cataloged the hardcover edition as follows:
Morgenroth, Kate.
Jude / Kate Morgenroth.—1st ed.
p. cm.
Summary: Still reeling from his drug-dealing father's murder, moving in with the wealthy mother he never knew, and transferring to a private school, fifteen-year-old Jude is tricked into pleading guilty to a crime he did not commit.
ISBN-13: 978-0-689-86479-7 (hc.)
ISBN-10: 0-689-86479-5 (hc.)
[1. Crime—Fiction. 2. Mothers and sons—Fiction. 3. Prisons—Fiction. 4. Politics, Practical—Fiction.] I. Title
PZ7.M826695Ju 2004
[Fic]—dc22
2003020475
ISBN-13: 978-1-4169-1267-5 (pbk.)
ISBN-10: 1-4169-1267-3 (pbk.)

For my parents

Part I

1

THE POLICE ARRIVED, then the paramedics, then the police photographer, and after that Jude lost track. There were so many officers and technicians and medical personnel that they spilled out of the small kitchen and into the hallway beyond. They knew what to do with the body lying on the kitchen floor. They knew how to secure the area to preserve evidence. They knew the procedure cold. But no one knew exactly how to handle Jude.

Jude sat in the darkened living room staring at the television. He was aware of what they must be thinking. What kind of kid sat watching TV when his father was lying dead in the next room? That's what they were saying in the kitchen. He knew the smart thing would've been to act like they expected him to. He should have cried or something.

They had taken his statement, then one of the policemen—the youngest, the one who couldn't pass the buck—was assigned to stay with him in the living room. The policeman didn't sit. He chose to stand, like a guard, near the doorway.

Jude could feel the officer glance at him every once in a while, but he kept his eyes carefully focused on the television—so he didn't notice another figure in the doorway until he heard someone clear his throat.

When Jude looked up, he saw a man in a suit. The suit was the tip-off. *Detective,* Jude thought.

The man jerked his head at the young policeman, and the officer beat a quick retreat down the hall. Then he looked back to Jude and said, "Hey."

"Hey," Jude replied.

The detective seemed to take the brief acknowledgment as an invitation, and he crossed the room to stand beside the couch. He glanced over at the muted television. "What are you watching?"

Jude shrugged. "Crap."

"It's all crap," the man said. "But I watch it anyway," he added. "Mind if I sit?"

Jude shifted slightly, as if to make room.

The detective sat on the end where the springs were broken, and he sagged almost to the ground. He grunted but didn't comment on it. At that level Jude could see that he was balding at the crown.

They sat without talking. Jude pretended to be staring at the screen, but he was really watching the man next to him out of the corner of his eye. Just as Jude thought the man was about to speak, a sharp voice echoed down the hallway.

"Where the hell are you, Burwell?"

Another man appeared in the doorway of the living room. This man was as thin and sharp as his voice—except for his face, which had the drooping, wrinkled look of a hound dog.

"I thought we were doing the walk-through

first," he said to Burwell. His eyes slid over to Jude. "Is this the kid?" he continued, without waiting for an answer to his first question.

Jude turned back to the television. He didn't like how this second man talked about him as if he weren't even in the room, but Jude's pointed movement failed to offend him; it just drew the man's attention to the television.

"You guys watching *Leave It to Beaver* or something?"

"We're just hanging out," Burwell said, glancing at Jude as if to include him in his answer.

The second man moved into the room to get a better look at the television. "Hey, I love this show," he said. "Turn up the sound for a minute."

Jude lifted the remote and changed the channel.

Instead of getting angry, the man broke into a smiling chuckle. "I see you've got a smart-ass here," he observed, but he said it as if it were a compliment.

"Hey, Grant, why don't you go back into the kitchen and make some notes about the scene. I'll be back in a couple," Burwell suggested.

"Okay, partner. Whatever you say." Grant looked over at Jude and said, "Don't let my partner fool you. He likes to play the jolly fat man, but he has the soul of a shark." He winked, pivoted on his heel, and disappeared back down the hallway.

"Don't mind him. He's an asshole," Burwell said in explanation. He paused, then asked delicately, "I need to ask you a few questions. You okay with that?"

"I guess." Jude tugged nervously at a ragged patch of fabric on the arm of the sofa.

Burwell pulled a notebook and a pen from his jacket pocket. "Were you the one who called in?"

Jude nodded.

"Okay. What's your name?"

"Jude."

"How old are you, Jude?"

"Fifteen."

"Can you tell me who that is in the kitchen?"

"That's my dad."

Burwell had been scribbling, but then he stopped. "I thought so," he said. "I'm sorry about your loss."

It was a common enough phrase, and the man said it without fuss. Jude realized that the detective must have repeated it a hundred times before. It was just part of a day's work for him. For some reason the thought that the loss of his father—the only person Jude had in the world—was just another corpse in a long line of bloody cases made his throat close up.

"Do you have any relatives we can call for you?"

Jude shook his head.

"None?"

"No," he said. "There's no one."

"Where's your mother?"

Jude looked back at the TV. "Dunno. She split when I was a baby." He waited for the man's pity, but

Burwell just made a note and plowed on with his questions.

"Were you in the apartment when the shooting occurred?"

"Umm . . . yeah."

Burwell didn't overtly react, but he watched Jude more closely as he asked him the next question.

"Where exactly?"

Here was where it got tricky. Jude had spent the last half hour trying to decide what his story would be. He decided that he couldn't lie about being here. Too many people had seen him on his way home, and he had passed a neighbor when he came into the building. So he said, "I was here, watching TV."

Burwell wrote for a few seconds. "We'll go over this more later, but right now I want you to tell me about what happened. Do you think you can do that?"

Jude figured his best course would be to keep it simple. "I heard someone bust in the door," he said. He paused and had to clear his throat before going on. "They went down to the kitchen and I heard something, like a *pop* or something. Then they took off."

"They?"

Jude covered quickly. "I heard them talking when they were walking down the hall."

"Only two?"

"I'm pretty sure."

"So they never came back in here?"

Jude shook his head.

"And you didn't go into the kitchen?"

"Not until they split."

"Then you went in?"

"Yeah."

"And what did you do when you went into the kitchen?"

"I called 911."

"Immediately?"

"Pretty much."

"And how long after that did the police arrive?"

"Less than ten minutes," Jude guessed.

"Do you know why someone might have wanted to kill your father?" Burwell asked, flipping the page in his notebook and still scribbling.

"Yeah." Jude had made the decision to be honest here.

Burwell glanced up. "Oh?"

"He was skimming too much from his shipments," Jude said. Now that they had gotten away from what happened, he felt a little steadier.

"His shipments of what?"

"Heroin and coke mostly." Jude changed the channel on the TV.

"Did he get a shipment tonight?"

"Yeah."

"You saw it?"

"Yeah."

"Did you see who dropped it off?"

Jude shook his head.

"Do you know who he got it from?"

"Uh-uh."

Burwell rested his notebook on his knee and looked at Jude, his plump face unreadable in the light from the television.

Jude expected another question, but this time it didn't come.

"So, you think you're pretty tough, I guess," Burwell said mildly.

The comment caught Jude off guard. He didn't know what to say, so he didn't say anything.

Burwell took his silence as agreement. "Well, I'll let you believe that for a little while. I'm going to have one of the men take you down to the station, and we'll come down when we finish here. So you have maybe"—he checked his watch—"an hour or so to think about how tough you are before we get there."

He folded up his notebook and tucked it back into his pocket, sliding the pen in beside it.

"See, I'm ready to be sympathetic and under-standing here, but if you don't tell me the truth, you're forcing my hand. I've been doing this too long not to smell bullshit when it's served up to me. The officers asked your neighbors if they heard anything. They're not too helpful—apparently no one saw a damn thing—but your neighbor Mrs. Ramos was pretty positive about one very interesting detail. She said she heard someone kick in the door. She didn't call the police or go out and check because she didn't want to get involved, but she was worried enough that they might try her door next that she stood and listened for them. Mrs. Ramos claims that whoever went into your apartment didn't come out for nearly ten minutes. She was real positive about that. Willing-to-testify kind of positive, if you know what I mean. So maybe you should think about whether you want to tell me what was going on in here for those ten minutes. Ten minutes you say you were here in the TV room and they were shooting your father, and you didn't see a thing."

Jude scrambled desperately to think of something to say—something convincing, something believable.

Burwell waited a moment, and when Jude didn't respond, he said, "You see, this detective thing isn't that hard because people aren't that smart." He stared at Jude.

Jude tried to stare back, but he found he couldn't hold it.

"Listen, you're young. We don't send kids to jail. If you had something to do with this, it's better to tell us. Then we can help you. Maybe it was a friend of yours come to take care of things for you. You've got a nasty bruise there, and your neighbors told us that you tend to get a lot of bruises. We take those things into account, you know. We understand about things like that."

"You don't understand anything," Jude said.

The detective seemed to hear the catch in his throat, and his next question was gentler. "Okay, maybe I don't, but how can I understand if you don't tell me? Listen, if you're scared about them coming after you, remember, we're the police. Protecting people is what we do."

If Jude had only been worried about his safety, he might have caved in and told the detective everything he knew. But the man had trusted him. He had trusted Jude to keep his word and had left him alive. He wasn't going to be like his father, Jude told himself fiercely.

When the silence stretched out, the detective nodded as if Jude had said something that confirmed all his suspicions. "Right. Let me explain something to you, Jude. Maybe you didn't have anything to do with this, but if you know something about your father's murder and you don't tell us, that makes you an accessory to the crime. That means you're partially responsible, and if we can prove it, we can cart you off to juvie, and the boys there will make a tough kid like you look like cotton candy. So think about that for a little while, and see if you can remember anything else."

Jude thought about it.

He was still thinking about it in the interrogation room more than two hours later. One of the policemen had taken him down to the station to wait for the detectives, and the longer he sat there, the more he felt like he wanted to jump out of his skin.

He jumped up and paced the room, back and forth, back and forth. The mirrored window caught his eye, and he realized that someone—maybe even the detectives—could be on the other side watching. Waiting. Figuring out when he was softened up enough. They already knew he was lying. His story hadn't held up for even five minutes. What would happen if they questioned him for two hours? Would he hold out . . . or would he break down and tell them the truth?

2

THE TRUTH WAS that Jude shouldn't even have been there in the apartment. He was never home that time of day. It was all because of his shoe.

Normally Jude stayed after school to shoot hoops, but that morning the rubber sole of his sneaker had torn away from the toe. Throughout the day he kept catching it as he walked, the rubber doubling under his foot and making him stumble. By the end of the day the sole smacked the pavement like a reverse flip-flop, and there was no playing ball with it like that.

He lingered for a few minutes, watching the others shouting and jostling out on the court. One of the kids spotted him standing there. "Come on, Jude. We need you," the kid called, pausing in his jog downcourt. "We're getting killed out here."

Jude was always first choice for center because he was bigger than the others—though the other guys teased him, saying white boys can't jump. It was true, he had no legs, but he was tall and strong and quick, too—an all-around good player. He wasn't the flashiest out there, but his team tended to win.

"I can't today," he said.

"Ah, come on," the kid coaxed.

From down the court someone else yelled, "Get your butt out here, man."

"Can't," Jude said again.

"That's it. We're toast." The kid shook his head and turned, and a second later he was yelling for the ball, "Yo-yo-yo, over here."

All the others pounded up and down the concrete in Nikes and Adidases. Jude remembered when he had arrived at the court last spring with his "new" pair. His father had bought them, and he was so proud of his purchase. Jude had been talking about wanting a pair of Nikes, and here was this pair of Nikes and, his father announced, they'd cost only four dollars at the thrift store. Unfortunately, Jude could see why. They didn't look like they'd been worn, but they were *old*. Instead of laces they had Velcro, and fluorescent stripes down the sides. When he wore them to the court, everyone pointed and laughed and tried to tease him. He just shrugged as if he didn't care, and the guys soon gave up on the jokes. He noticed that in the next few weeks several other kids showed up with old sneakers like his. Jude assumed they were making fun of him. He didn't even begin to suspect that they'd bought shoes like his because they admired him, and that they mistook his silence for confidence. They thought he was different. They didn't know that all he wanted was to be like everyone else.

In everything, Jude did his best to blend in. Like most of the other kids, he dressed in long, baggy shorts and a basketball jersey with a white T-shirt underneath. The only difference was that he usually wore long sleeves, even in the surge of Indian-summer heat. The long sleeves covered the fading bruises, dark and mottled on the pale skin of his arms.

He hung on the fence a few more minutes, scuffing his good sneaker in the high grass. But just when he was about to leave, he spotted his best friend, R. J., jogging across the parking lot toward the court. Jude raised a hand and R. J. swerved toward him.

Two years ago—when Jude had moved to Hartford with his father—R. J. had jumped him on his first day of school. Jude had been the new kid too many times to be surprised by it; he and his father had moved at least a dozen times over the last fifteen years. They usually moved into rough neighborhoods—usually because of lack of money; now because, though his father had money from the dealing, he had to stay in central Hartford to be close to the business. Jude didn't mind. It was what he was used to. He knew what to expect—and part of what he expected was a fight on the first day of school. It was as certain as a handshake after an introduction.

The new kid was usually an easy target, but Jude had the advantage of experience. He had ducked R. J.'s wild punch and started his swing from the knees like his father had taught him. He had loosened R. J.'s front tooth, so that afterward he could wiggle it a little with his tongue—and they had been friends ever since.

"Yo, man, why aren't you out there?" R. J. called as he approached.

"Can't today."

"Why the hell not?"

He lifted his foot and showed R. J. his sneaker.

"Man, didn't I tell you that you *got* to get you some new kicks? Your old man will have to spring for them now."

"I was gonna get me some last week, but they didn't have the ones I wanted in my size," Jude said.

"Yeah, whatever. You might be able to lay that shit on the guidance counselor, but it don't work with me." He grinned and Jude smiled back. That was why R. J. was the only person who he confided in—he was the only one who saw through Jude's bluff and cared enough to call him on it. "So what's the problem? Your dad's got cash—I mean, he's gotta if he's skimming. What the hell is he doing with all of it?"

Jude made a face. "I think he's just cheap. But he says he's saving it for my college education."

"You're kidding me, right?"

Jude shook his head.

"Oh shit." R. J. burst out laughing. "You better hope he's just cheap, 'cause he'll be lucky if you graduate high school."

"It's not funny," Jude said, but he couldn't help laughing too.

"Hey, listen, if he won't spring for them, or you

don't wanna even go there, I can try my brother. If I catch him at the right time, I could score a hundred easy."

"Nah, man, you don't need to do that," Jude said. He knew how much R. J. hated asking his big brother. A year ago his brother had gotten heavy into the junk and started dealing to support his habit, and most of the time R. J. stayed as far away from him as he could.

"That reminds me, I didn't forget your birthday's comin' up. I got something for you," R. J. said.

"What is it?"

"I'm not gonna tell you, stupid. Then it wouldn't be a surprise. But hey, did you go to Miss Perez's class today?"

"I cut," Jude said. "I didn't do the homework."

"Me neither, but I heard there's a test tomorrow."

"Shit, I forgot about that."

"Listen, Frankie told me that Perez uses the same tests every year. So I'm gonna go through my brother's old shit. My mom kept all that stuff. She thought he was a regular scholar—not that it does him any damn good now. Meet me at my locker the period before, and if I find it, we can memorize the answers. You up for it?"

"Definitely," Jude said.

"Catch you then." R. J. raised his fist and Jude hit it lightly with his own.

But he wouldn't be there tomorrow, or the next

day, and the gift R. J. had for Jude would sit on the shelf in his locker for weeks.

WHEN JUDE LET HIMSELF into the apartment and flapped down the narrow hallway into the kitchen, he found his father at the table emptying a plastic bag of white powder into a metal mixing bowl.

Jude stopped in the doorway.

"What?" his father demanded.

"Nothin'," he said quickly, crossing to the fridge.

His father grunted.

Jude retrieved a jug of orange juice and, standing with the door of the fridge propped open, tipped back the container and took a swig.

"That is a disgusting habit," his father said.

He swallowed, wiped his mouth. "You do it all the time," he pointed out.

"That doesn't mean you should. Pour yourself a goddamned glass and go get me the baby powder from the bathroom."

Jude pinched up a corner of his shirt and carefully wiped the mouth of the jug. "You think it's a good idea to pull this again so soon, Pops?" Jude tried to speak casually to cover the sickening lurch he felt at his father's request. His father had cut the last four shipments. This would make the fifth in a row. You could get away with it once in a while, but each supplier had the name of his product stamped on the dime bags, and if quality was bad, the word spread.

The packets his father filled were stamped with the words FIRST CLASS, and it usually was. On the street it had the reputation for being the purest cut you could buy, and it was always in demand. Or rather, it used to be. The junkies, who didn't notice if you stumbled over them on the street, noticed if you messed with their high. You couldn't cut five shipments in a row and keep your customers. Five in a row was stupid. Even worse, five in a row showed disrespect.

"I think you should keep your mouth shut about things you don't know anything about," his father snapped.

But the fact was that Jude knew all about it. Not from his father, but from the neighborhood where deals went down on most street corners, and the favorite topics of conversation routinely involved who was dealing, who was snitching, who was dipping, who was dead. R. J. had actually been the first to pass along the warning. Because of his brother, R. J. was usually the first to hear the rumors.

"You're telling me you think the other guys aren't doing it?"

"Sure they are," Jude admitted. "But not like this, and if they're doing it this much, they're not getting away with it."

"But I am," his father said. "We are. Now, go get me the damn baby powder."

"Pops, I don't think . . . ," he started.

It was his own fault. He should have known better.

His father was up in a moment. It took only two steps for him to reach Jude, and then he was grabbing Jude's shirt. His father's fist cocked back, and then Jude's head exploded with light and he was knocked back against the counter. The juice carton flew from his hand and landed on its side, liquid pumping out its mouth.

Jude felt the hard edge of the counter against his back, and the first pulse of his heart brought the flower of pain beating in his cheek. His father dropped his hand and turned away, and Jude felt the urge to hurl himself at that silent, disdainful back. It took all of his will to hold himself still. Then after a second Jude pushed himself upright, and leaving the juice to spill itself on the floor, he walked out of the kitchen and down the hall to the bathroom.

The baby powder was in the cabinet above the sink. He retrieved it, shut the cabinet, and caught his reflection in the mirror, cloudy and splattered with sprays of toothpaste. There was already a red welt rising on his cheek, and his father had nicked open the skin with the plain gold band he wore on the ring finger of his right hand—but that didn't interest Jude as much as the eerie expression of calm the mirror reflected back at him. From his expression someone might assume he didn't care. He remembered when he had practiced for hours just this blank look. He'd thought that maybe if he didn't show the fear and shame and anger, then maybe he wouldn't feel it either. It hadn't worked.

When he returned to the kitchen, his father was mopping up the juice with a wad of paper towels. Jude set the powder container down hard on the table; it must have been open, because a cloud huffed from the top.

Jude was about to exit the room again when his father called to him in a very different tone, "Hold on a second there."

He stopped but didn't turn. He heard his father open the door to the freezer.

"Better put this on your face." His father circled around him and held out an ice pack.

"It's not that bad," Jude said, but he took the ice pack anyway.

"You know, you should just slug me back. You're as tall as I am now, and when you put on a little muscle, you'll be bigger than me." His father draped a casual arm over his shoulders and gave him a little squeeze.

Jude felt sick with disgust—both for the way his father tried to make it up to him and with himself for putting up with it. It was all so predictable and so pathetic, but he forced a smile and said, "I couldn't hit an old man."

"Who're you calling old man?" His father released his shoulders and playfully jabbed him on the arm. "You're a tough guy, you know that?"

It was his father's highest compliment. "I'm gonna go watch some TV," Jude said, starting down the hall.

He followed the narrow corridor to the living room and settled down in the corner of the brown couch. They had rented the apartment furnished, and they had the brown couch and a green armchair in the living room, a metal folding table and four mismatched chairs in the kitchen, and a narrow twin bed and dresser in each bedroom. They had been living there two years and had added nothing but a TV, which rested on the seat of the armchair.

Jude didn't even notice the bareness of his surroundings. It was what he was used to. Before moving to this apartment they hadn't lived anywhere much longer than a year; they had moved from one city to another with the speed of the guilty, and since they never stayed, they never accumulated anything. Once, Jude had put up a poster in his room—of Michael Jordan in midair, stretching toward the basket—but his father tore it down during a fight, and Jude didn't try to hang another.

Jude flicked on the TV and sat there surfing through the channels and holding the ice pack to his face until it lost its chill and turned to a soft gel. By then his stomach was rumbling, and he decided to brave the kitchen to get something to eat.

His father must already have added the baby powder, because when Jude returned, he was bent over the mixing bowl filling one of the tiny wax-paper envelopes. Even though Jude's flapping shoe announced his arrival, his father didn't look up. That meant the spurt of regret had passed. Everything was back to normal.

Jude opened the freezer and inspected the contents. "You want something to eat?" he asked.

His father placed the dime bag in a small pile with the others he had filled and picked up an empty. "Not hungry."

Jude removed a Salisbury steak TV dinner, stuck it in the oven, and set the timer. He found a roll of duct tape in a drawer and wound it around the toe of his shoe. Then he sat back down at the kitchen table to wait for the buzzer. Since there was nothing else to do, he watched his father fill the glassine bags. His father's fingers were short and thick and clumsy. The clumsiness came from the knuckles—swollen and lumpy with arthritis from the fighting he had done as a young man. Jude knew that not only was it difficult for his father to cut the shipments, it was also painful. Normally he would have offered to help, as he was almost twice as fast, but his cheek still throbbed in a painful reminder, so he just sat.

And that's exactly where they were when the two men arrived.

3

JUST AS THE SMELL of the Salisbury steak started to fill the room, Jude heard the sharp *crack* of wood splitting. Their door must have taken only one good kick to buckle in its cheap frame, because a second later he heard the footsteps.

Jude glanced over at his father. He was sitting bolt upright in his seat.

When Jude looked back, there were two men standing in the doorway to the kitchen. They were both old—one gray haired, the other bald—but despite their age they were still powerful men, bulky under their overcoats. The gray-haired man entered first; he held a briefcase in one hand. The bald one followed; he carried a rifle.

The second man raised the rifle to his shoulder . . . then looked at his companion.

So Jude looked too.

The gray-haired man was gazing at Jude's father. It was almost as if the man looked sad, Jude thought—but that was crazy.

The man nodded slowly, meaningfully.

Jude glanced over at his father just in time to see him return the nod. Then his father turned to meet Jude's gaze. It was as if his entire life had been moving toward that moment in the small, grubby kitchen.

"You were right," he said to Jude. "You were right."

It was the only time his father had ever said those words.

With the silencer the noise of the rifle was barely louder than a cork popping from a bottle.

His father was looking at Jude as the bullet hit. His father's eyes widened in surprise, then they went suddenly flat, as if a connection had been abruptly severed.

Jude watched as he tilted slowly sideways, slipped off his chair, and landed facedown on the floor. Though his limbs were bent uncomfortably beneath him, he didn't move, and as Jude stared a pool of deep burgundy spread from beneath his chest, like the tide washing up across their linoleum floor.

With the gun still propped on his shoulder, the shooter looked at Jude. He had nothing of the wild, glazed look Jude had noticed on the faces of the neighborhood men who usually took care of these things. The old man's hands were steady and his eyes were calm. He was waiting for orders, Jude realized. Just like a soldier.

"Should I take the kid out?" the shooter asked.

"He wasn't supposed to be here," the gray-haired man said. "You said he stayed at school to play ball."

"Sorry, boss. He always did before. What do you want me to do?"

Jude could feel the thud of his heart as if his whole body hammered with it. He tried to say, "Please." His lips moved, but no sound emerged.

The silence stretched out, and the man with the rifle seemed to take that as answer enough. Jude could see him fit the gun more snugly into his shoulder and sight on him with one eye.

But just then the other man said, "Wait. Not yet."

The shooter lowered the rifle and shot a puzzled glance at his companion.

Jude blinked, took a shaky breath, and held himself perfectly still as they moved into the room—as if they might forget about him if he kept quiet enough.

The one holding the gun skirted the table and looked down at the body, probing it with a toe. The other—the boss—put on a pair of gloves, then lifted his briefcase onto the kitchen table across from Jude and opened the catch.

If someone was going to take out his father, it should have been Benny or Mike or even Willis, Jude thought. They were the ones who took care of stuff like this—not strangers, and certainly not these strangers. They both looked over fifty, and there weren't too many people in the business that were still around at thirty, much less fifty—at least not in Jude's neighborhood.

The boss began swiftly loading the pile of dime bags into the briefcase. A few had drops of blood beading on the wax. He set those aside and packed the rest. Then he looked up at Jude and said, "Paper towels?"

Jude pointed at the cabinet under the sink.

The man turned toward the cabinet, then stooped, retrieved the towels, kicked the cabinet closed again with his foot, and came back to the table with the roll in hand. He tore off a couple sheets and delicately mopped at the blood on the remaining bags. Then he loaded them up and wiped down the table.

Jude kept his eyes on the man in front of him—kept his eyes away from the motionless figure on the floor.

The man put the paper towels back and returned with a roll of tinfoil. Pulling out a long sheet, he picked up the metal mixing bowl and tapped the remains of the powder into the middle. He twisted it up like a doggie bag, packed that also, and closed the briefcase with a *snap.* Then he returned the tinfoil to the cabinet where he'd found it . . . and paused there by the sink. He said, "Do you smell something burning?"

The other man sniffed. "Maybe the oven."

The boss opened the oven door. "It looks like we interrupted dinner. I'll turn this off for you, okay?" He didn't wait for Jude to answer, but spun the dial setting for the oven. Then he turned again to the shooter. "Go and keep an eye on the door for me, will you? Make sure no one gets nosy."

"We should get going, boss."

"I'll be there in a minute."

The big man gave his boss another look but left the room without another word.

Once the shooter had gone, the man crossed back to the table and took a seat opposite Jude. "You're Jude," he said.

Jude was so shocked at the sound of his name that he didn't answer, but it didn't matter because it wasn't really a question.

"You look just like your father when he was your age. You got the girls running after you like he did?"

Jude shook his head, wordless.

"I don't believe it, a good-lookin' kid like you. Listen, I want to ask you something, and I want you to answer me truthfully. You understand?"

Jude nodded.

"I want you to tell me what your father meant when he said 'You were right.'"

"I told him," Jude said, and his voice came out hoarse, little more than a croak.

"Told him? Told him what?"

"I told him that he was taking too much."

"I see. So you were expecting this?"

No, Jude thought, *not this. I couldn't have been expecting this.* But he nodded again. Because he had been expecting this, only without really thinking it would ever happen.

"I wish to God your father had listened to you, but

I'll tell you this. You gave him something I couldn't. You gave him some warning—and I'm glad. It clears my conscience a little. I don't like having to take out old friends."

"Old friends?" Jude repeated. His father didn't have any friends that Jude knew of. The only person his father had was him.

"We grew up together," the man said. "We're not exactly friends, but when you go that far back with someone, that means you do something for them if you're in a position to. He called me, and I got him this gig. It was the least I could do. Your father did me a couple of favors before you were born, when things were different for him."

As Jude was listening to the man talk about his father, he was also aware of the creep of the blood as it spread out from his father's body. The floor in their kitchen wasn't level, and the blood was making its slow way downhill toward Jude's feet. He hooked his sneakers over the rung of his chair and tried hard to concentrate on the man's words.

"You know, life's a funny thing. You think you know where you're going—you think that you can plan it all out, but it doesn't work that way. Back when we were kids and playing ball together in the empty lot on the next block, you think we ever imagined that we were gonna end up here? Like this?" The man leaned over, resting his head on one hand. "I guess that it was our choices that brought us here—mine and Anthony's both—but it doesn't feel that way. You know what I mean?"

Jude didn't hear the question. He was stuck on the sentence before. "Who's Anthony?" Jude asked. His father's name was Frank.

"I meant your father. He used to go by Anthony when he was a kid."

Jude tried to understand this, but the man kept talking, and it took all of Jude's will just to follow the words.

"I guess what I'm trying to say is that I'm sorry it had to come to this. I didn't want to take him out, but he didn't leave me a choice, the stupid bastard. But here's the thing. If I was smart, I'd take you out too."

The fear was there again, snatching his breath from his lungs.

The man sat for several seconds. "How old are you?" he said finally.

"Fifteen."

"Big for your age," he observed. "My boy's seventeen, and I was just thinking what he'd be doing if he was in your situation right now. You know, I think he'd be puking, he'd be so scared. So I'm wondering why you aren't."

Jude couldn't believe the man couldn't see that he *was* that scared. Then he remembered the frozen calm of his face in the mirror—how he seemed to assume the mask automatically now, without his willing it into place. He was scared so often he had just learned to live with it, like some people learned to live with pain.

"Ten years ago, even five, this wouldn't have been a problem. I'm getting soft," the man muttered. "Let me ask you this, if I let you go, how do I know you're not gonna turn around and rat me out the second I walk out of here? Your old man didn't keep his word, how can I trust you?"

Jude's answer came out in passionate denial. "I'm not like my father."

The man cocked his head, as if listening to the conviction in Jude's voice.

"I told him not to dip out so much," Jude insisted. "I told him what was gonna happen."

"Yeah, I know. I hope that means you also know what will happen if you say anything about tonight. I may be getting soft, but I do what I have to when people force my hand." He glanced meaningfully down at Jude's father.

Jude followed his glance automatically but looked away quickly. "I'm not like my father," he repeated desperately. "I'll keep my word. I won't say a thing. I promise."

The man studied him. Then he stood up. "I'm giving you a shot," he said. "Don't blow it," and he disappeared through the doorway. A moment later Jude heard low voices from the hallway, then nothing. He was alone.

4

WHILE JUDE WAS PACING the interrogation room, Detectives Grant and Burwell were picking through the apartment. Grant would have been content to pull open the drawers, glance through belongings inside, and get back to the station. But Burwell insisted on methodically removing all the contents of each drawer.

"Come on," Grant said. "It's not as though you're going to find a note naming the murderer."

"You never know what you might find," Burwell said.

The next drawer that Burwell opened wasn't filled with rumpled clothes—it was filled with junk. Grant would simply have swirled his hands through, but Burwell carefully removed the drawer and emptied its contents on the bed. When he flipped it over, he saw the envelope taped underneath.

"I found something," Burwell said.

Grant glanced over and his eyebrows shot up in surprise. "Well, get a load of that. Let's check it out."

Burwell pulled off the envelope and extracted some sheets of paper. He shuffled through them.

"Anything interesting?" Grant asked.

"You could say that."

"I don't imagine it happens to say who whacked this guy?"

"No. Nothing to do with the murder."

"Well, what is it then?"

Burwell ignored the question and instead asked one of his own. "You know Anna Grady?"

"Yeah, 'course. She's the county DA for West Hartford. Are you suggesting we call in West Harford to collaborate on this? That would be a first. They usually ask for our help, not the other way around."

"Well, I think we're going to need to call her in, but not exactly for help. That kid we have down at the station . . ."

"Yeah, what about him?" Grant prompted.

Burwell silently handed over the papers. Grant glanced at them, then looked more closely. "Holy shit," he murmured.

"Yeah," Burwell said. "Can you believe it? The friggin' DA is his mother."

THE NEXT MORNING Anna Grady was shown into the observation room adjoining the interrogation room. The station's chief and the two detectives watched as she crossed to the one-way glass and stood gazing through. The men had a good view of the back of her expensive tailored suit, but all they could see of her face was a quarter moon of jaw.

She said, "Is that him?"

Burwell answered. "That's him."

Outside those two little rooms the station was

buzzing with gossip. No one could figure out why the West Hartford DA was being called in on a drug hit. The crime hadn't even occurred in her district.

West Hartford was the affluent suburb bordering the depressed and crime-ridden city center. The shooting itself had happened in Eastside, one of the most dangerous neighborhoods in Hartford. It was a neighborhood where you could hear automatic gunfire any night of the week. There were fifty to sixty homicides a year, and in a city of less than 150,000 that made it the highest homicide rate in New England. Drug-related killings were a dime a dozen, so why, the station personnel wondered, was the DA sitting in on this one? And if it was a big-deal hit, why wasn't someone from the Hartford DA's office there as well?

Anna Grady stood on the other side of the glass and looked at the son she hadn't seen in fifteen years. She didn't speak, and the silence stretched on so long that eventually the chief had to break it with a cough.

Still staring through the glass, she said, "Does he know anything?"

"No. We thought it would be better coming from you."

She turned to look at him. After a long moment she said, "I meant does he know anything about his father's murder."

"Oh." The chief blinked. "Well, you can ask the

detectives. They were the ones who interviewed him last night."

She turned her gaze on Grant and Burwell. Burwell said, "He says he didn't see anything."

"But?" she prompted.

Burwell shifted uncomfortably. "There are a few discrepancies in his story. We think he may be covering for someone."

"So you think he might have been involved?" she asked.

There was a silence. Then the chief said, "Tell us how you want us to handle this."

"I want you to handle it as if it were any other investigation," she responded tartly.

"He's not a suspect," Burwell said.

"You said yourself that he's lying about what he knows," she replied.

"I said there were inconsistencies," Burwell corrected her.

She held his gaze until Burwell flushed and looked down.

"If the Hartford DA is satisfied with our work, that should be good enough," the chief said, reminding her, as mildly as possible, that she wasn't there in an official capacity. "But of course if you discover anything different, please feel free to pass it along."

Her eyes narrowed. "I see," she said. "Okay, I'll talk to him."

"If you need anything else, I'll be in my office," the chief said.

"And we'll be in the squad room," Burwell added.

"I'd prefer it if you stayed," she said. "If I'm able to get any information from him, I'd like you to hear it."

Grant and Burwell shot desperate looks at the chief, but he gave a little shake of his head. Then he said, a little too heartily, "Of course. Grant and Burwell are at your disposal. Call me if there's anything else I can do to help." And then he escaped the room.

JUDE WAS WORKING on adding his name to the dozens scratched into the metal surface of the table when the door opened. He went over the *J* with the edge of his key, digging the letter deeper into the metal. Then he tucked the key away and looked up. He had been expecting the detectives back for another round—not a tall, elegant woman.

He waited for her to introduce herself, but she just closed the door and sat down in the chair across from him. She watched him but didn't say anything.

He fidgeted, trying to find other places to look in the room, but he found it was hard to avoid someone who was staring at him so fixedly. Eventually he gave up and stared back, but still her gaze didn't waver.

"What?" he demanded.

She didn't respond.

Jude had never spent much time around women. His only real contact with women was with his teachers—but he never had to be alone with them; he was usually sitting in the back of the room, separated by five rows of desks and thirty other kids. And this woman was very different from the women who taught at his school. She looked like something out of a magazine. Her blue blazer and skirt were so crisp it looked as if she might have just cut the tags off. Her nails were perfect ovals, brushed with a light pink polish. Her hair was glossy and smooth. And her face was steely and unreadable. Everything about her was intimidating.

Finally she said, "Do you know me?"

Was that why she hadn't introduced herself? Because she expected him to know who she was? "No. Should I?" he asked.

She smiled at this, a tight little smile, as if she thought his question was somehow funny. She said, "I'm Anna Grady." When he didn't respond to the name, she added, "I'm the West Hartford district attorney."

He wondered exactly what kind of trouble he had gotten himself into.

"Do you know what a DA does?"

"I know they don't usually show up at two-bit drug hits," he said.

"Is that how you feel about your father's murder?"

Something in the way she said it got through his defenses and stung him. "That's none of your business."

But she nodded as if he had answered her, as if he had just as much as told her that he was frightened and lost and that way deep down—and this is what scared him the most—deep down there was a part of him that felt exactly that way about it. A cold, calculating, revengeful part that felt that his father had gotten what he deserved.

"What do you want?" he demanded, spooked by this woman in a way that the two detectives hadn't managed.

"I thought you might want to tell me about the men who shot your father."

"I already told the detectives," he said. "I was sitting in the living room when—"

She cut him off abruptly. "That's not what happened."

"Oh yeah?"

She nodded again in that self-assured way of hers, as if, Jude thought, she knew everything about him.

"You were there. We know you saw everything. Why don't you just tell us who did it?"

"I told you I was in the living room. I didn't see a thing."

"I know what you said. Do you want to hear how I know you're not telling us the truth?"

Jude rubbed the pad of his forefinger over the ruts of his name carved in the table.

"Number one, the report says that whoever killed your father took enough time to wipe down the table, so I think they might have taken the time to stroll down the hallway—especially if they could hear the television, which you claimed you were watching at the time. Two, you never mentioned what you did when you heard the shot. Did you just sit there on the couch till the program you were watching ended? Or did you get up and run and hide in the bedroom? Or did you get up and run into the kitchen to see if you could help your father? That is, if you were really in the living room in the first place, which I tend to doubt. And finally, I just can't get over those ten minutes your neighbor mentioned. Why would she lie about that? She has no reason to. You do. You know who killed your father. So now my question is, why aren't you telling?"

He kept his eyes down. "I already said—"

"Do you want to be a liar like your father?" she asked quietly.

"What the hell do you know about my father?" he said.

"I know a lot more than you do, Michael."

"You're so full of it. And you can't even get my name right. It isn't Michael, it's Jude."

"I know," she said. "It must be short for Judas. Your father always did have a nasty sense of humor."

"Stop talking about him like you know him," Jude said savagely. "You don't know anything about him."

"I don't?"

"No." He glanced at her again and said, a little less certain, "You couldn't."

She tapped one fingernail against the metal table. *Tap. Tap. Tap. Tap.* Staring at him. *Tap. Tap. Tap.* Just when he thought he couldn't stand another second, she stopped abruptly.

"Detective Burwell found something in your father's apartment last night," she said.

"Yeah?" He tried to keep his voice from breaking.

"It's the reason I'm here today."

Oh God, he thought. What had his father done?

She slid a yellowed, crumbling envelope across the table toward him. "Take a look."

Jude stared at it. Reluctantly he reached out and picked it up. When he raised the flap, tiny pieces crumbled off in his hands. Glancing up, he saw that she was looking in the other direction. He removed the papers from inside. The first was a birth certificate for an Anthony Arvelo. It meant nothing to him until a memory sparked in his brain. The man who killed his father had called him Anthony. He checked the date and saw that it was the right year, though the wrong day. Or at least it wasn't the day they had celebrated as his father's birthday.

"So my father changed his name. Big deal."

"There's more."

Jude shuffled to the next piece of paper, and he discovered that this one was a marriage certificate.

And it also contained the name Anthony Arvelo.

"So? It's my father's marriage certificate," he said. "I figured he probably married my mother."

"Did you look at the other name?" she said.

He hadn't even thought to look. He glanced down. His father had never told him his mother's name. Jude saw the name on the line next to his father's. It read ANNA GRADY. Then he made the connection. She had introduced herself as Anna Grady.

"It's a coincidence, right?" he said.

She shook her head.

He fixed his eyes on the name etched in the metal surface of the table. He felt the same sense of unreal calm he had felt as he watched his father slide sideways in his chair and fall to the floor.

"I'm your mother," she said.

5

DETECTIVES GRANT AND Burwell were waiting for Anna in the observation room. The moment she entered, she knew she'd made a mistake in asking them to stay and watch the interview. All she needed was one look at the detectives' faces to know that it had been a bad idea.

They weren't looking at her. They were looking at Jude. Anna followed the direction of their gaze, and she saw what they saw—a boy sitting slumped in his chair, his faced turned away. He seemed suddenly very young. When she'd been in the room with him, all she could see was his father's face. The resemblance was so strong it took her breath away every time she looked at him. He had his father's Italian good looks—the square jaw, the thick, wiry black hair, the heavy-lidded eyes. The only difference was that Anthony's face had never been that still, his eyes never that flat. Anthony's eyes had always been crinkled and sparkling with fun, or slitted and shining with anger, but had never had that wary blankness. But now she saw past the shell: She saw the frightened boy. What had she just done?

She reached for her briefcase, hoping they didn't notice that her hand was still trembling. "He's been through a lot," she said abruptly. "There's something he's not telling, but we might all be better served if he got some rest before doing anything else. But it's your case. Tell me how you want to proceed."

"For now we'll see what we can uncover through other avenues," Burwell said. "You can take him home. We'll just need your number in case we have any further questions for Jude."

"Fine." She pulled a pen out of her briefcase. "Do you have other papers for me to fill out?"

"We can send those to you if you'd prefer," Burwell offered.

She accepted the courtesy without comment.

"And we should be able to give you a few days' buffer from the press. After that the investigation will likely make it necessary for everything to come out."

"In that case, I'm going to ask Harry Wichowski to call," she said.

"I'm sure the chief will be happy to talk to him about any of his concerns."

She nodded. "I'll be speaking with you."

Grant and Burwell watched her leave the room. They remained silent as she returned to the interrogation room and spoke to the boy, but her voice was so low they couldn't hear what she said. Whatever it was, Jude stood and followed her out without a word.

"That was a hell of a family reunion," Burwell said. "I mean, if your kid shows up after fifteen years, don't you think you'd at least pretend to be happy to see him?"

"She's a cold bitch, that one," Grant said. "But if you stick around a little longer, that'll look like nothing. I've seen a lot of messed-up shit in my career. I seen a mother who killed her three kids. So I guess a mother who doesn't really want a son she hasn't seen since he was a baby doesn't exactly shock me."

"Still, I feel sorry for the kid."

"Oh, he'll be all right," Grant said. "Better off than he was with his father, at least. And certainly better off than in the foster homes he would have ended up in. And it's all thanks to you finding that envelope."

"I wonder if she'd thank me," Burwell said.

Grant grinned. "You want to know what I think? I think this is a thankless job."

6

JUDE FOLLOWED ANNA down a deserted corridor and out an emergency exit that led into the parking lot.

"Just over here," she said, threading her way through the cars. They reached a silver BMW. "This is it," she said, hitting the locking system on her key ring.

He slid gingerly into the leather seat.

"Nice car," he said.

"What?" She was already fitting her key into the ignition. "Sorry, but I want to get out of here before people see us."

Jude didn't answer.

"I mean so we get at least a little bit of time before the media hits," she explained quickly.

"Yeah," he said.

"I just didn't want you to think . . ." She let the sentence drift off.

Anna started the car and pulled out of the parking lot. She didn't speak again until they were well away from the police station, and then her voice sounded different. She sounded almost hesitant. "Can I call you Michael now?"

"My name is Jude," he said.

"But your real name—"

"I've always been called Jude," he repeated.

"I know," she said, and he noticed that her

knuckles rose in craggy relief from their grip on the wheel. "By your father. I would rather call you anything else."

"I don't see why. He had every right to name me. You're the one who left us," he pointed out. He was able to keep the anger out of his voice even though he could feel it rising in the back of his throat.

She swerved to the side of the road and slammed on the brakes. It was so sudden Jude was thrown forward against his seatbelt. The car behind them leaned on its horn as it cut around them, barely missing their bumper, and they could hear the man shouting as he drove by.

Jude sat, still tensed from the sudden violent response, waiting for . . . he didn't know what.

"I didn't leave you," she said. "He took you."

Then Jude's world sharpened—as if he were looking through a blurry telescope that was unexpectedly thrown into focus. In a way it was more shocking to him than the moment she'd told him who she was. In all his imaginings he had never thought to question what his father had told him. He had never envisioned his mother coming back and saying, "It was all a lie. I never really left you," although if he had imagined it, she would have been crying and telling him how much she had missed him and how wonderful it was to have him back.

Instead she said, "I forgot what a bastard he could be. He could at least have told you I was dead."

"He said that he wished you were," Jude told her.

"What a comfort."

Jude looked out the windshield as he asked, "What happened?"

"He took you right from your crib when you were barely three weeks old, and that's the last time I saw either of you. Your father used to be a cop, if you can believe it." Her laugh was harsh. "So he knew how to avoid being found."

"So you tried?" Jude couldn't help asking.

She turned toward him, but instead of answering him, she just reached out. Ignoring the seatbelts and the steering wheel and the distance between them, she pulled him into her arms. And then Jude didn't care what had happened before. His dream had come true.

7

JUDE COULDN'T BELIEVE the house when he saw it. It was modest by West Hartford standards, but it looked like a palace to him. Anna led the way inside. Then she called out, "Harry, you here?"

There was a muffled response from deeper within the house.

Jude stopped, and Anna, sensing his hesitation, stopped as well.

"Oh," she said. "I forgot to tell you about Harry. Harry is . . . he's my very good friend," she finished rather lamely.

"You mean your boyfriend?" Jude clarified.

She turned a little red but said, "Yes. I guess you could call him that."

They found Harry just inside the door of the kitchen on his way out to meet them.

From the moment he set eyes on Harry, Jude automatically compared him with his father. Both Harry and his father must have shared the same build once. He knew his father had been tall and broad in the shoulders, but for the years that Jude had known him he had seemed to shrivel into an old man, his muscles slackening, his shoulders hunching as if he were drawing in on himself. Harry was also tall and broad, but while Jude's father had wasted away,

Harry had thrived. His shoulders were still wide and thrown back, and instead of losing bulk, he had added to it. He had taken on an extra layer, thickening his whole body without quite making it fat.

In his neighborhood Jude had gotten good at identifying the men who held power and the ones who were just pretenders. All it took was one glance at Harry to see he was the real thing. His age was harder to determine. Jude could tell from his face that he certainly was not young. The skin was leathered and his nose had a crooked lean. There were deep lines running from nose to mouth, but he had the look of a man who could still go ten rounds.

Harry smiled, and the lines around his mouth that had made him look so stern a moment ago now deepened into welcome. He extended his hand to Jude and looked so genuinely glad that Jude's heart leaped a little in response.

"I can't tell you how great it is you're here, Michael." He squeezed Jude's hand. "Your father was a good friend."

"You knew my father?" Jude asked.

"Anna didn't tell you? He was my partner on the force for years."

"Oh." Jude didn't know what to say, but they both were looking at him, so he said the first thing that came to mind. "Are you still a cop?"

"Sort of. I moved up in the ranks a bit. I'm deputy commissioner now."

"Oh," he said again. His father could have been deputy commissioner. His father could have been the one with Anna now, while Harry might be dead. Anything could have happened, he thought senselessly.

"I'm really sorry about what happened to your father," Harry said. "But don't you worry, we'll catch the bastards. Right, Anna?"

But Anna didn't answer right away, and when she spoke, she didn't answer the question. Instead she said, "I'm just glad they found Jude."

Jude looked up sharply and found her smiling at him.

"I don't care about the rest," she said.

Harry looked back and forth between them. "Found Jude?" he said. "Who's Jude?"

They both looked at Harry, then back at each other, and burst out laughing.

8

ANNA GAVE JUDE a tour of the house—now his new home. It looked like something from a magazine or a movie set—because those were the only places he had ever seen houses this perfect. On the first floor there was a dining room, a family room, a sitting room, and a study. The dining-room table was a rich, gleaming mahogany, and the matching sideboard bore up under the weight of an enormous silver tea set. In the sitting room the love seat and chairs were a stiff, snowy white. The family room had a leather couch and chairs arranged comfortably around a low pine coffee table, and the television was tucked discretely in a cabinet in the corner. Only the study showed any signs of habitation. In there papers were stacked on the big wooden desk, and books had been pulled off the shelves and heaped in piles on chairs.

"Sometimes I bring things home from the office and work here," Anna said, apologizing for the mess.

"Sometimes?" Harry snorted.

They climbed the stairs to the second floor. There were four bedrooms. Anna had the big one at the front of the house, but she told Jude he could choose from the other three. Jude picked the room that had a fireplace. It hadn't been used in years, but Anna promised they'd get it working—and they'd buy all new furniture. Whatever he wanted.

And that's what his new life was like. He could have whatever he wanted. They bought new furniture for his room. And basketball posters—framed this time. And a stereo, along with a couple dozen CDs. And enough new clothes to fill the new dresser.

It was literally a dream come true. All of a sudden he had the mother he'd always missed and all the things he'd ever wanted. He didn't have a father, but he had Harry, and Harry was almost better than a father—he was a friend.

The only shadow on his happiness was the memory of the night his father died. The investigation, Jude knew, was sure to come around to him again. As if by mutual consent, for the first few days no one even mentioned that night, his father, the investigation, or anything to do with the future. But they couldn't ignore it forever, and Harry was the one who finally brought it up, in a roundabout way.

It was the evening of the third day. Anna said she had to stop by her office, but she promised to pick up dinner. Jude spent the time upstairs in his room listening to his new CDs, but he kept an eye on the window, and he saw her pull into the driveway. When he got to the kitchen, he found Anna and Harry unpacking cartons of Chinese food, and Jude immediately sensed a certain tension in the room. After years of monitoring his father's moods he was sensitive to that kind of thing. But when he entered the room, Anna looked up and smiled at him.

"I hope you like Chinese," she said. "I forgot to ask you what you wanted to eat tonight."

"Chinese is my favorite," he replied. Mexican was really his favorite, but he figured this kind of lie was okay.

"Well, come in and get some," Harry said. "If you don't hurry, you might be out of luck because I swear I could eat it all myself."

Jude crossed to the counter and picked up a plate. There were a few moments of heavy silence, then Harry returned to the conversation they'd obviously been having before Jude entered.

"You're going to have to face it, Anna. Sooner or later the press is going to get wind of this. You need to take the initiative and control the situation, and that means going public."

"Oh God." She let the serving spoon clatter onto the counter. "I thought we might be able to put it off just a little longer."

"You know better than that. In fact, this is what you're best at. You manage the press all the time in your job."

"It's different when it's my personal life. I still remember how bad it was last time. Don't you?"

"That was a long time ago," Harry said.

"But it lasted almost an entire year. There was barely a week that went by when I didn't have some reporter calling. I don't know if I can go through that again."

"You won't have to. That was all tragedy and drama. This is the happy ending. They'll cover it in a week—two at most. Then they'll move on to the next disaster story."

"They're vultures," Anna said.

"They're just doing their job," Harry corrected her. "Just like you and me. If you're smart, you can use them at the same time they're using you."

"Like before," she said.

"Just like before," Harry agreed.

They both looked at Jude, who pretended to be absorbed with picking out the pieces of beef from the container of beef with broccoli. He wanted them to keep talking so that maybe he could pick up more of what had happened last time.

"Just get it over with and break the story tomorrow," Harry said.

She said nothing.

"Food's getting cold," he added after a moment.

"Well, eat it, then," Anna retorted.

But Harry didn't move. "It's your call, Anna. I'm just telling you what you already know."

She relented. "I know, Harry. You're right. I'm just not looking forward to going through this whole media circus again."

"It'll be fine. Listen, we'll give an exclusive to the *Courant,* and you should call Alan Goldstein in to write the story. Then you can explain the situation, and the two of you can work out together how to present it, and that will set the tone for the rest of the coverage. We'll just say no TV interviews together— to protect Jude, what with all he's been through. So, what do you think?"

"We'll do it tomorrow," she capitulated. "If that's all right with Jude."

They both looked at him. "Is that all right with you, Jude?" Harry asked.

"Sure. Okay by me."

"He doesn't have any idea of what's going to happen," Anna said. "How can you know unless you've been through it?" She paused. "And he's going to need to know the whole . . . story." She was obviously uncomfortable even referring to it.

"We could give him the clippings," Harry suggested. "Then he'd be prepared—and they'd give him a better picture of what happened back then *and* what might be coming up."

"I suppose you're right," Anna said. "But let's leave it until after dinner."

"After dinner it is," Harry agreed.

They brought their plates over to the table. Then Harry got forks while Anna put out the napkins and Jude got the glasses. Dinners before this had been lively; they'd talked mostly about silly things, but they'd laughed a lot. Now it was as if a spell had been broken, and dinner was subdued. They were all preoccupied with their own thoughts. Jude couldn't help dwelling on the fact that in just a little while he would know exactly what happened between his parents.

After dinner Anna sighed and said, "I guess I should get the clippings for Jude."

"I'll get them," Harry volunteered. "They're in the attic, right?"

"I think you're the one who stored them," Anna said.

"I think you're right. Be back in just a sec."

When he left, there was an awkward pause. Jude wondered if she was thinking about what was in the articles. Would she want to tell him anything before he read them?

But when she spoke, she didn't say anything about his father. "The next few days are going to be pretty rough," she told him.

"I can handle it," he said, trying to reassure her. "I've probably been through worse."

She looked away. "I'm sorry."

"What for?"

"For lots of things," she said. She hesitated but was about to continue when Harry announced from the doorway, "I found them. I put them all in a box, and it was right where I left it." Harry blew dust off the top and slid it across the table to Jude. "This should help explain some things. I don't know if either of us could give you an objective version, so maybe this is the best way for you to hear the story."

A minute later Jude was climbing the staircase with the box tucked under one arm and his heart beating fast. When he got to his room, he set the box down and switched the desk light on. The pool of light was bright on the desk, but the corners of the room remained gloomy. Jude sat in the chair, removed the lid, and lifted out the small, ragged stack of clippings. Then he picked up the first article and read.

City Prosecutor Files Abuse Charges in Her Own Office

CITY HALL—In a stunning development yesterday Anna Grady, the city's lead prosecutor in the newly formed Domestic Violence Prosecution Unit, herself filed papers against her husband of one year, city police officer Anthony Arvelo, alleging that Arvelo had physically abused her over a six-month period. The police commissioner's office said yesterday that Arvelo, 29, would be placed on paid leave pending the outcome of the investigation.

Grady, who kept her own name after marriage, filed charges alleging that Arvelo repeatedly abused her. Officers at the 17th Precinct, where Arvelo works, said they were shocked to hear of the charges. "Anthony's a regular guy and a great cop," said one officer, who requested anonymity. Phone calls to Arvelo's desk at the precinct were returned by the Police Benevolent Association's lawyer, Paul Cottingham, who declined comment until he could review the charges. City officials confirmed that Arvelo, a ten-year veteran of the force, had a clean record.

Coworkers in the Domestic Violence Prosecution Unit, formed as an arm of the district attorney's office two years ago, were similarly surprised by the charges but acknowledged that Grady did appear to have recently been injured. Kenia Martin, a coworker of Grady's, confirmed that Grady had shown up at work with bruises, which she said Grady claimed were due to a soccer game. Other members of the prosecutor's office, who requested anonymity, said that Arvelo and Grady met while the two were working on a domestic violence case more than a year ago.

When asked about the irony of Grady's filing charges in her own office, Martin said, "Well, it does seem amazing. I know Anthony, and he doesn't look like an abuser, but we find all kinds of people hit their wives, and that's what this office is here for." Martin cited the reluctance of many victims of domestic abuse to file charges against their husbands or fathers and said that Grady's filing charges might encourage other women to come forward.

Anna Grady joined the DA's office four years ago, after graduating summa cum laude from Cahill Law School. When the city formed the Domestic Violence Prosecution Unit two years ago, Grady was chosen as one of the prosecutors, and after a year was promoted to head the team. Martin said that Grady had a reputation for long hours and fierce dedication to her work. Martin also cited Grady's care for her clients and her competitiveness. Grady was unavailable for comment, and phone calls to the Arvelo-Grady residence were not answered late yesterday.

Jude laid the article gently, facedown, to one side. The clippings were in chronological order, so that as he went through them he got the story as it had been covered by the press. First there were two other articles, much the same as the first, but which had run in different papers. Then there was a whole bunch of editorial pieces and letters from readers in response to the story. Jude ended up only glancing at these; he couldn't figure out why everyone seemed to think it was such a big deal.

When he got to the accounts of the trial, he read more closely, though it wasn't so much for the outcome (guilty) as it was for some description of his father and mother together. There was nothing. The articles described his father as impassive and his mother as poised. He wished he had a dictionary, but even when he was able to look up the words, it still didn't tell him anything.

After the descriptions of the trial there was another bunch of opinion pieces. From these Jude gathered that a lot of people were angry that his father hadn't gotten a heavier sentence. Then there were a few profiles on his mother's career after the trial. He was glancing through these when he turned over an article and saw the picture. It was a photograph of Anna cradling a baby in her arms. He realized with a shock that the baby was him. He studied the picture more closely. It had obviously been staged—Anna had a forced, self-conscious smile as she displayed him for the camera. Jude remembered Harry had told him that Anna was never a motherly type, even when he was born. *Had she even minded when his father took him?* he wondered bitterly, and quickly turned it over.

That's when he came across the article that explained the rest.

Prosecutor's Son Kidnapped, Husband Missing
Convicted Police Officer Sought as Suspect

CITY HALL—City prosecutor Anna Grady reported yesterday in a frantic call to police that her three-week-old son, Michael, had been kidnapped from her house in Longmeadow late last night. It is the latest shocking trauma in her highly publicized divorce.

The police confirmed late yesterday that Anthony Arvelo, Grady's husband of almost two years, is being sought as a suspect. Arvelo was recently convicted of abusing Grady during their marriage. The police said that Arvelo apparently cleared out the apartment where he had been living since the beginning of the abuse trial, and that a car he had borrowed from a fellow police officer was found at a train station near Grady's residence.

Police commissioner Joseph Lauria said in a prepared statement, "[The police department regrets] that Officer Arvelo is a suspect in this case, and we ask that any person with knowledge of Officer Arvelo's whereabouts contact the department immediately." Lauria added that if the child was kidnapped, the Federal Bureau of Investigation may become involved in the search. "We ask that Officer Arvelo turn himself in immediately," Lauria said, "to avoid any more-serious consequences."

Detectives found evidence that a ladder was used to gain access to the second-story window of the room where the baby slept, the police said. The screen on the window had been cut with a knife or box cutter, and it appeared the child was taken through the window and down the ladder while the mother and a housekeeper were downstairs, police said.

Anna Grady was unavailable for comment.

The police department recently dismissed Arvelo after his conviction for domestic battery in a widely publicized case one month ago. Grady, the city's prosecutor for domestic violence cases, had filed charges with her own office almost a year ago, stating that Arvelo had abused her verbally and physically. Other reports later confirmed that she had been pregnant with Arvelo's child at the time. Grady gave birth to her son, Michael, three weeks ago at St. Luke's Hospital. Grady's courage in confronting domestic abuse in her own situation has made her a celebrity and a champion of women's issues. "I was silent for too long,"

Grady said in an interview, "and the right thing to do was to come forward and tell the truth."

Arvelo was convicted of one charge of domestic battery. He was placed on probation for one year and was under a restraining order. Yesterday some members of the DA's office, who requested anonymity, questioned the prudence of that decision. "This was just another case of a police officer getting special treatment," said one prosecutor.

Lauria said he has appointed Harry Wichowski, Arvelo's partner of eight years on the force, to lead the investigation into the alleged kidnapping. Wichowski said that he volunteered to head the investigation because he believes he knows the suspect the best. "Anthony and I were friends—are friends—and if this allegation is true, then I'm going to encourage him to come forward, or to find him if he doesn't," Wichowski said.

Harry hadn't succeeded. Jude didn't need to look at the rest of the articles to know that despite his best efforts he had gotten nowhere in the investigation.

Jude carefully replaced the articles, then he tucked the shoe box under the bed. He decided that if his mother or Harry asked for them back, he would tell them that he was keeping them, but it turned out no one but Dolores, the housekeeper—who dutifully moved them to vacuum every week—touched them for years.

9

"CAN I COME IN and talk to you for a minute?" Harry asked, cracking open the door of Jude's room.

Harry and Anna had been closeted in her study for most of the morning, preparing for the press. Jude had watched some TV, occasionally wandering out into the hallway to see if they'd emerged yet. Finally he had retreated up to his room. He was feeling strange—aimless and out of place. This must be what it had been like before he arrived—just Anna and Harry. Before today both Anna and Harry had been careful to include Jude. He'd felt part of things. That morning it seemed they'd forgotten about him, so he felt a burst of relief when he heard the tap on his door.

"Sure, come on in," Jude said, sitting up on his bed and punching the volume on the stereo lower with the remote control.

Harry entered and pulled the desk chair over next to the bed.

"What's up? Is everything okay?" Jude asked.

"What? Oh, yes, fine," Harry said. "We were just talking about strategy. But I thought I'd come up and clear up a few details."

"Details?"

"About the night your father was killed."

The relief he felt at seeing Harry disappeared and was replaced by a knot in his stomach. Jude didn't know what to say to that, so he didn't say anything. He just shrugged an okay.

"Anna thought it would be better if I talked to you about it. She still feels badly about how she treated you at the station. She thinks it's best if she stays completely out of the investigation, and I agree."

Jude nodded.

"Listen, I don't want you to worry. This isn't an interrogation, and I'm not here as deputy police commissioner. I'm here as your friend. I want to help . . . well, smooth things over for you. You know, clear some things up. Does that sound okay?"

Jude nodded again.

"Anna mentioned there was an . . . ah . . . mix-up with your story. You were probably just confused and scared when you talked to the detectives, right?" Harry looked to him for agreement, and Jude nodded one more time.

"That's what I thought. But Anna tells me the detectives may have gotten the wrong idea. They thought you knew something—or even that you might have been involved. So I just need you to tell me they're wrong and that you didn't have anything to do with it."

"I didn't," Jude said promptly.

"That's good . . . that's good, I didn't think you could have. Even though I know your dad was probably a little tough to get along with some-times—hell, he was my partner for years. But I told you that, didn't I?"

"Yeah," Jude said. "I remember."

"Right. Now, I just want to get this thing cleared up for you and your mother. Can you give me a reasonable explanation for what happened in the apartment?"

"It happened like I said," Jude told him. He'd considered this and decided even if there were holes, it was best to stick to the same story.

Harry leaned forward in the chair. "Jude, trust me," he said. "I can help you. I think you don't want to tell me because you think I'm going to report it, right? But I'm not. I swear to you. I think you and your mother have been through enough."

He paused and looked closely at Jude. "I understand why you did it," he said. "Your father used to hit your mother, too, you know. And I don't see why either of you should have to go through any more because of him. I don't want to see you put through a trial, and it could be even worse for Anna. That kind of publicity could seriously compromise her career, and I think she's destined for big things. So if you'll just admit to me that you had something to do with it, I can help. I can make sure that the pressure eases off and no one ever bothers you again. It will be almost as if it never happened, and no one will ever know. No one but me and you. I won't even tell Anna."

Jude had been determined to deny everything, but as he listened to Harry's speech he got an idea. He knew that Harry's offer of protection extended only to Jude. If he told Harry the truth and said that he didn't have anything to do with it, Harry wouldn't cover for the real shooters. But if he made Harry believe that he was involved, Harry would cover for him. There would be plenty of time to tell the truth—later, when things were better. In the meantime, if Harry could really do what he claimed, it would solve everything.

"You can get the detectives to leave me alone?" Jude asked.

It was almost an admission.

"I'm pretty sure I can," Harry said after a moment.

"And you won't tell Anna? You promise?"

"I promise."

"And you won't ask me for the details?"

"I just need to know the truth," Harry said.

Jude took a deep breath. "Okay."

"Okay what?"

"Okay, you're right."

Harry nodded. "Just one more thing. Will the police find anything? I mean anything conclusive? There's no chance anyone else is going to come forward and . . . talk, is there?"

Jude was confused for a moment, then he realized, of course, Harry knew from the details of the case that even if he had been involved, he hadn't acted alone.

Jude shook his head.

"Are you sure?"

"Pretty sure," he said. If innocence couldn't protect him, he thought, then nothing could.

Harry leaned back in his chair and sighed. "Thanks for being straight with me. I'll see what I can do to get the heat off you. Just stick to whatever you've been telling them, and I'll take care of the rest."

AND HARRY WAS as good as his word. Jude had to see the detectives only once more—a couple of days later—but this time they met at Anna's house, not down at the station, and Harry was there with him and did most of the talking. He orchestrated the meeting with Burwell and Grant with a subtle blend of flattery and threat. He said he wasn't working in his official capacity. He claimed he was acting merely as a representative for Anna, but even Jude could tell that the power of his office was there, understood if not invoked.

"Jude didn't see anything," Harry said firmly, and he made it clear that no one on the investigation was to make even the slightest suggestion that he had. Then Harry asked them if they were close to making an arrest.

Burwell laughed and said, didn't he think that he was getting a bit demanding? Maybe they'd be closer to an arrest if they could get a little help. Maybe Jude could give them a hint.

Sorry.

Grant suggested that they could give Jude the names, and he could just pick one. Whichever struck him.

Harry shook his head.

Burwell said they didn't know when they'd have an arrest. The investigation wasn't going as well as they would like. Leads were thin. They didn't have much beyond the next-door neighbor's statement. Then he mentioned that the chief was concerned about public pressure for an arrest when the story hit the papers.

Harry appeared to consider the problem, but when he spoke, it was clear that he had already anticipated this possibility. He said that he could probably help them with the press. He might even be able to engineer it so that there was almost no pressure at all.

"Not possible," Burwell said, but he said it hopefully, as if he were asking Harry to tell them he was wrong.

Harry obliged. "Consider it done," he told them.

And it *was* done.

The articles that were published on the case made the murder look almost like an act of God. Jude read them, and they all described Jude's father as a man who had beaten his wife, stolen her child, and become a drug dealer. It was never directly stated, but it was certainly implied that the victim in this case had deserved what he got, not to mention that his murder was what ultimately brought mother and son back together again. There was usually one short paragraph at the end about the ongoing investigation, and that was it.

There wasn't even a hint in any of the articles that Jude knew anything. The way it was presented, Jude could do no wrong. According to the papers, evil was vanquished and this was the happily-ever-after ending. According to the papers, it was a triumphant reunion and they had settled down peacefully as a family, as if fifteen years had been merely a blip on the radar.

And that had seemed to be true—for those first few days. But now the paradise the papers described had disappeared. After the story broke, life turned strange, almost surreal. Cameramen, photographers, and reporters camped outside the house. Anna spent most of her time either on the phone to her office, huddled over the kitchen table with Harry, or talking to reporters. Jude sometimes hung around the kitchen, listening to their conversations, but eventually ended up retreating into the family room and watching TV.

Harry and Anna were so busy handling things they didn't have much time for him. They apologized, but he was left very much on his own. The only one who really talked to him during the day was Dolores, Anna's housekeeper. Dolores was a short, squat woman who always spoke in commands—

"Don't put your feet up on the couch when you're wearing shoes," "Don't leave your glass of orange juice out on the counter," "Don't leave your wet towel on the floor of the bathroom."

Living with his father, he had always been the one to pick up the clothes and papers from around the apartment, or to stand over the sink cleaning the dishes when he got home from school. He always thought that having someone else to do it for him would be great, but he hadn't reckoned on Dolores.

By the evening of his first day with Dolores in the house he had decided to tell Anna that it was either Dolores or him. She'd have to choose. But he changed his mind that evening—when he tasted her cooking. For fifteen years Jude had lived on canned and frozen food. The last few days they'd survived on takeout. Dolores's food wasn't fancy, but it was home cooked and tasted great. The first night he went through two servings, and there was barely enough to go around. Dolores grumbled but made twice as much the second night, and there was enough for him to stuff himself until he felt like he could barely get up from the table—and when he glanced over at Dolores as she was clearing the dishes, he thought he almost caught her smiling.

THE WORST OF the media blitz was over in a week. All together Jude had been living there less than two weeks, but he had almost forgotten about his old life until one evening when his mother turned to him during dinner and asked, "Where did you used to go to school?"

Jude suddenly realized that he hadn't thought about the fact that school was going on without him. While all this stuff had been happening, the guys were still back there cutting class and playing ball. R. J. must be wondering what had happened to him. Then Jude realized that they probably knew what had happened. Someone would have seen the papers. It would be all over school by now.

"I go to Hartford High," he told her.

"And how did you like it?"

"It's all right," he said. "I've got this one good friend, R. J., and we have a lot of classes together, so that's pretty cool."

Jude liked Hartford High better than any other school he had attended, mainly because he'd been there for a couple of years and most of the kids didn't do much better in the classes than he did. Jude had always struggled in school—they had never stayed in one place long enough for him to feel comfortable. Whenever they moved, the new class seemed to be at a different point. Either they were in the middle of a lesson and he had to work to catch up, or they were learning something he'd already done—which meant he got only half of some things, while he got others twice, and some he missed completely. As time went on, he fell further and further behind.

"When do you think you'll be ready to go back to school?"

Jude shrugged. "I could go whenever."

"I'm asking because I can't take off any more work. I'd love to spend more time with you, but with my position . . . you understand, right?"

"Sure," Jude said. "Course."

"I have to go back to work on Monday, but if you need some more time, you can stay home. Dolores will be here during the day."

"I could go back Monday, but I'll probably need a note. I missed a bunch of tests." He thought of R. J. and wondered if he had managed to dig up his brother's old history tests. If he had, and Miss Perez really did use the same tests every year, Jude might actually be able to get a good grade in the class.

"But Jude, you *do* know that you won't be going back to your old school, don't you? You don't live in that school district anymore."

"So where am I gonna go?" Jude asked.

"I talked to the headmaster of Benton Academy. He's agreed to waive the entrance exam as long as you're willing to work hard."

Even Jude had heard of Benton Academy. It was an exclusive private school in West Hartford, more like a college campus than a normal high school, and it had been a regular joke back at Hartford High. Whenever one of his friends had passed a test or was caught studying, they'd tease him and say, "What, you trying to get into Benton or something?" Never in a million years had he thought he would have a chance of going.

"I can't go there," he almost whispered.

"Why not?" Anna said.

For the first time Jude realized that his mother had no idea what his life had been like up to that point—she couldn't possibly know if she didn't see why it was impossible for him to switch from Hartford High to Benton Academy. But he didn't know how to put it into words, so he said simply, "I'm not smart enough."

"Of course you're smart enough. No one expects you to get A's. You'll have a lot of catching up to do, but that's why I think Benton's the best place. You'll get a lot more attention there."

Jude didn't doubt that. The question was whether it was the kind of attention that he wanted.

ON HIS FIRST DAY Jude sat through his classes slouched so far down in his seat that his head barely topped the back of the chair. Half the time he didn't understand what was being discussed. In Spanish class—usually his best subject—he couldn't follow a thing. At Hartford High his Spanish teacher made them conjugate verbs, or if she was feeling adventurous, she took short dialogues from the book and had the students read them. In the class at Benton the teacher spoke completely in Spanish. Jude caught a word here or there, but that was it. At one point hands went up around him, raised to answer a question, and Jude hadn't even realized that the teacher had asked one. Math and biology, his other morning classes, weren't much better, despite the fact they were in English.

There was *one* good thing about the day. The school had assigned Jude a buddy to take him around for the first week. His name was Simon, and he was surprisingly friendly. Jude could tell Simon was trying to make him feel welcome, but Simon must have been warned about asking too many questions, because he kept starting sentences and leaving off abruptly in the middle.

Jude had been dreading lunch, but after his last morning class Simon was waiting. He walked with Jude to the cafeteria and brought him to sit at a table with all his friends. One kid asked Jude how he liked Benton so far, then there were a few awkward minutes when no one said much of anything. Finally they seemed to get used to him; they started talking to one another, and Jude was able just to eat and listen. Simon's friends mostly talked about classes and homework, and Jude realized that they must be the smart kids. Maybe they would be able to help him with his schoolwork, he thought. Maybe Benton wouldn't be so bad after all.

JUDE GOT INTO his first fight at school two weeks later. For the first week he had Simon—who dutifully came to pick him up at his classroom to deliver him to the next. At the end of the week Simon said, "So, you know your way around now?"

Jude told him he did, and then he was on his own. To his surprise, no one bothered him. He walked from class to class alone, though Simon still waved him over to his table at lunch. Kids stopped staring quite so much, and Simon and his friends started to loosen up and ask him about his old neighborhood. Jude found that they were fascinated with his stories about life in the rougher part of town. It seemed like Simon's friends must have spread the stories, because suddenly there were a lot of kids hesitantly asking him to come over and sit at their tables. Then Jude started to think that Anna was right and that Benton was different.

It was the beginning of his third week that it happened. He was heading toward the cafeteria for lunch when he passed a group of boys lounging against the lockers and he heard one of them call out, "Hey, you."

Jude kept walking. There were footsteps behind him and a hand grabbed his arm.

"Hey, I'm talking to you."

He stopped and turned to face the kid. It was a boy from his English class—Jude thought his name was Mike or Matt or something.

"What do you want?" Jude said.

"What do I want? He wants to know what I want," the boy called over to his friends, and they snickered.

"I'll tell you what I want. I want to see how tough you really are, ghetto boy. You talk real big, but I think you're a fake. I think I can kick your ass. "

"You're welcome to try," Jude said calmly.

The kid stepped forward, and his shove sent Jude stumbling back.

When Jude regained his balance, the boy beckoned him tauntingly. "Come on, pussy. What you gonna do?"

Jude swung, and his fist landed right on target. He'd had his own nose flattened a few times, but he thought from the boy's shriek that it was probably the first time for him.

The school called Anna in for a conference that afternoon. They had Jude wait outside the office while they talked, and when Anna emerged, she looked grim. She said, "Come on, I'm driving you home," but she didn't look at Jude when she spoke.

She led the way to the car, and Jude followed a step behind. He waited for her to break the silence, mainly because he didn't know what to say, but she didn't speak again. When she finally pulled up in front of the house, she put the car in neutral but didn't shut off the engine.

Now she's going to yell, he thought. But she didn't. It was worse than that. She said, "I'm disappointed in you, Jude."

He tried to explain, to defend himself. "But he started it," he protested.

"You should have just ignored him and walked away."

"He shoved me."

"In that case you go get a teacher. You don't break his nose. That's not the way to solve things."

It was the way he had always solved them in the past, but he didn't think he should bring that up.

"I need to get back to work," she said.

"Okay."

He started to open the door, and she added, "I hope this won't happen again."

He shook his head no. But it did.

Two days later, in retaliation for his attack on their friend Matt, a group of boys jumped him in the bathroom during lunch. It was four against one, but Jude had been fighting all his life and they weren't any better fighters than Matt. The two boys who tried to grab his arms found they could barely hold on, and they hadn't counted on the reach of his feet. The struggle lasted less than a minute. The two who were supposed to be doing the damage took off after Jude landed a few good kicks. Then one of the boys holding his arm escaped, but Jude didn't let the other go as easily. Jude didn't break his nose, but if anything, this boy looked worse—he ended up with a black eye and a split lip that bled all over his shirt.

This time Anna didn't come right away. Jude spent the afternoon in a chair outside the principal's office, across the hallway from a room full of secretaries. He was very aware of the fact that he had some blood from the kid's split lip on his white button-down shirt.

They wouldn't let him go home on the bus, and one of the secretaries had to stay late to wait for his mother to come pick him up. The woman packed her bag and put on her coat, so when his mother finally arrived, the woman was out the door before Anna finished apologizing. Then they were alone.

Jude started to say, "It wasn't my fault—"

"Not here," she snapped, but this time he didn't have to wait until they got home for her to speak. As soon as he shut the car door behind him, she said, "They're thinking of expelling you."

"Fine with me," he muttered.

"Fine with you? What, do you want to end up like your father? Is that what you want? Because that's right where you're headed."

She couldn't have known that she was touching on his greatest fear. He answered with fury. "I'm not like my father. I'm not a bit like him."

"Oh yeah? Two days ago you broke a boy's nose. Today the principal said that you bruised three boys and that a fourth was badly beaten on his face. That sounds just like Anthony to me."

"I was defending myself," he said. It had been a point of pride with him that he never made the first move.

"Fists aren't the answer. They're never the answer."

"If someone comes after me, I'm not going to just

stand there and take it. I did that for a long time," Jude shot back. "I'm never going to do that again."

Anna, who had an answer for everything, didn't seem to know what to say to that.

Strangely enough, it was Dolores who came up with the solution. Dolores said that her nephew had been in trouble in school, but he settled down when he started taking boxing lessons. The gym where the lessons were offered made it a requirement that the kids pledge not to fight outside of the ring. If they did, even once, they were out of the program. Dolores reported that they had great success with the rule.

Anna hated the idea, but she agreed to try it.

Jude went reluctantly, but he found that he liked it. It was the first thing he had found that he was really good at. He didn't think about what that might mean.

10

As MUCH AS his mother had disapproved of his fighting, Jude became a minor celebrity after his two victories. The fact that Jude had beaten up four kids at one time made for instant popularity. It seemed like suddenly everyone wanted to be his best friend. It should have been wonderful, but instead he discovered that you could be lonely even when you were surrounded by people.

Jude decided the feeling came from the fact that he was so different from most of the kids at Benton. As far as he could tell, ultimate tragedy for them was getting a B- on a test. They thought he was tough because he beat up a couple of kids. They lived less than ten miles from one of the most violent neighborhoods in the country, but it could have been ten thousand. It was so far out of their experience they couldn't even fathom it.

Out of all the boys in his grade the one Jude thought he would have the most in common with turned out to be the only one that kept his distance. His name was Nick, and Nick's pack was the cool crowd. They were the group that everyone wanted to join. Jude wasn't the only one who watched them from the corner of his eye as they laughed and smacked the table in the cafeteria with their palms, and he wasn't the only one who studied the way they draped them-selves over their desks in the classrooms, daring the teachers to tell them to sit up and pay attention. Everyone in the tenth grade watched Nick and his gang, and they knew it. They wore clothes like Jude's friends from Hartford High—loose, baggy pants and black ski caps. Sometimes one of the kids brought out a boom box and they played rap and hip-hop. They faked basketball moves in the hallway, though Jude never saw them go out to the court to throw up a ball.

Then one day Jude looked up from his lunch and Nick was standing there.

"Hey, you're Jude, right?"

"Yeah."

"I'm Nick."

"Yeah, I know," Jude said.

"Hey, I wanted to ask you something."

"Sure," Jude agreed.

"Not with these dweebs listening." Nick jerked his head toward Simon and his friends.

The kid next to Jude whispered, "Asshole," but not quite loud enough for Nick to hear. Nick turned and started walking away. He didn't even look over his shoulder to make sure that Jude was following. He led the way out of the cafeteria and into the bathroom, and checked the stalls to make sure they were empty before he spoke.

"Hey, I was thinking you might be able to help me and my buddies."

Jude leaned against one of the sinks. "Help you with what?"

"We want to pick up some weed. We thought you might be able to score some."

Jude could do it easily enough. He went back to the old neighborhood to play ball and hang with R. J. at least once a week. He would have gone more often if he could, but things were different now. The first time he returned to the old neighborhood, the guys stopped the game when they noticed him standing by the fence. The court emptied in seconds, and they were all around him, pounding him on the back, slapping his hand, bumping fists. R. J. shouldered his way through and tackled him in a bear hug. They all wanted to know about the good life. They thought Jude had it made, and they teased him about Benton and pretended to be scared of his mother. Then they returned to the court and played ball until it got dark, and afterward Jude and R. J. sat on the court, their backs against the chain-link fence, catching up.

It was a great day, but after all the guys had made such a big deal about his new life, Jude found he couldn't exactly go back every afternoon. It wouldn't look right. So Jude went back when he could, and he watched Nick's group from across the cafeteria. They were the ones Jude wanted to know, so of course they were the only ones who pretended to ignore him.

Until now.

"So you gonna help us out?"

Would it be such a big deal if he just took Nick over to the old neighborhood? He wouldn't actually be selling or anything. He could just take Nick there, as if for a game, and point him in the right direction. It seemed like such a little thing. On the other hand, there was his mother to think about.

It was a struggle, but finally Jude said, "I can't. Sorry."

"I thought you were in the game," Nick coaxed.

"Nope, sorry."

"Awright." Nick shrugged. "Well, catch you later."

"Yeah, later," Jude said, and watched Nick walk out of the bathroom. The door swung closed slowly behind him.

AT THE TIME things had been going well at home despite the fights at school. On the days Jude didn't have boxing or tutoring, the bus delivered him home at four. Dolores stayed until Anna came home around six or six thirty, and then Jude and his mother would sit and eat dinner together. Sometimes Harry would join them. After dinner Anna needed to work, but there was an extra table in her study, which she cleared off so Jude could do his homework. She had a small radio that she kept tuned to the classical station.

The homework assignments seemed practically

impossible to Jude, but he liked how it felt to be sitting there working next to his mother. It was as if he were playing at another life—almost as if he weren't the same person that had lived with his father for fifteen years. The boy who sat in the study hunched over schoolbooks couldn't possibly be the same one who had sat slumped on a succession of old ratty couches in front of the TV most nights, the books left unopened in a bag.

Then there was one night that Anna didn't get home until seven. A week later there was a night she didn't get home until eight. The week after that it was nearly nine three nights in a row. On those nights he ate dinner with Dolores, listening to the sound of her loud chewing, the scrape of her knife on the plate, the *tink* of the fork hitting her front teeth, and all the time she kept checking her watch and shaking her head.

Anna apologized when she got home. She told them about whatever crisis had arisen, trapping her in the office. Dolores listened to the nightly excuses in silence. At the end she'd give a little nod, pick up her purse, retrieve her coat from the closet, and bark good night at him. On the third night in a row that Jude's mother didn't get home until nine, Dolores didn't grab her coat and leave. Both she and Jude stood there in the kitchen watching Anna pick at her reheated dinner. Then Dolores said, "I know I said I'd stay with the boy, but I can't keep on with these kinds of hours."

Jude waited for Anna to appease her. He waited for her to say that it would get better—that she wouldn't always be this late, but she didn't. She said, "I know, Dolores."

"You should be at home with your son," Dolores said.

Jude was angry at his mother for not coming home, but he certainly didn't want Dolores criticizing her. He immediately rose to his mother's defense. "She couldn't help it. Besides, it's only a couple of hours after school, and I'm old enough to be on my own now."

Anna turned to him in relief. "Would you be okay with that?"

"Sure," Jude said. "Yeah."

"Great. That is such a help to me."

Jude felt a glow of pride. "No problem."

His mother turned back to Dolores. "You can go home at the normal time, Dolores. Jude will be okay on the days I'm a little late."

Dolores frowned, her lips pinching together in disapproval, but she didn't say anything.

When Jude got home the next afternoon, Dolores met him at the door and said, "I know your mother told me I should go home, but I think I will stay."

"I'm fine," he told her.

"Your mother should be here with you," Dolores said. "Not at the office till all hours."

"I'm okay, Dolores," he assured her. "Don't worry about me."

So she went, and Jude was left in the big, sprawling house by himself. That first week there was only one day that Anna managed to get home before seven, but she apologized and said that it was just a bad week and that it should get better. But if anything, the second week was worse. Her explanation that time was that autumn tended to be a very busy season. After that it happened so often she stopped giving excuses. The fact was that Anna had gotten swept up in her work again, and Jude spent the evenings alone, usually in front of the TV. The homework seemed too hard for him now. What was the point? Anna wasn't around to impress anyway.

Then one day, on a whim, Jude went up to Nick in the cafeteria. "I can help you with that thing," he said. He told himself that it wasn't like he was selling it or anything, and it would be only this once. What could it hurt?

Part II

11

"JUDE, MY MAN, you comin' or what?" Nick called out, slamming his locker closed.

Jude wanted to say, "No, I'm not coming." Even better, he'd like to punctuate the words with a fast sucker punch right to the head. After more than a year of being Nick's "homeboy" the role was getting a little old.

It had started with that first trip back to the old neighborhood with Nick to get him weed. Jude had arranged to meet R. J. and buy from his brother. They did the deal, and Jude got them both out of there as fast as possible. He could tell that R. J. didn't think much of Nick, but Nick hadn't noticed. He was excited by the trip and impressed by R. J. and his crack-smoking, dope-dealing brother. Nick kept saying, "This is some real street shit. This is off the top," and he wouldn't stop talking about it the next day in school. He kept telling the other kids, "It's all about the 'hood." And that Jude was his "hustler," his "connection." Whatever they wanted, Jude could get it for them.

Jude had tried to protest, to say that he didn't do anything but give him a tour, but Nick rolled his eyes and said, "The hell you say. You the man." In the end Jude let it slide. He had pinned his hopes for a real friendship on Nick and his buddies because they had seemed to be the most like his old friends. Now he couldn't imagine how he had been so stupid. Pretty soon he'd found out that all they ever did was get high and try to act like they were from the 'hood instead of what they were—rich white kids from the suburbs. He tried to remember the first time he had looked at Nick and thought, *What an asshole.* Maybe it was when Nick bought his first bag of heroin.

Jude had meant to take Nick back to the neighborhood to buy just that once, but that once had turned into once a month. The one time Nick had ventured there without Jude—taking one of the crew with him instead—they had come home with oregano instead of pot. After that Nick insisted that Jude come along. "You're my passport," he said. "I need you, man."

The ironic thing about it was that Jude felt less and less comfortable in his old neighborhood. His visits back to play ball petered out after about six months, when his old friends had, one by one, started dealing, or using, or both.

R. J. held out for a while, but finally he started dealing too; he told Jude that you couldn't stay in school just to get some shit minimum-wage job after graduating, when all the other idiots were out there bringing in a couple of thousand a week. Jude didn't say anything. What was there to say? But he felt sad, thinking how just over a year ago they had talked about how they weren't going to end up like all the other dumb suckers. They had vowed together that they were going to make it. Now Jude looked at R. J. and he felt guilt and relief in equal portions because he knew that he, too, probably would have ended up doing the exact same thing. If his father hadn't started skimming, if he hadn't died, if the detective hadn't turned the drawer over—the chain of events was such a thin barrier between R. J.'s life and his. He was the lucky one.

They were still friends on the surface, but now Jude couldn't mention failing the trig test, when R. J. was talking about a buddy who got gunned down in the street. He had tried to tell R. J. about his boxing, but his friend had laughed and said, "Yeah, see how far your fancy moves will get you when the other guy has a MAC-10."

R. J. didn't touch the stuff he sold—they had that much in common—so Jude could still pretend to be able to talk to him, but these days he only went back to take Nick, and recently he found himself looking over his shoulder when they walked the short distance from the car to the benches. He had changed in the last year, and he felt more comfortable at Benton than in his old haunts, but everyone in Nick's crew still treated him like he was from the 'hood. Maybe it was the boxing. To Nick and his friends the gym he went to had the air of the street. Maybe it was the fact that Jude failed half of his classes. That seemed to impress them, as if he failed because he didn't care. Maybe it was the fact that nothing ever seemed to bother him, because of that blank expression he had worked so hard to achieve. So when Nick called out, "Jude, my man, you comin' or what?" Jude tried to come up with an excuse.

"I got boxing today, man."

"Don't worry, I'll get you back in time for you to wipe out at least three guys," Nick promised.

They went in Nick's car. He pulled up along the curb just outside the projects where R. J. worked the benches. It had a small courtyard, bounded on three sides by low brick buildings. Trash lined the walls and piled up in drifts in the corners. There were some concrete tables with checkerboards carved into them and park benches lining the outskirts. These were mostly filled with teenagers and young men perched on the backs of the benches, like spectators at a match. It was considered a good spot because it wasn't easy for the cops to watch.

Nick peeled off to connect with one of R. J.'s boys, and Jude headed over to the benches opposite the entrance, where R. J. sat like a king on a throne. He clasped Jude by the hand and said, "My man."

"Hey, R. J. How's business?"

"Good. Pretty good. Hey, check this out," R. J. said. "I think I'm gonna get me a Mercedes. It's used, but it looks mint. I need better wheels, especially as now I might have to make some trips over to your side of town."

"Oh yeah?" Jude said. "You gonna come over for dinner?"

R. J. broke up laughing. "Oh yeah. Shit, me and your mom would sure have a lot to talk about. Nah, man. I was thinking of setting up a pipeline right into that ritzy school of yours. Those kids got money to burn, and they won't know the difference between good stuff and shit that's been stepped on so bad there's barely anything left but filler. I was telling my boss that it's a sure moneymaker. They'll be able to buy in the comfort of their own fucking homeroom. It's gonna be serious cash, you sure you don't want in?"

"Thanks, but I can't. You know."

"What's the problem? The cops ain't gonna touch your ass."

"Sorry, man."

"You pussy," R. J. said, and he was only half joking.

Just then Nick joined them. "Hey, R. J."

R. J. just nodded at him.

"You ready?" Jude said, turning to go, but R. J. stopped him with a question.

"What about this punk? Could he handle the business? Could he handle being a runner?"

"I can handle anything you got," Nick answered for himself.

"I sincerely doubt that," R. J. said. "Jude, what do you think?"

"I guess. Yeah, he probably could."

"I'll have to talk to the boss about it," R. J. said. "I'll get back to you."

Jude and Nick headed back to the car. On the way they passed a beat-up van that hadn't been there on the way in. Jude averted his eyes. He knew that the two men sitting in the front seat were undercover cops. And he knew that as surely as he had recognized them, they had recognized him as well.

12

JUDE KEPT HIS gloves high, protecting his face. His opponent circled, bouncing on his toes, ducking and weaving like an idiot. Jude knew if he waited and threw a few jabs to keep the kid moving, pretty soon his opponent would tire himself out and it would be quick work to finish him off, but Jude didn't want to wait.

It drove the coaches crazy. They told him that he could be great if he just used his head. They told him he was a natural. They told him he might have a career if he wanted one. He liked to hear it, but he still didn't take their advice. Instead of waiting, Jude threw a wild, desperate roundhouse. He *wanted* the kid to come inside. He *wanted* the kid to land one, but Jude's glove connected. He knew what it felt like when the ground seemed to tilt under your feet and the mat rushed up to meet you. The kid dropped like a stone, his shoulder and head smacking the canvas.

When Jude got back to the house, it was dark and quiet. He flipped on the hall light and called out, "I'm home." He often did that, though he wasn't exactly sure why—he knew there wasn't anybody there. There never was these days.

Jude dropped his bag by the stairs in the hallway and wandered into the kitchen. He opened the fridge—as usual, there were two plates on the shelf, covered with tinfoil. Dolores fixed them and left them in the fridge during the day. One for him, the other for Anna.

He picked one up and peeled off the foil. Just his luck—it was the one meal Dolores made that he couldn't stand. Liver. He could have told her he didn't like it, and she probably would never have made it again, but he didn't have the heart to hurt her feelings. So Jude scraped it off into the garbage, retrieved a frozen pizza from the freezer, peeled off the wrapping, and put it in the oven.

He was eating the last quarter off the shiny metallic cardboard when he heard Anna's key in the front lock. She must have tried to add the day's mail to the huge pile on the table next to the door, because he heard a slithering crash and Anna's "Shit." It happened every few weeks. The mail piled up until the stack grew too high and toppled. Only then did she reluctantly gather it up and wade through it.

In a minute Anna appeared at the doorway to the kitchen, her briefcase tucked under one arm, another bag slung over her shoulder, and the pile of mail untidily gathered in her hands. She dumped it on the kitchen table, let her briefcase and the other bag fall to the floor, and sank into one of the chairs.

Jude watched her from his perch on a stool at the counter.

She looked up at him, then at the remains of the

pizza in front of him. "Don't tell me," she said. "Dolores made liver, right?"

She was joking, which meant she was in a good mood. Jude nodded.

"Any more of that in the freezer?" She gestured toward the empty pizza box.

"I don't think so."

"Well, I'm not that hungry anyway." She stood and went to the cabinets, retrieved a wineglass, and opened the fridge. She pulled out a bottle of white wine and uncorked it, pouring almost to the rim. She brought both the glass and the bottle back to the kitchen table and started opening the mail. Most of it was junk, which she dropped on the floor next to her chair.

"So how was your day?" she asked him.

"Fine."

"Any tests this week?"

"Three."

"And?"

He shook his head, and her good mood evaporated. "Oh, Jude."

He hated when she said his name like that. He could feel his shoulders tightening just like they did right before he threw a punch.

He put down the last piece of pizza. He didn't want it anymore. The argument they were having now was an old one—the same one, in fact, over and over.

"Did you go to the gym again today?" she demanded.

He didn't answer because she already knew.

"If you spend all your time there and you don't even pick up a book, how do you expect to pass anything? You've got to work for what you want. If you'd only put some effort in . . . you know, if you don't straighten up your act, I'm going to have to put a stop to your boxing."

He kept his eyes on the half-eaten, congealed remains of the pizza. She could threaten all she wanted, but she wouldn't do it.

"I'm serious about this. You're a junior now, and you don't have much more time to mess around."

He could predict these fights so well now. Recently he'd given up on his part, but Anna still rolled through her lines with gusto. He supposed that there was something admirable in this. He thought it was almost like reading a tragedy over and over in the hopes that one of these times you'd somehow get a happy ending.

"I hoped for better from——"

"Hello? Anybody home?" Harry shouted from the hallway.

She stopped in mid sentence, looking sheepish. Then she said, "Oh. I meant to tell you. I asked Harry to come over." And Harry swept into the kitchen carrying a bottle of champagne in one hand and his hat in the other. He hadn't even bothered to take off his coat.

"Congratulations," Harry said, handing over the bottle with a flourish and giving her a big, smacking kiss. "Shall I open it, or do you want to do the honors?"

"But I just opened a bottle of wine," she protested.

"It's a champagne night." He picked up the wine bottle, recorked it, and started working on the champagne. "So, what do you think about it?" he asked Jude.

"About what?"

"About the big news, of course."

Jude looked at Anna.

"I didn't get a chance to tell him yet," she said.

"Well, what are you waiting for?" Harry prodded. "Tell him the good news."

"We won the *People v. Reznik* case today," she said.

People v. Reznik was the biggest case to hit the city in ten years. Martin Reznik was a junkie who, in the middle of a robbery, had shot a policeman through the heart. The officer—a man with a wife and a three-year-old son—had died at the scene.

Anna had taken a big risk in deciding to prosecute the case herself. The tricky part was that it wasn't enough for the jury simply to convict him—anything less than the death penalty would be considered a failure. The last death penalty sentence in the state of Connecticut had been handed down in 1976—more than two decades ago.

For the last three months she had been working even

later than usual. Ten P.M. was an early night. One or two A.M. was more normal. Jude realized that he should have known that something was up. It wasn't even eight.

"They convicted him?" Jude said.

"And we got the death penalty," she added.

"And that's with seven women on the jury," Harry said. "It's all over the news. Have you seen?"

"We were watching it at the office," Anna said.

"Champagne because someone got the death penalty?" Jude asked.

"No, the champagne isn't for that," Harry said. "It's . . . no, you tell him, Anna."

"All right. Well, it's something I've been thinking about doing for a long time, and I decided that if I got the conviction on this case, I would go ahead with it." She paused, smiled. "I'm going to run for mayor of West Hartford in the next election."

"Isn't that great?" Harry said, peeling the foil off the neck of the bottle.

Jude just stared at her.

"It's goddamned exciting," Harry continued. "Now, wouldn't you say that deserved some champagne?"

Harry worked the cork, rocking it back and forth in the neck till it gave with a *pop*.

"Anna, if you do the honors, I'll get the glasses. I think this is a special occasion and that Jude should join us," he said, lining up three glasses on the counter. "How old is he now, anyway?"

"He's fifteen."

Jude looked up sharply. He had turned sixteen several months earlier. One glance at Harry showed that he was aware of the slip before Anna caught it.

Jude stood up abruptly and left the kitchen. On his way out he could hear Anna saying, "What? What did I say?"

ANNA FOUND HIM in the basement punching the practice bag he had hung there. She carried two champagne glasses down the stairs and sat on the bottom step. She put one of the glasses on the step beside her and sipped from the other, watching him go through the motions of an uppercut, teaching his muscles to move in just the right way so when he sped up, they would retain the correct form.

"You forgot your champagne," she said.

He didn't respond, concentrating fiercely on the bag in front of him.

"Jude, I know you're sixteen."

He hit the bag.

"I know you're sixteen," she repeated. "I just forgot for a second. For God's sake, I forget how old I am every time my birthday rolls around."

He slammed the bag harder.

"So don't you want your champagne?"

Out of the corner of his eye he could see her sitting motionless on the steps, but he couldn't make out the expression on her face.

"I can't do this, Jude. I can't make up for the past, so it's useless to keep on trying," she said.

That stopped him. "Keep on trying?" he said. "Since when did you start?"

"Now, that's not fair."

"Maybe not, but it's true," he said.

"If only you'd stop for a second and put yourself in my shoes, you'd realize that this past year has been hard on me. And maybe I'm doing the best I can. You should think about that and try to be a little more understanding."

"You mean like how you are with my grades?" he said. "Understanding? Supportive?" He didn't even bother to ask her how her year could have been harder than his, and why she didn't try putting herself in *his* place.

"Well, if I expect a bit more from you, it's because you're young."

"That is such bullshit," Jude said.

"I thought—well, I hoped—that you'd be happy for me."

She waited for his response.

He struggled with the desire to please her, but he managed to stifle it. Instead he said, "You might have asked me."

"Asked you?" Anna was surprised.

"You wouldn't have done it without asking what Harry thought, would you?"

"That's completely different," she said. "I asked

Harry for his professional opinion. I'm going up against the incumbent, and he'll be tough to beat." She looked at him and sighed. "Okay. Jude, what do you think about me running for mayor?"

"I think it stinks," he replied promptly.

She dropped her hands. "This is going to be a really tough time. I hoped that you would help me through it, but that's okay." Then she started to push herself up off the bottom step.

"Why?" He stopped her with his words. "At least tell me why."

She sank back down on the step. "Why am I going to run for mayor?"

She repeated the question gravely, as if really considering her answer, and when she gave it to him, it had the ring of truth and the weight of a confession.

"Is there anything you're afraid of?" she asked him. "I mean something that keeps you up at night?"

"Yeah," he admitted.

"What is it?"

He hesitated. He couldn't tell her that he was afraid that he would always be a disappointment to her. Instead he said the closest thing to the truth. "That I'll never do anything great."

"Then you should understand why I want this so much. You know what keeps me up at night? I worry that I don't have what it takes. I want this more than I've ever wanted anything. If I got this, it would make up for . . . all the other things that haven't gone right in my life. It would feel as if there was a reason for them. And right now, having won this latest case, I probably have about the best chance I'm ever going to have. It's an outside chance, but it's a chance, and I have to take it. It's now or never, and I can't face the idea that it might be never. I've come too far and worked too hard for it to end here."

"Ask me again," he said.

"What?"

"Ask me again what I think," he repeated.

She started to smile. "Jude, what do you think about me running for mayor?"

"I think you're a shoo-in," he said.

They grinned at each other.

She picked up his champagne glass and held it out to him. "Let's drink to that."

13

WHEN ANNA ANNOUNCED her intention to run for mayor, the press attention reminded Jude of when he first came to live with his mother and of the media blitz that followed. It seemed so long ago now. Only a little more than a year. Only a lifetime.

Jude knew this move would ultimately take Anna even further away from him, but she wanted it, so Jude was determined to do his best. He might not actually be able to help her, but at least he could make an effort not to hinder her.

With that in mind Jude resolved not to take Nick to the projects to buy. This time he'd stand up to him and just say no. He waited for Nick to ask, but it turned out that he didn't have to worry. R. J. was as good as his word, and he set up a pipeline straight into Benton's hallowed halls—and it was Nick who agreed to play the middleman.

In a certain respect Nick had always played the middleman—when Jude had taken him to buy, he'd brought back a supply for everyone. But Nick was smart. He didn't want to buy too much at one time, and he didn't want to be seen going to Jude's old neighborhood too often, so their access had been restricted. Suddenly Nick's crew had access to as much as they wanted, and where they had once kept it to weekends and the occasional after-school high, now they started snorting in the bathroom before lunch, after gym, between classes. They were high all the time.

Jude saw it, noticed the signs, and he used it as a way to distance himself. It was almost a relief to be alone again. It made it easier to deal with what was going on at home.

The media splash was big after Anna announced, and the reporters dug up all the old stories—the trial, the kidnapping, Jude's return. The difference was that now it was just background; the real news was Anna's work. Instead of camping out on the lawn, the reporters hovered around her office and the courthouse, speaking to her employees, to her detractors, to everyone who might have an opinion. Everyone except Jude.

He had been dreading the attention, but now that it hadn't materialized, instead of being relieved, he felt curiously forlorn. He found himself skimming every article for a mention of himself or his father. It came up less and less.

The topic of choice was debating how the race would shape up. Mayor Deberry was an old, grizzled veteran who talked like a mob boss and had fought his way into the office by tooth and nail. He played to win and wasn't squeamish about fighting dirty if he had to. The last two elections had ended up deep in political mudslinging.

Local news was slow, so the papers filled the space with speculation about the upcoming election. There were a couple of skirmishes between Anna and the mayor, played out in the pages of the *Hartford Courant,* but they were on topics like taxes and education. For two months the candidates stuck closely to the safe, uncontroversial political issues. The articles observed that Anna was playing it very straight, and reported that the incumbent's staff had advised him to go along with it. If she kept purely to issues, his incumbency would carry the day by a comfortable margin. The papers started predicting a tame election race in the upcoming year.

As with so many predictions, it was wrong.

A COUPLE OF MONTHS later, just after the spring break, Jude was on his way back from lunch when he rounded a corner and hit a crowd of kids milling around the hallway. There were several teachers trying to corral the students into classrooms, but every time the teachers turned their backs, the kids slipped right back out of the rooms they had been ushered into. The first lunch period had just ended, and more students were arriving by the minute on their way from the cafeteria to their classes.

Curious to see what was stopping everyone, Jude shouldered his way through the crowd until he could see a row of desks that had been pulled from a nearby room to form a barrier across the corridor. There was a policeman standing on the other side.

"Back into your classrooms, now," the officer was saying, though without appreciable effect. The students near the desks weren't budging. Jude pushed his way closer until he could see down the hallway to where another cop was unrolling crime scene tape. He was cordoning off the boys' bathroom. There were other policemen in the hallway tending to a group of students. Jude recognized Toby, one of Nick's closest friends. Toby was trying to shield his face, though by the shaking of his shoulders it was obvious that he was crying. There was a cop bent over him with a comforting hand on his back. A few steps away there was Brian, another member of the crew, not crying but looking white and shaken.

"Does anybody know what happened?" Jude asked.

One boy looked around. He was in Jude's class, and he had once asked Jude if he could interview him for the school newspaper. Jude thought his name was David or Davis or something.

"It's your friend Nick."

"What about Nick?" Jude asked, his stomach flip-flopping.

"Well, they're saying that he's dead." The kid could hardly keep a straight face as he said it, the statement was so outrageous.

"Dead?" Jude repeated.

"Yeah," the kid confirmed. "They say he just fell over and started spazzing out. Like he had a fit or something. Isn't that wack?" he said, trying to elicit some sort of reaction from Jude.

But Jude simply turned and started to fight his way back through the crowd. The word was traveling quickly, and there was a relentless pressing toward the barrier of desks. The teachers were shouting for the students to turn around and go back to the cafeteria, but everyone except Jude seemed to be going in the opposite direction. The corridor was filled with the noise of hundreds of students talking excitedly, spreading the news. The roar of all those voices bouncing off the hard, slick walls came crashing down on him like a waterfall. Jude started using his elbows to get away from the crushing mass of bodies. Some of the kids got an elbow in the ribs and turned to confront him, but when they saw who it was, they thought better of it.

Jude escaped the throng and slipped into a classroom. There were only a few students inside, mainly grouped around the door. Once he got past them, he was able to sink into a desk in the back corner of the room. He put his head down on his arms and closed his eyes. He heard someone say, "Look at Jude. A kid's dead, and he's taking a nap."

But he wasn't sleeping. He was thinking of what would happen when his mother found out. There was no way his name wouldn't come up. She'd never forgive him.

14

JUDE REMAINED IN the classroom until teachers came through and herded the students into the auditorium. The principal made a brief announcement that there had been an "accident" and they would be sending the students home early.

Jude got off the school bus at his stop. Then he walked a block to the public bus stop and caught the next one headed downtown. From there he used a pay phone on the corner to call R. J.'s beeper. He had to beep him five times before R. J. called him back.

Jude picked up the pay phone after barely one ring.

"Who the hell is this?" R. J. said.

"It's Jude," he whispered.

"Why you whispering, man?"

Jude didn't know. When he spoke next, it was in a normal tone. "R. J., I think Nick overdosed at school today."

"Aw, shit," R. J. said. "Shit. I knew it."

"Knew what?"

"I thought I might have given him the wrong stuff. Some of the junkies came to me complaining that my product was crap and didn't have no heroin in it. I musta given Nick the street cut."

"How much did you usually mix the stuff you sold him?" Jude asked.

"I stepped on it till there wasn't barely nothin' left in there. I just told him to snort, like, triple the dosage, and even then it barely gave them a buzz."

"And how pure was the street stuff?"

"I sell good shit. It's the purest you can get."

"And Nick snorted at least three times the regular dosage."

"Damn," R. J. said. "He gonna be all right?"

"R. J., he's dead," Jude told him. "And I don't know if he told any of his friends who was supplying him."

"I told him he better keep his big mouth shut."

"Yeah, well, I don't know what he said or didn't say. I just wanted to give you the heads-up. You might want to lie low for the next few days."

"Are you kidding me? I'll be going on a little vacation tonight, I think."

"I don't know if you need to leave town," Jude said dubiously.

"He was a rich white boy, right? No offense, but he wasn't one of the scholarship students or nothing, right?"

"Yeah, right," Jude said.

"Then I'm outta here. The shit is gonna hit the fan with this one."

Later Jude wondered how R. J. knew, and he didn't.

"I owe you big-time, man," R. J. said. "I'd better get moving. Catch you later."

"Yeah. Later." Jude hung up the phone and walked back over to the bus stop.

It was still only two when Jude got back to the house, and Dolores was vacuuming in the living room when he came through the front door. She saw him pass by on his way to the stairs, and she switched off the machine.

"What, did you get tired of school? Decide you had enough?" she called out.

Jude just kept going, and after a moment the vacuum started up again.

He realized that he had left his book bag at school, so he couldn't do any work even if he wanted to. He thought about going to the boxing gym, but somehow that didn't feel right. So he lay down on his bed, and the next thing he knew, he opened his eyes and it was dark outside. He must have been asleep for hours.

"Jude," a voice said. He blinked and lifted his head. The light from the hallway silhouetted Anna's figure in the doorway.

"What time is it?" he said groggily.

"It's late. It's past midnight," she said.

He rubbed his eyes and sat up on the edge of the bed.

"You still have your sneakers on," Anna observed.

He rubbed his face. "Yeah. I don't know, I just fell asleep."

"Well, no wonder. You must be . . . I can't imagine what today must have been like for you."

"What?"

"With what happened." She stepped into the room, and she must have caught his puzzled expression by the light from the hallway. She snapped on the desk lamp. "With Nick Hackley. He was in your class. Was he a friend of yours?"

"How do you know about what happened?" he asked, his mind still slow with sleep.

"I'm the DA, remember?" she said.

"But you don't usually hear about these things this fast, do you?"

"This isn't a usual case." She sat down in the desk chair next to the bed. "We're going to be working closely with the police on this one to make sure that everything's done right."

"I guess," he said, uneasiness blooming in his gut. "I've been talking to reporters for hours now."

"Reporters?" he repeated.

"It's a big story, and the reporters want to talk to me because I've been vocal about the drug policy. These drugs are destroying lives. How are we—" She stopped abruptly, made a small gesture of apology. "I'm sorry. I don't want to lecture. I really just wanted to come in and see how you were." She put a hand on his arm.

"How I am?" he echoed.

"They're organizing a talk tomorrow at your school to help everyone deal with what happened, and afterward you'll break up into discussion groups, but we're also encouraging parents to talk to their kids. I wanted to make sure we talked."

This would have been the moment to confess to her. He knew he should tell her everything, but the light, comforting hand on his arm stopped him. He couldn't bear the image of her snatching it back as if she couldn't stand to touch him. So he said, "I'm okay."

"You sound upset. You sure you don't want to talk about anything?"

"I'm fine," he repeated.

"Okay." She stood up but didn't make a move to leave. "Jude . . ."

He thought it was all up then. He thought she was going to ask him if he had something to do with it, and he resolved that if she asked, he would tell her. She didn't. She said instead, "I hope . . . I mean, you wouldn't do drugs, would you?"

"No," he said.

She smiled in relief. "I didn't think so. I was pretty sure that you wouldn't have anything to do with them, but I wanted to make sure."

It was worse than he could ever have imagined.

THERE WAS AN assembly the first thing the next morning. First the principal got up and explained what had occurred—as if there were a student in that auditorium who didn't know. Then a doctor spoke to them about the physical dangers of drugs. He was followed by a volunteer who worked in a clinic for addicts and talked about what drugs did not just to your body, but to your life. They capped everything off with a speech from a counselor about expressing grief, and they assigned the students to discussion groups to talk out their feelings.

In the afternoon the students were sent back to class, but the discussions continued. Each teacher felt a need to address it—none felt comfortable diving back into trigonometry or the history of the Reformation after the morning's activities.

What Jude found most interesting were the questions. The most frequently asked was "Why?" In Jude's opinion, it was a stupid question without an answer, but the teachers gamely tried to answer it anyway. "Bad things sometimes happen to good people." "God's will." And Jude's favorite: "Sometimes it's hard to see all the reasons at first, but as time passes you will come to understand why it happened." That just meant that as time went on people would come up with justifications. In his old neighborhood they answered the question truthfully. There they just shrugged and said, "Shit happens."

The second most popular question was "Who is responsible?" It seemed to Jude that since Nick was the one who had snorted the heroin, he was responsible, but as the day progressed Jude realized that there had to be a scapegoat, and it couldn't be Nick. He was already dead, so there would be no one to punish and no one to blame.

As time passed, it was this second question that

turned out to be the most pressing. The papers chewed it over daily, and the police were working overtime. They were concentrating their efforts on trying to discover where Nick had gotten the drugs. Jude heard the updates from Anna—that is, on the days she got home before he went to bed.

Jude kept waiting for his name to come up. Every night he waited for Anna to say something when she reported the day's frustrations. He was sure she would hear it from someone. With a case this big everything was certain to come out eventually.

15

JUDE AND ANNA WERE just sitting down to breakfast
Friday morning when Harry stormed in. They heard
his car screech to a stop outside, heard the front door
slam, heard his footsteps almost running along the
hallway. When he appeared in the doorway, his face
was red and he was out of breath.

"Have you read this morning's paper?" he demanded.

"We just sat down to breakfast," she replied. "I
was about to—"

"Well, read this!" and he slapped the front page
down on the table in front of her.

"It can't be *that* bad," she said.

"You tell me. Because I don't know what the hell
to think." He was pacing the kitchen, and he hadn't
even so much as glanced at Jude.

Anna frowned. "Jude, get Harry some coffee, will
you?" she said, and picked up the paper.

Jude wanted to read the article, but he got up,
filled a mug with coffee, milk, and sugar, and handed
it to Harry. He quietly retreated to the back of the
kitchen to get out of the line of fire.

"The son of a bitch," Anna said. "That political,
backstabbing liar."

Then Jude knew it must be something to do with
the mayor.

Right after the death of the student the mayor's office had come out with a rare show of support for the DA's office in general, and for Anna in particular. She mentioned to Jude that she was surprised and gratified that the incumbent had risen above his politics and had gotten behind the cause. Harry was there at the time, and he said that it was a brilliant strategic move. The mayor wasn't going to benefit from going up against Anna and her popular, tough-on-drugs policy. The man knew the public didn't want to see the mayor and the DA jockeying for polling points when they should be working together on what was obviously a threat to the city's youth.

But even Harry didn't foresee the possibilities of the mayor's position. When a week had passed and there still hadn't been any significant headway in tracking down the dealer who was responsible, the mayor was able to begin expressing concern about the way the case was being handled. It began with just a quote here and there, but it escalated every day that went by without an arrest.

The mayor's campaign had begun the past Monday, exactly a week since the accident. By Thursday he was hinting that maybe the DA wasn't as tough on crime as she claimed. Today—Friday—he dropped the bomb.

As Harry and Anna talked, Jude gleaned the contents of the article, and he understood the reason for Harry's panic. The opening punch was a knockout. It said that undisclosed sources hinted that the lack of progress in the investigation wasn't the fault of the police, but that it stemmed from impropriety on behalf of the DA's office.

He knew what they must be referring to, and he couldn't believe he hadn't thought of it. He had assumed that eventually someone would tell Anna. He hadn't considered that the mayor's office might get the information first. His brain froze. He couldn't think.

"What the hell is all this about?" Anna demanded.

"I was hoping you could tell me," Harry said.

"You think I've got something to hide?" Now Anna's neck flushed up to her jaw. "You believe this crap?" and she threw the paper at him. It fluttered to the floor between them.

Harry immediately softened. "Of course not," he said. "I know you would never do anything, but I thought that someone on your staff . . ."

"And that I knew about it and covered it up?"

"No," Harry said. "You're right, of course, but there has to be something. I can't believe that even Deberry would have the nerve to just make it up."

"And that's what everybody in the city is going to think too," Anna said. "Hell, you did. If you believe it, what chance do I have?" She stooped to pick up the paper and refolded it neatly, but the headline was still visible. She stared at it a moment, then reached out and folded it once more, corner to corner, as if in defeat.

"Don't worry, we're not beaten yet," Harry urged, finding a little confidence now that Anna had apparently lost hers. "I know some people in their camp that owe me a few favors. I'll get to the bottom of this," he promised.

Jude watched from the back of the kitchen, gripping the counter behind him as if he needed it to keep from falling. He meant to speak. He meant to open his mouth and confess everything, but he hesitated. His courage failed him, and then Anna was up and gathering her things, and Harry was talking again, and they were gone. Gone, along with his last chance to confess. Now he was just waiting to be found out.

He didn't have to wait long.

IT WAS SUNDAY afternoon. Anna was at the office—where she spent most of her weekends now. Jude was in the study with the curtains drawn. The sun seeped into the room around the edges of the window, outlining it in light. The TV was on but muted, and Jude was dozing on the couch, a stack of schoolbooks unopened on the floor beside him.

The soft *click* of the door woke him. When he opened his eyes, he saw Harry standing there. "It's you," Harry said softly.

Jude quickly sat up, but he didn't reply; he knew what Harry was referring to.

Harry crossed the room and took a seat near the

couch. There was a long, heavy silence, then Harry spoke again.

"I have to admit I underestimated you, Jude. You had me fooled. I didn't realize how much you hated her. Have you been planning it for a long time? I'm just curious."

Harry was so calm. Jude had not expected him to be this calm. Jude felt anything but calm.

"No, I swear, you've got it all wrong," Jude protested. "All I did was take this one kid from my school to my old neighborhood."

"Took him to your old neighborhood to buy drugs," Harry completed the sentence. "You knew about Anna's drug policy. You knew that if it ever got out that her son was dealing, she would be ruined. So what exactly did you think you were doing? Helping?"

"No . . . I mean . . ."

Harry waited a moment, but Jude couldn't think what to say.

"You know, I've always stood up for you, Jude. When you got in those fights, I took your side and told her that it was the way you grew up and it wasn't your fault. Then when your mother got frustrated with your grades and your attitude, I told her that you were trying your best. But this time . . ."

"Wait, Harry, let me explain. I didn't sell them the drugs," he said in a rush. "I didn't mean to hurt her. Nick came and asked me to take him where he could get some, and I swear it was going to be just that once. I thought it couldn't hurt if I took him once, but then he kept asking me, and he was my friend . . . but when I found out she was running for mayor, I stopped. That's when Nick started dealing himself. I didn't have anything to do with it. I know I shouldn't have taken him back there, but I never sold him anything. You've got to believe me."

Harry listened in silence. When Jude finished, he said, "It doesn't much matter if I believe you or not. It doesn't matter that you didn't actually sell it—if that's the truth. The real issue is what the public will think when they find out that you were the one who made it possible for Nick to get his first hit. The mayor's people are still gathering their facts. My friend tells me that it'll be a few more days before they have enough legal proof to go ahead with the story, but then they're going to spring the whole thing. Apparently the cops have seen you going to a known drug location a number of times."

"But Anna never knew about that," Jude said.

"It doesn't matter. The fact is, the police never reported you because you're the DA's son. Even if people believe that Anna didn't know, what does that say? Her own son is helping his friends to buy drugs, and the biggest plank on her platform is her antidrug stance. How does that make her look? Like a good candidate for mayor? Like someone who's going to be able to run an entire city?"

"I didn't mean it. I'm sorry."

"It's too late for sorry. You should have thought of that a long time ago. Or at the very least, you could have said something right after it happened. Then maybe I could have done some damage control. Now I can't think how it could be worse. I'm going to have to advise her not even to bother filing for candidacy. Truthfully, I don't think she'll be able to hold on to the DA's position either."

"Harry, tell me what to do. I'll do anything. I swear. I'll tell you who sold the drugs to Nick. It was an old friend of mine, and he left town, but you could probably find him."

"We could have used that a week ago, but it's too late for that now."

Jude should have been relieved that he wouldn't have to betray R. J., but he wasn't.

"Then what can I do? There's got to be something," he insisted.

Harry shook his head.

"Anything."

Harry paused for a moment. "Well . . ."

Hope sprang up. "Tell me," Jude pleaded.

"I don't think that you'd be able to do it."

"I could," he said eagerly. "I swear. Anything."

Harry uncrossed his legs now, planted his elbows on his knees. "You'd have to let Anna discover that you were the one who sold Nick the drugs."

"What? But I didn't."

"It doesn't matter whether you did or not. The point is you make her think you did, and not only that, but let her discover that you're still selling."

"You're kidding, right?"

Harry leaned back in his chair. "You wanted to know what you could do. Well, that's what you could do. That's the only way. I didn't think you'd have the guts."

"Wait, I didn't say I wouldn't do it. What happens when I make her think that I'm selling?"

"She sets you up for a sting, and you let her do it."

"Then what? I go to jail or something?"

Jude was joking, but Harry said, "That's the idea, but you're only sixteen. It would be juvenile detention."

"But how would it help?"

"First of all, the mayor's people won't take it to the press if there's an investigation in progress. Then they won't be able to claim that the DA isn't pursuing it."

"So why can't you just have an investigation and have them discover that I didn't do anything wrong?" Jude said.

"I already explained why that wouldn't work. You took your friends back to buy drugs. You might not have actually sold to them, but that won't make a difference. Anna's run for mayor will be over. But if you let her discover that you're involved and she turns you in, then there's no way that the mayor would be able to make her look too weak for the job. If the press is handled correctly, it will show how far she is prepared to go to make West Hartford safe from drugs."

"Have you already talked to Anna about this?" Jude asked uneasily.

"Absolutely not. Anna doesn't know anything about it. She *can't* know anything about it. For this to work she has to think it's real."

"You mean that she'll really think . . ."

"That you're dealing. Yes, for a while she would have to think that."

"That's worse. That would be like everything you said before was true. For me to be dealing, and to keep on doing it even after Nick . . . How can I let her think I'd do that?"

"Like I said, it's going to take some guts."

"I don't know," Jude said. "Isn't there anything else, Harry?"

"Nothing. A week ago, maybe. Now there's nothing else. Don't think about what she's going to feel when she finds out you're dealing. Not only will you fix the situation, the coverage on this could get her elected, and it would be because of you. Think of that."

Jude thought of it. Hadn't she said that she wanted to be mayor more than anything? He could give her that. Then she'd have a reason to say, "Thank God those detectives found that envelope. I don't know what I would have done without you, Jude."

Then something else occurred to him. "Wait, how long would I have to spend in juvie?"

"Only until after the election," Harry said. "A month or two at most. Then we'll get you a new trial, and with the real evidence you'll be acquitted."

Jude returned to the issue that bothered him even more than the time in juvie. "Can't we let Anna in on it from the beginning?" he asked again.

Harry shook his head decisively. "No way. She'd never go for it. Plus she's a terrible liar. She has to believe it. I'm not going to sit here and tell you it's going to be easy. I'll do my best to make sure that you don't see her much, but I can promise you that there will be times you'll want to tell her everything, and you won't be able to. You need to look beyond that."

Jude thought about what it would be like when she found out the truth. He would just have to keep thinking about that moment. That would make it all worth it. "Okay," he said. "I'll do it."

16

JUDE SAT AT the desk in his room staring at the web of budding branches outside his window—waiting. The air was so still that he could have been looking at a picture instead of a window. He checked his watch, though he knew the time wouldn't tell him anything. Harry hadn't said when the phone call would come. Just that it would be tonight.

Through the branches Jude could see patches of gray sky. In the afternoon his room usually got a ray or two of light from the sun before it disappeared, but today was overcast, and the light faded almost imperceptibly until he realized that he was sitting there in the dark. Jude switched on the light. Harry had said that everything needed to look right—and a dark house wouldn't look right.

The light changed the room, and it suddenly seemed impossible to continue to sit there doing nothing. Jude opened the backpack at his feet, fished out his math book and a pad of paper, and was just opening the book when the phone rang.

Even though he had been expecting it, he jumped at the sound. Jude stood up quickly, almost knocking over the chair.

Jude reached the phone just as the first ring died away, but he waited. It was crucial to the plan that the answering machine picked up before he did. Then the whole conversation would be audible through the speaker, and if Harry got the timing right, that's just when Anna would be coming in through the door.

It rang a second time. He heard the machine downstairs click on and Anna's voice saying, "You've reached . . ." He lifted the receiver to his ear.

"Hello?" He heard a voice say something, but he couldn't make it out over Anna's voice saying, "We're not home right now. . . ."

"Hold on," Jude said, "the machine's going."

He waited for the message to finish. Anna's voice said, "Please leave a message after the beep."

"Hello?" Jude said, and he could hear his voice, picked up by the machine, echoing through the downstairs. He thought he also heard the sound of a key in the lock.

"Jude?" It *sounded* like a boy's voice. Harry hadn't told him who it would be. He had just instructed Jude to act like he knew the kid.

"Yeah."

"It's me. Listen, I'm calling because I need some smack."

"I thought I told you not to call me here," Jude said.

"Yeah, I know, but I'm having a party this weekend."

"What are you trying to do, get me put away?"

"I know, I know, but I figured your mom wouldn't

be home yet. I wouldn't have called, but it's an emergency."

"I told you I'm holding off for a while until everything calms down."

"But that was, like, two weeks ago," the voice wheedled. "And I've got a bunch of friends that want some too, so it would be a big purchase. We'd make it worth it for you, I promise."

No matter how he strained his ears, Jude could hear nothing from downstairs. Not a sound.

"How much would you want?" he asked.

"We'd buy an eight ball."

"That much? You know if you OD on this shit too, I'll kill you," Jude said.

"Nothing like that's gonna happen. I swear."

Jude gave in, as scripted. "All right. You're so pathetic, I'll do it."

"Thanks. Thanks, man."

"But not at school. I'll meet you in the park. I'll be at the statue near the northwest entrance."

"Could we do it tomorrow?"

"The day after," Jude said. "At twelve."

"Great. Thanks again."

"Whatever. See you Wednesday."

"Yeah, Wednesday. I swear I won't forget this."

Jude hung up. As he took his hand away from the receiver, he found that it was shaking. Heading slowly for the stairs, he thought he heard the sound of the front door closing. When he reached the hallway, he couldn't help it. He looked through the front window just in time to see a car—Harry's car—disappearing around the corner. That's how Harry had managed the timing; he'd been the one to drive her.

Jude turned away from the window and crossed to the answering machine and deleted the message.

PER HARRY'S INSTRUCTIONS Jude followed his regular routine that night. He forced himself to eat at least part of the dinner Dolores had left for him. Then he sat in front of the TV until eleven. From nine o'clock on he couldn't have said what he watched. He was waiting for Anna to return home.

But she didn't come.

Jude went to bed at eleven thirty, but he didn't sleep. He just lay in bed and watched the clock: twelve, twelve thirty, one, one thirty, two. At two twenty he heard her. She moved around downstairs for a few minutes before he heard her climb the stairs. Then the door to her bedroom clicked shut.

The next morning when Jude woke, again he didn't vary from his regular morning habits, but when he descended the stairs, his heart was thumping as if he'd just run a marathon. When he rounded the corner into the kitchen, there was no one there. He took three steps to the table and sat down, his legs suddenly shaky. There on the table in front of him he found the note. It read: "Had an early-morning meeting. Might not be back until very late tonight. Don't wait up."

He crumpled it in his fist.

He found he couldn't face the idea of breakfast. Instead he remounted the stairs to collect his things for school. His math book was still open on the desk, the blank sheet of paper beside it. He stuffed the book into his bag and hurried back down. All at once he couldn't wait to get out, even if he had to wait at the bus stop in the cold for half an hour. The house seemed unnaturally quiet. He grabbed his jacket from the closet and headed toward the front door, but just as he was reaching for the knob it turned on its own and the door opened.

Jude took a step back, but it was only Harry.

"What are you doing here?" Jude said. "I thought we were supposed to meet later." Then in almost the same breath, "So how did it go?"

Harry looked over Jude's shoulder. "Is Anna here?"

Jude gave him a disgusted look. "What do you think I am, stupid?"

"Did you see her this morning?"

"She left before I came downstairs," Jude said.

"Okay, let's go talk in the kitchen," and Harry walked past him to the back of the house. Jude followed.

Harry went to the counter and got out a mug. He felt the side of the coffeepot, made a face, and put the mug back. "Left a good while ago, did she?"

"I don't know," Jude said.

Harry moved to the other cupboard and took down a glass this time. "So . . ." He opened the fridge, got out the orange juice, and poured himself a glass. "Better for me than coffee anyway," he said. He took a sip and leaned back against the counter. "Well, it worked."

"Oh?" Jude replied, but what he wanted to say was, "What the hell does that mean?"

"It's the reason I'm here now instead of meeting up later. There are going to be a couple of plain-clothes watching the house starting this morning—in case you change the meeting place. Though they're depending on the fact that you said you're not going to do it in school. They can't exactly follow you from classroom to classroom. It would be a bit obvious, wouldn't it?"

Jude didn't realize he'd been holding his breath until he tried to speak. "So she reported it to the police?"

"Yes, of course. Though I have to admit I was worried for a bit there. When she came out of the house and got back into the car, I thought that something had gone wrong. She was quiet, so I knew that she'd heard something, but she didn't say anything, and I couldn't exactly ask her. She waited at least ten minutes—we were almost back at the office—before she told me. I was already trying to think of a back-up plan. I never in a million years imagined that she would think of covering for you for ten seconds, much less ten minutes."

Ten minutes. Ten whole minutes she hadn't spoken. Even Harry, who knew her better than anybody, never thought she'd hesitate. Jude felt a surge of emotion . . . until Harry offered an alternate explanation.

"But more likely she didn't say anything because she was worried about her career. Same thing happened back when your father was beating up on her. She didn't want to go public with it because she was afraid of what it would do to her career to admit that she was a victim of domestic violence at the same time she was prosecuting domestic violence cases. I was actually the one who convinced her she could turn it to her advantage. And the timing was perfect—with her being pregnant with you. It made a nice little story. Mother protecting her child and all that."

"*You* convinced her?" Jude said.

"Yes, but that's not important now," Harry said. "I don't have a lot of time, and I came here to give you this." Harry tossed a bag of white powder on the table.

"Holy shit," Jude said, eyeing the bag. He picked it up and weighed it in his palm. "Jesus, Harry, I don't need anywhere near that much."

"To make the story plausible, you need some stock."

"Not this much," he protested. "Not unless you want everyone to think I'm doing a pretty brisk business."

"But that's exactly what we want them to think."

"You want them to catch me with that?" His voice broke high on the question.

"No, not that much . . ."

Jude was about to heave a sigh of relief when Harry continued.

"Not initially. There wouldn't be any reason for you to carry all your supply with you to the sale. The rest of it you can leave in your room. They'll find it later." He must have caught something of what Jude was feeling in the expression on his face. "What did you think? That you'd go out with a gram or two? That's hardly worth it. We might as well just let the article run in that case—we'd benefit so little. We have an opportunity here to turn a potential disaster into an advantage, but in order to do that you have to think big, take a few more risks. Let me put it this way," Harry said. "It's the difference between simply avoiding ruining Anna's career and actually helping her." He paused, looking at Jude expectantly. He seemed to be waiting for an answer.

"Fine," Jude said. "Okay, whatever you say."

Harry shook his head. "That's not good enough," he insisted. "This is going to be hard. Harder than you probably think. There'll be things that we can't predict that might come up and make you think twice, even three times, about what you're doing, and you won't be able to ask me about them because after this morning we probably won't be able to talk. You need to really commit to this, so I need something more from you than 'whatever you say.'"

"What do you need?" Jude asked.

"Some assurance that you're going to see this

through. I may not be on the front lines with you, but I'm risking a lot—maybe even more than you, as I have more to lose."

Then Jude understood why he was getting the hard sell. Harry was worried that he'd get scared and spill the beans.

"When I say I'm going to do something, I do it," Jude assured him.

"And your word is good?"

"I never told anyone who killed my father," Jude replied. He thought he saw a flash of something in Harry's face, but it was gone in the next second, before Jude could read his expression.

"All right then." Harry took a seat at the kitchen table. "There are a couple of things you need to know about, after you're charged."

"Yeah?"

"Your lawyer, if he's any good, is going to tell you to plead out. To make a deal. This is important—under no circumstances should you agree to that, no matter what they tell you. If you admit to it, it will be much harder to get you a new trial when the time comes. Witness testimony is one thing, but I don't know what I could do about a confession. Do you understand?"

Jude understood, and the very thought took his breath away. He nodded.

"Secondly—and this is just as critical—you absolutely cannot say anything to Anna about what's really going on. I don't care how much you're tempted—

don't. There'll be plenty of time afterward, but it will ruin everything if you tell her too soon. I don't think she'll be able to go through with it, and that will look even worse than the article. Even if she did follow it through, Anna is a lot of things, but she's not a very good actress. So it won't be *real*."

"Okay," he said.

"I want you to give your word." Harry was staring at him intensely.

Jude rolled his eyes. "Fine," he said. "I promise, okay?"

"Good." Harry stood and picked up his coat, which was folded over the back of a chair. "Enough talking. Now it's time to do something."

"What if I need to get in touch with you?" Jude asked.

"Too risky," Harry said.

"But what if it's an emergency?"

"I can't imagine what could happen that would be so bad it's worth the risk of contacting me. How about this—if I see anything that I'm concerned about, I'll contact you. If you don't hear from me, you'll know that I've got it covered. Okay?"

It wasn't exactly okay, but Jude didn't have much choice other than to agree.

"You ready?" Harry said, shrugging into his coat.

"Sure," Jude agreed. What else was he going to say?

17

AT SCHOOL THAT day Jude took a Spanish test that he had forgotten about, scribbled notes in English on *Julius Caesar,* which he hadn't read, and had to stay after class in math to listen to his teacher's reprimands because for the second week in a row he had failed to hand in his homework. Throughout, he somehow managed not to think about Anna or Harry or what was going to happen to his life after tomorrow.

When he let himself back into the house that afternoon, he stood a moment by the door listening to the silence, loath to move. Sounds seemed to echo when the house was empty, bouncing off the walls and reverberating in his chest, as if that, too, were empty.

Jude left his book bag at the bottom of the stairs and went into the kitchen to get the things he would need to break the heroin into bundles. Then he retrieved his bag and climbed to his room. He didn't even bother to close the door; he knew Anna wasn't going to be home anytime soon.

Jude crossed to the desk, then set the supplies down and fished out the plastic bag from the drawer. It could be just a bag full of baby powder they had given him. He almost hoped it was, but when he opened the plastic, dipped a finger in, and touched the tip to his tongue, he knew that it wasn't. He knew the bitter taste from the years with his father.

He set about packaging some of the stock. It had been a year and a half, but his hands remembered what to do, though at first they were clumsy with lack of practice. He remembered his father's thick, awkward fingers sealing up the little bags, sealing up his fate.

Jude didn't have the glassine bags his father had always used, but tinfoil would do as well, and soon he fell into a kind of rhythm, so that he'd wrapped many more than he needed before he realized it. It didn't matter. In fact, it would look even better to have a whole bunch wrapped and ready to go here in his room. It was all just for show anyway.

Jude put what he needed in his book bag and looked around the room for a place to hide the rest. He had to remind himself that there was no need to hide it. It was meant to be found. He ended up just sticking it back in one of the desk drawers under some old notebooks and papers.

Then he should have gone back downstairs again, watched some TV, eaten dinner—or at least he should have thrown his dinner out to make it look as if he had eaten it, but all of a sudden he felt too tired to get up. It was barely dark outside, but Jude lay down on the bed. When he opened his eyes again, it was morning; he'd slept straight through the night.

He rolled over to look at the clock and practically leaped out of bed. There was no time for a shower or breakfast. He just threw on the first clothes that came to hand, checked his bag to see that he had the stuff, and took the stairs in twos. As he grabbed his jacket and yanked opened the door, he could see the school bus rounding the corner. He flew out the door and down the path, reaching the bus stop just as the last kid was climbing the stairs.

Jude dropped into an empty seat near the front, panting. His oversleeping and his frantic dash were really a blessing. He was so flustered and out of breath he didn't notice that the car parked across the street from his house had started its engine as they trundled by.

When the bus pulled up in front of the school, instead of heading to English, Jude went to the cafeteria to get some breakfast. He bought a rubbery bagel and an apple juice and carried his tray over to a vacant table at the back of the long room. As he sat there chewing the bagel, he watched the other tables, filled with kids scribbling madly to finish copying the homework assignment before it was due, talking about last night's ball game, huddling around a book for some last-minute exam cramming. He already felt as if he were a million miles away from these kinds of worries. He didn't even bother going to his morning classes. He sat in the cafeteria until it closed for lunch preparation, then he went and sat in the library. He took a book off the shelf and opened it on the desk in front of him, but he didn't read. He just waited for the clock to tell him that it was time, and when the hands reached eleven forty-five, he got up and started toward the park.

He entered through the northwest gate and made his way to the statue. There was a man with a pretzel cart, so Jude bought a pretzel and a Coke to wash it down. He drank the Coke but ended up feeding most of his pretzel to the pigeons. He threw out a few pieces to three birds that were pecking among the puddles in front of the bench, and then birds seemed to descend from all sides. It gave him something to do—watching the crowd of birds fight over the hunks of dough while he waited for someone he knew wasn't ever going to show up.

But he played the game, as Harry had instructed him, and made a show of periodically checking his watch, then glancing around as if expecting someone. The air was warming toward spring, but there was still a sharp winter wind. He got up and stamped around in a small circle before returning to the bench again. He waited forty-five minutes past the appointed meeting time before he pretended to be fed up and rose as if to leave.

Harry had told him that both the police and the DA's office had agreed that they would take him even without the sale. Jude got only about ten feet away from the bench before they came for him. They descended like the pigeons, seemingly from nowhere.

The only one he had seen—the first one to reach him—was the pretzel man. He flipped a badge at Jude and shouted, "Police."

Harry had wanted Jude to pretend to panic and try to run, but he found he didn't have the heart for that kind of charade. He didn't want to be tackled and brought down in the muddy puddles that dotted the walkway. So he simply dropped his bag and raised his hands.

"You have the right to remain silent," the pretzel man said, advancing.

Jude felt someone come up behind him, catch his upraised arms by the wrists, and roughly muscle them down behind his back. He felt the burning cold of metal cuffs, which had been chilling in the air for the last hour, close over his wrists.

"Anything you say can and will be used against you in a court of law," the pretzel man continued, while another officer retrieved his bag from where Jude had dropped it. The man peeked inside and brought out a handful of the tinfoil-wrapped packets. "Bingo," he said.

"You have the right to an attorney—"

"And you're gonna friggin' need one," the cop behind him added.

18

JUDE MET WITH his lawyer in a tiny room at the precinct. It reminded him of the interrogation room from the night of his father's death—it had taken only a year and a half to end up back where he started.

Jude had been sitting in the room for more than an hour when his lawyer walked, or rather edged, through the door. She lowered herself cautiously into the chair across from him.

Jude couldn't help staring; his lawyer was the heaviest person he had ever seen. She seemed as round as she was tall. Her arms didn't hang at her sides, but instead were supported by her bulk as if on armrests. The cruelty of it was heightened by the fact that while the size of her body was staggering, her face was only plump—and it was pretty. Or it would have been pretty if she'd smiled, a real smile, not the sour twist that she substituted for it.

She caught his stare before he could glance away, and she responded to it in a dry, sarcastic tone, "It's not catching, it doesn't affect my brain, and unfortunately we're stuck with each other."

At her speech Jude felt a sudden wave of pity. It was the last thing he had expected to feel at that moment—or at least he hadn't expected to be pitying anyone but himself. He searched for something to say and came up with, "Why unfortunately?"

She eyed him shrewdly. "Anybody who wants this case wants it for the wrong reasons. That's why your mother hired me. I don't want it."

"Great, just what I need—a lawyer who doesn't want my case," he said.

"Let's get something straight. I'm not here to hold your hand. I'm here to help you clear up this little mess you've made."

"Little mess?" he repeated. "Is that what you'd call it?"

She pursed her mouth. "I was trying to be gentle," she admitted. "By the way, I'm Maria Powell. Call me Maria."

She held out her hand and he took it. It was surprisingly soft and delicate.

"Let's get down to brass tacks, because I'm sorry to say I don't have a whole lot of time right now. This is just a preliminary interview to go over a few things."

Jude nodded.

"I don't mean to scare you, but it doesn't look good." She glanced at Jude's impassive face and said, "What the hell, let's be honest here. I do mean to scare you. They're planning on charging you with possession with intent to distribute. They've got you on the possession, and from the amount of heroin involved they've got a pretty solid case for intent to distribute. For good measure, they're also tacking on the charge of criminally negligent homicide. I don't see how they're going to pull that off, but that's what I hear."

Jude said nothing, but he wasn't quite able to meet her probing stare. He could sense that he wasn't going to enjoy lying to her. He had never quite gotten the hang of doing it easily with people he liked.

"Do you know about mandatory minimum sentences for possession with intent to distribute?" she asked him. "Even without the criminally negligent homicide charge you're looking at four years without parole. Minimum."

That startled him enough to look up. "But I'm a minor," he protested.

"The first thing they're planning to do at the arraignment is to submit a motion to have you tried as an adult. I don't agree with it, but more and more often the law is going after kids and treating them like adults, and I'm afraid that with the criminally negligent homicide charge—plus the amount of heroin involved—they have a good chance."

"Who decides that?" he asked.

"Decides what?" she said.

"Who decides to submit that . . . the motion?"

"The DA's office." Now it was her turn to avoid his eyes.

He decided to drop it. Her discomfort was answer enough.

"So we need to talk about what we're going to do," she went on briskly.

Usually somebody using the word *we* this way would have annoyed Jude, but here Maria sounded as if she meant it.

"The senior assistant DA is handling the case, and he's tough but not unreasonable. Now, I think that in view of your age and your . . . um . . . history they might go for a plea bargain. I think with some coop-eration on your part we can arrange for you to go to juvenile detention and plead you down to eighteen months, maybe two years." She held up a finger when Jude opened his mouth. "Don't answer me yet. I want you to think about it."

Jude shook his head.

"I said think about it, and I didn't mean for three seconds."

"It's not that, exactly."

"What then?"

"It's the first part. That means I would have to plead guilty, doesn't it?"

"Yes, of course."

"But I'm not going to make a plea bargain," he said.

"You're not . . . what?"

"I'm not going to plead guilty."

She blinked, her mouth slightly open. "That's crazy," she said.

"I know," he agreed.

"They caught you with more than three ounces of heroin."

"Yeah."

"If you're convicted, the judge would have to sentence you to at least four years, Jude. Real prison. What I'm talking about, you go to juvenile detention and could be out in less than two."

"I know," he said. "I know."

"So tell me you're joking."

He looked out the window to a view of the alley. "I'm not," he assured her.

"Why, for God's sake? You've got to at least have a reason."

He shook his head. He didn't know what to say to her.

"This is about as stupid a stunt as I have ever seen. If you plead not guilty, this thing goes to trial. Let me make this very clear to you now. You don't want this to go to trial. You don't know—you can't imagine—how ugly that would be."

"I do," he said.

"No, you don't. Because if you did, you wouldn't consider it, not even for a second. Not for a millisecond. But I don't have time right now to paint the picture for you." She checked her watch. "I've got a hearing for another case. Listen, I'm not going to blow sunshine up your ass and tell you it's all going to be all right. It's not. Best we can do is damage control. You think about that. You've got some time—

we won't be talking about a deal until after the arraignment, but after that I'll arrange a meeting with the assistant DA, and we'll need to be on the same page. You got me?"

Jude nodded.

"I'll be seeing you at the arraignment," she said. "Most people might tell you not to worry, but you know what? I want you to worry."

Then, in order to get up out of her chair, she had to place her palms on the table and give a little push. She caught him watching, but instead of being angry, as he might have expected, she just gave him that twisted smile. "We're all prisoners, you know," she said. "In one way or another."

WHEN JUDE ARRIVED at the courthouse the next day, he was tired and despondent. He didn't remember the police lockup being so uncomfortable. He guessed that back then, compared with what he was used to, it wasn't so bad. He'd gotten soft in the last year and a half. He hadn't even realized it, but he'd gotten used to luxury.

At the courthouse he was delivered into the hands of his lawyer. Maria pushed open the door that led into the courtroom, but she didn't step through immediately. "Good Lord," she whispered.

Jude looked in over her shoulder. The room was packed.

Someone at the back noticed their arrival, and it

rippled through the crowd. Heads twisted, craning to get a good look at him.

"Reporters," Maria hissed. "I didn't expect this many. There weren't even this many for the Reznik case, and he was a cop killer."

"Thanks," Jude whispered back. "You really know how to make me feel better."

"Don't say I didn't warn you," she said. "You'll take the deal when we get it."

Before he could reply, she waddled into the room, and with all the eyes on them it must have been almost as difficult for her as for him, Jude thought. Somehow that realization gave him the courage he needed to follow her.

When they reached the front, they found there was no room for them. Two men in the first bench rose to give up their places so they could sit while they were waiting for their case to be called, but that freed barely enough space for Maria. A third had to get up, and Jude noticed that Maria's face was crimson.

Even with three spots vacated the space on the bench wasn't really big enough. Jude was wedged up against the end, and still Maria's leg pressed against his. They sat close enough for Jude to smell her shampoo— if clean had a scent, her shampoo would be it, Jude thought. He didn't want to consider how he must smell. In the overheated courtroom, with the radiators clanking just a few feet away, Jude could sense the stale odor of old sweat rising from his clothes.

When their case was called, Maria rose and led him to the front. The room quieted in anticipation.

Only then did Jude see the prosecutor, and he recognized the senior assistant DA. Jude had met the man a couple of times. His name was Andrew Comfort, though Jude knew they had another name for him around the courthouse. They called him Uncomfortable, and this referred both to his manner, which outside the courtroom was awkward and unpolished, *and* to his ability inside the courtroom to make a defendant very uncomfortable indeed. He was short and painfully thin, balding but with a boyish face that always seemed to hold a puzzled frown in the slight crease between his eyebrows. His appearance hid the ferocious will to win that he brought to every case.

The judge was a woman, barely tall enough to see over the bench. He wondered if it was deliberate— that the judge hearing juvenile arraignments looked almost like a child herself. She read the indictment in a conversational tone, seemingly unaffected by the large audience. "The charges are criminally negligent homicide and possession of a controlled substance with intent to distribute."

The judge looked at Jude and asked, "How does the defendant plead?"

Jude had worried that his voice might break or come out too loud, but he managed to get out the words "Not guilty" and have them sound relatively normal.

"Any motions to hear?"

Comfort spoke crisply. "I have a motion to have the defendant tried as an adult."

"I'll hear the motion Monday at three o'clock. Anything else?"

The assistant DA shook his head.

"Then we'll move on to bail recommendations. Mr. Comfort?"

"Your Honor, I request that bail be remanded."

"What?" Maria half stood in protest.

"We believe there is a certain flight risk with the defendant."

"This is ridiculous," Maria said. "He's a child."

"He's sixteen," Comfort corrected her. "And more than one million children run away every year. It's not an issue of age, but the flight risk isn't the only concern. There is also," he continued, "a bit of difficulty as to where he would stay if he were released on bail. It would be something of an awkward situation, if not an outright conflict of interest, to have the defendant living with the DA."

"Do you have anything to say to that, Counselor?" the judge asked Maria.

"I'm afraid this isn't something I've dealt with before," she said. "But I don't believe that my client should be penalized for being an inconvenience."

"I see your point," the judge said, "but unless you have a solution . . ."

"A foster home?" she suggested.

"There is also the high-profile aspect of the case to consider, Judge," Comfort added. "I think that a foster home wouldn't be able to protect the defendant adequately from the media, and there is still the flight risk."

The judge sighed. "It may not be fair, Counselor," she said to Maria, "but I don't see an alternative. The defendant is to be remanded without bail."

"In that case, I request that he be allowed to await trial at a juvenile facility for the duration, regardless of the ruling on the motion, *and* that he be given a private cell there, Your Honor," Maria spoke up.

"I have no objections to that," Comfort said.

"Well, we all seem to be agreed on this issue. I grant your request, Counselor. We'll set a court date at the hearing." The judge rapped her gavel, and Maria motioned for Jude to get up.

Jude obeyed, but he was still digesting the fact that he wasn't going home. In the next moment he wondered how he'd ever thought he could. What would that be like—living with his mother while her office prepared the case against him, and all the while Anna believing he was really guilty? He saw now that it was impossible. Harry must have known it too, but he hadn't said anything, probably fearing that Jude would back out. But he couldn't blame this on Harry. Harry had offered him a way to repair the damage, and if the cost was a little higher than Jude expected, how could he complain?

19

MARIA HAD SET up a meeting with Comfort after the arraignment. She intended to discuss a plea bargain. And they did discuss it—Comfort told Maria what he was offering: If Jude pleaded guilty to criminally negligent homicide and possession with intent to distribute, they'd give him a seven-year sentence and he could be out in five. Maria laughed because she thought he was joking. Then she realized he was serious. The meeting didn't last more than five minutes.

"I can't believe it." Maria was fuming as she and Jude left the room. "They want to hang you out to dry. I don't understa—" She broke off abruptly. As they emerged from the room, they found that the guard who was waiting for Jude now had company.

"I'm Harry Wichowski," Harry introduced himself to Maria. "I'm the deputy commissioner."

"I know who you are," Maria said. "What do you want?" She was still prickly from the confrontation.

Just then the assistant DA stepped from the room. "Hello, Harry," Comfort said coldly. "What are you doing here?"

Jude remembered that Harry and Comfort had never gotten along. Even Harry's charm could make no headway with the senior assistant DA—Comfort obviously distrusted Harry's ease with people. From what

Jude had overheard, he suspected there was some jealousy over the pivotal roles they each held in Anna's life.

"Anna asked me to stop by," Harry said. "I need to talk to Jude and his lawyer, if you'll excuse us." He wasn't exactly rude, but the effect was the same. Comfort bridled, and Jude could see that he was tempted to demand that Harry tell him what he wanted. Instead he walked away without another word. His assistant scurried after him.

Harry turned to Maria. "I'm sorry about that. I sometimes find Comfort . . ." He paused, searching for a word. "Inflexible. You probably agree with me after your meeting."

"I would think that the DA might have something to say about that," Maria suggested.

"It's a difficult situation all around." Harry sighed. "It's a serious case with serious charges, and it is also an issue on which she's made her views very plain. She can't be seen to go easy on him because he's her son."

"But she shouldn't be harder on him either," Maria retorted.

"You're in good hands, Jude." Harry spoke to him for the first time.

Jude studied the floor.

"How are you holding up?"

"Fine," he said.

"Anna asked me to bring this by for you." Harry held out a bag. "It has clothes, toiletries, a few books. . . ."

Jude took it. He could feel Maria looking at him.

"You mean she didn't stop by to see him last night?"

"I have advised her to wait until after the trial," Harry said.

Jude wondered if that was true—if Anna had really wanted to come—or if it was for Maria's benefit.

"But I promised her that I would come by and make sure he was doing okay. And I'd like you to feel free to talk to me about any concerns you may have," Harry continued. "I could try to smooth things on the other side."

Maria considered. "I might take you up on that."

Harry beckoned the officer over. "Take care of him," he instructed, motioning to Jude. "No cuffs on the way back, okay?"

"Sure," the officer agreed. "Come on, kid."

As Jude was led away, he heard Harry say to Maria, "Are you leaving? I'll walk out with you. . . ."

He looked over his shoulder, and they were already headed in the opposite direction. Harry happened to glance back at him, and Jude thought he saw him wink.

AT THE HEARING the judge granted the motion that Jude be tried as an adult. And suddenly he was facing time in a state prison instead of a stint at a juvenile facility. What saved Jude from panic was the fact that the trial was months away. It was set for late September, and Jude calculated that he wouldn't have long in an actual adult prison before the election, and after that Harry would get the conviction overturned and he'd be released. It was true that he was facing almost six months at the detention center, but in his solitary cell he was completely removed from the rest of the boys. The only thing he had to fear was boredom.

After the hearing Maria commandeered a room to sit down and talk.

"So things didn't go our way today, but then again, we didn't expect them to," she began. "I wanted to talk to you about the prosecution's case. I got the discovery yesterday, and I've been looking it over." She paused—ominously, Jude thought. "You didn't tell me about the phone call," she said.

"I don't know what you're talking about. What phone call?"

Of course he knew exactly what she was talking about, but he had to pretend he didn't. If it hadn't been staged, he wouldn't have known that his mother had been there to listen in.

"Apparently your mother overheard a conversation that you had with a . . . friend, and it was about selling him heroin. She said that the machine had picked up and you were upstairs, so when she came in, it was coming through the speaker and she could hear every word. Do you remember it now?"

"Oh, that."

"Yes, that. With that phone call their case for possession with intent to distribute is more than solid—it's practically impenetrable. The call also establishes your intent to sell to a minor, and your using the park as a meeting place puts the transaction in a drug-free school zone. Those details will add to the mandatory minimum sentence, and that's not the worst of it. The discovery also explains their reasoning in going for criminally negligent homicide. Apparently Nick told his friends that his dealer—allegedly you—said that the heroin he was selling was a special kind. It was special because it gave a better high, but you needed to snort more of it than the regular stuff. The police speculate that the dealer was taking advantage of a naive customer and, based on the amount that he was snorting, that Nick was buying a product that had very little actual heroin in the mix. Then they tested the stuff that killed him, and they found that mixture was almost sixty percent pure—which is about the best you can buy."

Jude remembered his conversation with R. J. and what he had said about mixing up the bags. "But it was a mistake," he said. "I mean, it must have been."

"That's what I thought. Only, then they tested the heroin they found in your bag."

"And?"

"Jude, the heroin in your bag was almost uncut."

"What?" he said in disbelief.

"It was over ninety percent pure."

Jude hadn't thought about where Harry got the heroin, but of course Harry couldn't just go out and buy it. He must have gotten it from some big drug bust, one of the ones where they nabbed it coming into the country. Who would notice a couple of ounces missing from several kilos?

"Jude, not only does it give them a case for criminally negligent homicide, it adds to the mandatory minimum. Uncut heroin gets stiffer penalties than a mixture. You're up to five years, no parole, even if they don't get a conviction for criminally negligent homicide."

"Five years?" he echoed. "It can't be that much."

"The average sentence for a first-time drug offender is almost seven years," she said.

"How much would the criminally negligent homicide charge be?" he asked.

"Four to six."

"You could get less for killing someone than for selling drugs?"

"Yes," she admitted, "in the case of criminally negligent homicide, at least. But listen, there *is* some good news as well. I've talked to Mr. Wichowski several times over the course of the past couple days, and I think he's sympathetic to our situation. He's said that he'll talk to your mother and to Comfort, and they may have a better deal for us."

Jude was surprised that Harry was going to trust him enough to offer a good deal, seeing as how worried he'd been that Jude would cave in and take a plea.

"We've got a meeting scheduled for tomorrow," she went on. "So it may not be as bad as it looks. It could work out for everyone."

"There's one thing you forgot."

"What's that?"

"I told you a while ago, I can't plead guilty."

"Yes," she said impatiently. "I remember, but that was before they formally charged you with criminally negligent homicide, and before you were definitely going to be tried as an adult, and certainly before we got the discovery evidence from the prosecution and found out that they have enough to bury you."

"It doesn't change anything. I still can't plead."

"You keep saying 'can't.' What do you mean, 'can't'?"

He shook his head.

"I can't think of a single reason why you 'can't.'"

"What about if I was innocent?" he said.

She stared at him over the table. "I've been doing this for almost ten years, and that's nine years and twelve months too late for me to believe that line. But you know what? Let's say—let's just assume—you *are* innocent. You want to know what I'd tell you?"

He knew already, but he humored her. "What?"

"After seeing that discovery, I'd say, 'Shout that you're guilty from the rooftops if they'll give you a good enough deal.' You hear me?"

"I hear you," he said.

"So?"

"I'm sorry," he said.

"Well, we're going to the meeting anyway. Then, if you haven't changed your mind, you can tell them yourself."

20

THE MEETING WAS held at the DA's offices. From the moment he and Maria got off the elevator, Jude could feel the people looking at him. Ahead of them the corridors were crowded with employees—hurrying from copier to fax, calling across the floor to other coworkers, hunched over their desks—but the employees stopped their work to watch them as they made their way to Anna's office.

Jude twisted his hands in the fabric of his jacket and tried to stay calm. This would be the first time he had seen his mother since she overheard the phone call.

When they entered the room, Jude saw that everyone was there. Comfort and his assistant were sitting at the table. Harry was standing just behind them, leaning casually against the massive desk, and beyond him, half blocked by his body, Anna sat in the high-backed leather chair paging through a file in front of her. She didn't even look up when they entered.

Comfort was the one who greeted them and motioned for them to sit.

"So we're here to try this again," Maria began. "To start off, I'd just like to say that I think we all have the same goals here."

"And what would those be?" Comfort asked.

Jude sensed that Maria held on to her patience for his sake. "I think we all would like to avoid the media circus of a trial and reach a fair and equitable agreement. It would save us time, the taxpayers money, and a lot of unnecessary pain for the people involved."

"I wish it were that simple, Ms. Powell, but you have only the interests of your client to think of. We have to answer to the people of this city, and I'm not so sure that they want this case swept under the carpet," Comfort said.

"It's called a plea bargain, and it's hardly sweeping it under the carpet. It is how ninety percent of the cases that pass through this office are resolved, and I was led to believe that you had an offer for me. I didn't know that we were coming all the way down here for you to tell us that you want to pander to the public's thirst for a bloodletting."

Comfort smiled—condescendingly, Jude thought. "Aren't you getting a bit melodramatic? The DA is a politically elected official and, as such, is held accountable by the people. The constituents are ultimately the ones this office has to satisfy—within the letter of the law. I believe that the district attorney has been quite clear about her views on the drug problem in our city."

Jude sneaked a glance over at Anna. She was listening, but her gaze was trained carefully on the papers in front of her.

"Plus, I think you're worldly enough to realize that the media spotlight on this case does change things. Maybe it shouldn't, but the reality is that it does."

"Why do I feel like you're setting us up?" Maria said.

"Well, you can judge for yourself. I'm willing to offer three years. He could be up for parole in less than two."

"That sounds—"

Comfort held up a hand. "On the condition that the defendant not only gives us his connection, but also agrees to testify against that person."

"And if my client isn't willing to testify? What are you offering then?"

"Nothing," Comfort said. "Not a thing."

"Before you said—"

"I've changed my mind. If your client isn't willing to give us a name *and* testify against that person, we will be going to trial."

Jude almost groaned aloud. He'd known it was going to be bad turning down the plea in front of Anna, but now she was going to think that he was turning it down because he wouldn't give up his connection.

"Can I have a moment with my client to talk about it?" Maria said.

"Of course."

Maria leaned over to him and spoke into his ear from behind her hand. She said, "Take it. For God's sake, take it."

He pulled back, looked at her, and shook his head.

She leaned in again. "Can we tell them we'll think about it?"

It was tempting to delay so he wouldn't have to be in the same room with Anna when he turned it down, but he didn't give himself time to consider it. "No," he whispered. "Just tell them no."

"Don't be stupid. Take it. I'm asking you to take it."

"No."

"This is it, you know," she hissed. "You won't get another chance."

"I know."

"Fine. I wish I could force you, but I can't. The one thing I won't do is tell them for you. I don't want any confusion here—I don't want anyone thinking I counseled you not to take the deal."

He wanted to say, "Please tell her for me. Please don't make me do it." But he thought of the day when Anna would find out the truth, and it gave him the courage he needed. "Okay," he said, and they straightened in their chairs.

"My client has made a decision," Maria announced. "But I am going to let him speak for himself."

Everyone looked at Jude. He wanted to know if Anna was watching him, but he didn't quite have the courage to check. So he ended up looking at Harry when he said, "No, thank you."

Harry couldn't repress a tiny smile. Jude saw it

because he was looking at him, but what he didn't know was that Maria saw it also—and puzzled over it for a long time.

But Harry's tiny smile was overshadowed by the snort that burst from behind him. Jude's eyes followed the sound, and he caught Anna's gaze. It was the first time she had looked at him, and the expression in her eyes made him flinch.

For a moment everyone was frozen, watching the two stare at each other. Anna rose from her chair, her eyes still on Jude. "I think we're done here," she said.

Everyone leaped up at the cue. Comfort's papers were in his hands, then his assistant was up and ushering Jude and Maria out of the room.

Jude could never remember the instant when he and Anna actually broke eye contact. It seemed to him that one second they were locked on each other, then she spoke and the next thing he knew he was outside her office.

Both Maria and Jude stood there beside the closed door, blinking at the swiftness of their eviction.

The door to Anna's office opened once more, and they both turned expectantly, but it was just the young lawyer with a folder that Maria had inadvertently left behind in the room.

Maria thanked him absently.

"Well," she said to no one in particular, "I guess that's that."

21

A WEEK AFTER the meeting Harry came to visit Jude at the juvenile detention center.

Jude was lying on his bunk dozing, even though the corridor rang with the shouts and arguments of the other boys awaiting trial. He had become adept at sleeping through almost any noise, and he found that it was the best way to pass the time. When he slept, he didn't have to think. He figured that if he could sleep enough, then one day he would wake up and it would be over, almost like a bad dream.

The clanking of his cell door woke him. He opened his eyes and there was Harry, saying, "What are you doing sleeping in the middle of the afternoon? I tell you, I'm thinking of going out and committing a few crimes myself to get some rest."

The guard who had opened the door laughed dutifully.

"Come on, Jude, they've given us a room where we can sit down and talk."

Jude sat up, swung his legs off the edge of the bed, and pulled his shirt straight on his shoulders, where it had twisted around his body as he slept. He stood, took a step over to the sink, and splashed water on his face, then over his hair to smooth it. Then he turned to follow the corrections officer out of the cell. He didn't say anything simply because he was out of the habit. Most days he spoke only a word or two, "Thanks" or "Okay" to the officer who brought him meals or escorted him to the shower.

Harry must have caught some of his silence, because he followed Jude and the officer down the corridor without speaking.

When the officer opened the door to the room, Jude said, "Thanks, Officer Lopez," and the man answered, "No problem, Jude." Lopez let Harry pass through and closed the door behind them.

Jude took a seat on one of the folding chairs, hunching over the table. Harry took the chair next to him.

"It seems like you're doing pretty well here," Harry observed. "Getting to know the guys."

"I'm okay," Jude replied listlessly.

"Have they been nice to you?"

"They're fine."

"Good."

There was a pause.

"You did great at the meeting the other day. You didn't lose your nerve."

Jude shrugged.

"I meant to come by earlier, but I had to wait for Anna to settle down."

It was amazing how quickly feeling could return. A moment before, Jude had felt like Harry could have said anything and it wouldn't have mattered, but the mention of Anna settling down made him sit up a little straighter. He wanted to ask about it but didn't know how. He didn't have to.

"She was pretty upset afterward," Harry said. "Even the public response hasn't cheered her up much. Have you seen the newspapers?"

"They don't give us the papers in here," Jude said, thinking about what Harry meant by "upset."

"Oh." Harry seemed nonplussed. "Well, the coverage has been phenomenal. The press has recognized that she is everything a public servant should be. In the *Independent* they wrote that she sacrifices her own desires to be an instrument of justice for the people." Jude didn't respond, so Harry went on. "The amazing thing is that it's not our connections anymore. I don't know the reporter who wrote that. Even most of Anna's enemies are laying off on this one. Only the *Courant* suggested that she's sacrificing you to her political ambition, but I heard through the grapevine that they received so much angry mail in response to that editorial that they haven't tried it again. I think the TV interviews have helped enormously. No one can possibly listen to Anna talk about her decision and not realize how difficult this has been for her. She did a great piece on channel four's news hour about the hard decisions we have to make as individuals that will affect the future of our country."

Jude made a noise at that, something between a "Huh" and an "Uhn."

Harry seemed to take it as encouragement.

"Some of the reporters are comparing her to the old class of political servants who worked for the system instead of making the system work for them. We've just released some information that we gathered about the mayor's personal abuse of the privileges of his office. It has made for a remarkable contrast, and the trial is going to be even better. The timing is perfect—right before the election. You should see the latest polls. Anna isn't exactly the underdog anymore. She has a real shot at it now, Jude, and it's because of you."

"That's good, I guess."

"And don't you worry about getting out afterward. I've got that all covered."

Jude nodded absently.

"You okay?" Harry asked.

"Yeah, fine."

Harry squinted at him. "You sure?"

Jude finally looked at him. "What did you come for, Harry? I'm sure it wasn't to find out how I am."

"It was part of it," Harry said defensively. "I was planning on coming anyway, but then Anna asked me to speak to you. She wanted to come herself, but I managed to convince her that it would compromise the case."

Jude was suddenly very still.

"Jude, she wanted me to ask you to reconsider."

"Reconsider?" Jude repeated, not understanding.

"The plea bargain," Harry explained. "I told her

that it wouldn't do any good, but she insisted that I try. Just in case she ever asks, I had better tell you the message." Harry hesitated, then continued. "She says, 'Please. Please do this one thing. If you can't do it for yourself, do it for me.' That's her message."

Jude could feel something breaking loose. It couldn't have been easy for her to ask that from him. "Can't we tell her—"

"It needs to be real," Harry reminded him. "Even if she did decide to go along with it, she can't be acting a part. It just won't work. So you need to hold on and be strong for her right now. Okay?"

Harry's gaze was level—without any trace of pity or disdain that Jude could detect.

Jude took a deep, shaky breath. "I'm scared," he said. It was such a relief to admit it. "It's all . . . more than I thought. More serious. More real. More everything."

"Hey, I warned you it wouldn't be easy," Harry said with a smile.

Jude smiled weakly.

"Just think about how it will feel when she finally knows the truth," Harry said. "What a moment that's going to be, right? Right?" he repeated, demanding an answer.

"Yeah," Jude agreed. "Right."

22

THE TRIAL PASSED in five hazy, droning days. When it started, Jude had spent more than 150 days at the juvenile detention center. Toward the end he even started to look forward to the trial as something to break the monotony.

On the day that the trial started Jude was awakened at six and given breakfast in his cell—the same as any other day—but this time he wasn't able to roll over and go back to sleep. He was driven to the courthouse and allowed to dress in slacks, a white button-down shirt, and a gray blazer. It was all freshly dry-cleaned, so there were no wrinkles in the coat and there were sharp creases down the front of his pants, but the crispness of the clothes didn't cover the fact that the jacket was tight across the shoulders and the pant legs were too short. It was as if the clothes were telling him that after almost six months in juvenile detention, he didn't quite fit into his old life anymore.

Maria was waiting for him in an adjoining room, and after he had dressed, they entered the courtroom together. Jude sat next to Maria; Comfort and his assistant were at the opposite table; and the seats were filled with potential jurors. The judge behind the bench was a stoop-shouldered old man with heavy bags under his eyes and thin white hair that tended to wave with static, especially after he rubbed his hand through it, which he had a habit of doing.

By eleven the heat from the hissing radiators made Jude's eyelids droop. They broke for lunch, and it was worse in the afternoon. He caught himself nodding off a few times, before jerking upright. He just couldn't seem to work up a proper interest. By the end of the day they had chosen twelve jurors and two alternates, and all he could think about was getting back to the cell, which he had been so anxious to leave, so he could lie down and go to sleep.

And it continued like that throughout the following days. Opening statements found him yawning through Maria's and Comfort's impassioned speeches. When Comfort described the case, he made it sound as if Jude was everything that was wrong with society today—a young man who didn't think of consequences, who hadn't learned the difference between right and wrong, who had consulted only his own wishes in his actions. In Maria's reconstruction of events she implied that he was a victim of his father, of his upbringing, of his environment. Jude had trouble concentrating on the arguments. If anyone had bothered to ask him, he would have said that he thought both Maria and Comfort were full of it.

In the afternoon the assistant DA called his first witness, Nick's mother.

Nick's mother talked about her son, recounting

stories of him as a child. She brought baby pictures, and she admitted that she hadn't talked to him about drugs. She said she thought that, at one of the best prep schools in the city, he would be safe.

She spent most of her testimony staring at Jude. Jude made the mistake of looking up, but only once. After that he kept his gaze trained on the tabletop.

After lunch Comfort called Toby, the student who had been with Nick when he overdosed. Toby testified that Nick said his dealer had instructed him as to the proper dosage for the heroin he was buying. Toby also admitted that he had done the recommended dosage and been fine. The day of the overdose, however, Nick had just made a new purchase. He used the new stuff, while Toby finished up heroin left over from an earlier buy. Toby noticed that there was something wrong only when Nick started having convulsions, and by then it was too late.

Comfort asked about how Nick had gotten the drugs. Toby said that for a long time everybody knew that Jude took Nick back to the old neighborhood to get them. For the final few months Nick didn't make any trips, but he seemed to have an unlimited supply. No, Nick had never said it was Jude who was supplying him with the drugs, but he'd often called Jude his "man" and his "connection."

After Toby's testimony the court adjourned for the day. The next morning Comfort called one of the officers who had arrested Jude in the park. He recounted the events leading up to the arrest and confirmed the amount of heroin Jude had in his possession. In the afternoon Comfort followed the arresting officer's testimony with the expert who had tested the heroin. He told the jury that it was 91 percent pure and took them through the implications of this discovery and the potential consequences.

In all her cross-examinations, Jude knew, Maria was trying her best for him. The truth was he hadn't given her much to work with. He couldn't tell her what really happened, and he didn't trust himself to sustain a credible story, so he chose to say as little as possible. As a result Maria's cross-examinations were short. The first witness, Nick's mother, Maria chose not to question at all. There was no point, she told him, of trying to attack a grieving mother—that was not the way to get the jury on your side.

Maria questioned Toby, but only briefly. She asked him if Nick had ever said that Jude had sold him drugs. Toby said no. She asked if Nick had ever identified Jude as his dealer in the last few months when they had stopped the trips back to the neighborhood, and Toby admitted that Nick hadn't.

Maria followed a slightly different tack with the expert witness. She asked him whether he could be sure that Jude knew the purity of his supply. The expert said that he couldn't be sure of that. Then she asked him how often heroin of that purity got sold on the street. He replied that he personally had never heard of it happening before.

Jude almost felt sorry for her—for her determined efforts to save what was clearly beyond hope. But he didn't feel sorry for long. Soon he found he needed all his pity for himself. At the end of that day's questioning Maria told him, "Tomorrow they'll finish up their case. We'll see if they call their last witness."

It was the tone of her voice that made Jude ask, "Who's their last witness?"

"Your mother."

23

THROUGHOUT THE OPENING days of the trial the courtroom had been full—but on the day of Anna's testimony it overflowed. The judge had to ask the people standing in the back, unable to find seats, to leave. Then he called the room to order, and Comfort called his last witness.

Anna rose from the second row of benches and made her way up to the stand. Here, in the courtroom, among all these people, she seemed smaller, but she held herself straight, and Jude felt a surge of pride. He was proud of the way Anna was holding up under the weight of so much eager fascination. She was sworn in, then smoothed her skirt as she took a seat. During her testimony Anna kept her eyes on Comfort as he asked her the questions. She didn't look at the jury, and she didn't look at Jude while she related the events that led up to Jude's arrest. She started with Nick's death and the futile search for the source of the drugs. Then she related the circumstances that led her to overhear his phone call, and described the steps she had taken that had ended in his arrest in the park. Throughout, her voice was even and dispassionate.

After establishing the facts of the case, Comfort steered her away from recent events and took her back to the time before Jude was born. Jude could sense everyone in the room sit up. The information that they'd been hearing—the phone call, the sting, the arrest, the search—they had already heard about in various forms from the arresting officers. They all wanted something more personal, and now they sensed they were about to get it.

"You were first in your class in law school, weren't you?" Comfort asked.

"Yes."

"You had your pick of jobs, didn't you?"

"I had a lot of offers," she admitted.

"Why did you seek out a position in the DA's office when you could have made two or three times as much in a private firm?"

"I . . ." She seemed to struggle with the answer. "I wanted to make a difference. It sounds so naive now, but I thought I could do something."

"Do what, exactly?"

She looked down into her lap, then up again, smiling a little self-consciously. "See that justice was done, but at the time I had no idea what that meant. I had visions of sending all the bad people off to prison—of making the world safe."

"And so you took a job in the DA's office."

"Yes."

"And what happened?"

"After two years of prosecuting misdemeanors I requested to work in the section that dealt with domestic crimes. It wasn't a popular place at the time, so I got to handle a lot of cases."

"And how did that go?"

"I did well there. I was able to convince many of the women to press charges, and we won a good number."

"And were you happy?"

"I thought I was doing what I had set out to do. So yes, I suppose I was happy."

"But then something happened that would change everything, isn't that right?"

"Yes."

"What happened?"

"I fell in love," Anna said.

Jude couldn't detect any emotion in her voice.

"His name was Anthony Arvelo, and he was a police officer who worked with me on a domestic violence case. The woman refused to press charges, and her husband killed her a few months later. Anthony was the one who called to tell me what had happened. He suggested that we go out for a drink, I said yes, and that was how it began."

"How did it end?" Comfort asked.

"He hit me, and for six months I let him. And for those same six months I was telling these women—my clients—that they had to press charges if they wanted anything to change, that they had to be strong and stand up for what they knew was right. It was the same speech I'd been making for years, and I kept making it, even when Anthony started hitting me where people could see. My coworkers didn't suspect anything. My coworkers bought my cover-up stories, but my clients knew. They looked at me and knew.

"Looking back now, I don't know how I did it. How I had the nerve to sit there and say those things to them, with a broken arm, with a black eye, and with a wedding ring still on my finger. It's not so surprising that I got fewer and fewer cases to try. They listened to my speech and thanked me politely but said they didn't want to press charges."

"What changed things for you?" Comfort asked.

"Actually, it was one of my clients. I got the case of a woman who had been married for thirty years; her husband had been hitting her for twenty-nine. He was a banker, and she was a housewife. They'd had four kids, two boys and two girls, but the kids were all grown up and moved out. She might have gone the rest of her life living with her husband and taking the beatings, but at Thanksgiving the wife of her oldest boy showed up with a broken collarbone and a bruise on her cheek.

"When I started to give this woman my usual speech, she looked at me and said, 'You can save your speeches for someone who needs them. When I saw my daughter-in-law, I decided.' And she pulled a loose-leaf binder out of her bag and handed it over. Inside she had gathered all her hospital visits, years of family photographs, diary entries, all meticulously ordered. 'Is it enough?' she asked me.

"That's when I began compiling my own file, because I had found out a few weeks earlier that I was pregnant, and as much as I could rationalize it away for myself, I couldn't do it for my child. Less than a month later I filed charges against Anthony."

"How did you go for so long?" Comfort asked.

"That's not a question I ask myself anymore. At the time it was the worst thing that had ever happened to me. Isn't it strange how the worst things in your life so often turn out to be the best? Or at least the most important. Because of that whole situation I finally understood something about justice. Justice isn't what they'd like you to believe. It isn't cool and impartial. It requires courage . . . and sometimes sacrifice. When I got out of school, I thought that justice was just about convicting the criminal. The problem is that those criminals aren't isolated. They are part of the fabric of our world, and that means that you're punishing somebody's father or somebody's husband . . . or somebody's son. And sometimes it's your own."

"You were the one who discovered your son's involvement, isn't that right?"

"Yes."

"And you chose to go to the police with that information."

"Yes."

"Was that a difficult decision?"

"It was the hardest thing I have ever done." As she said it, she looked at Jude, and if he had been in a room alone with her, he wouldn't have thought of his promise to Harry, or the possibility that the plan might fail and it all would have been for nothing. None of that would have mattered. If they'd been alone and she had looked at him like that, he would have told her the truth.

THEY BROKE FOR lunch and reconvened at two, but the courtroom was packed a full half hour beforehand. No one wanted to lose his or her seat for the cross-examination. The noise level was louder than normal, but when the judge banged the gavel, an almost immediate hush fell over the room, as if everyone had stopped in mid sentence.

Maria rose. She'd spent lunch talking to Jude, so he had an idea of what she was going to ask, but he was as anxious as everyone else to hear the answers.

During Anna's morning testimony Comfort had not asked about Jude's birth or his kidnapping by his father or his reappearance fifteen years later. Maria started by taking Anna through these events. When she had established the facts, she returned to the material of the morning—then she started with her real questions.

"You testified that soon after you were married, your husband started hitting you—isn't that right?"

"Yes," Anna acknowledged.

"And he continued to hit you regularly until you separated and pressed charges?"

"Yes," Anna said again.

"And why was it you didn't say anything before that?"

"I was ashamed. It's a common feeling among abused wives."

"But you of all people should have known that there was nothing to be ashamed of," Maria pointed out.

"I know. But I was anyway."

"Are you sure you weren't scared that it would affect your career?"

"Yes, I'm sure. Besides, if anything, it helped my career."

"Yes, it did, didn't it." Maria nodded. "Just like this trial is helping your career. It seems like a trend. Sacrificing the people around you to your career."

"Objection," Comfort hollered, jumping up in protest. "Is there a question here?"

"Ask a question, Counselor," the judge said to Maria.

"Did you put your husband on trial, and now your son, in order to advance yourself in your chosen profession?" Maria asked obediently.

"No, I did not," Anna denied hotly.

Maria merely regarded her for a moment, and in the resulting silence Anna's denial sounded a little too harsh. A little too emphatic.

His lawyer was very good, Jude thought. Too good. If he had actually given her something to work with, they might actually have had a chance. However, in trying to help him, she was undermining the point of his sacrifice.

After a long pause Maria chose a new angle of attack. "I wanted to clarify something you said in your testimony," Maria said. "Tell me if I understood you correctly. I believe you indicated that your husband's abuse changed you in a profound way. Is that an accurate statement?"

"Yes, I said that."

"And you were an adult at the time that it happened."

"I was in my late twenties."

"So would you say that it could have an even greater impact on a child?"

"I'm sure it would."

"So when Jude was restored to you when he was fifteen, did you ever ask him if his father had hit him?"

"No. No, I didn't."

"Why was that?"

"Because I couldn't do anything," Anna said, and her voice was so low that you could see the people on the benches straining forward, as if the extra few inches would help them catch her words.

"You couldn't do anything, so you didn't want to know?"

"But I did know," Anna said. "I didn't have to ask."

"So you knew that it had happened. You lived with your husband for one year, and it changed your life. Jude lived with him for fifteen. What do you think it did to him?"

She shook her head. "I don't know."

"Because you never asked."

"No, I never asked," Anna said. "I probably should have, but it was too hard, too painful. I didn't want to face what he must have gone through, so I didn't ask. You can judge me for it if you want to. That's your right. My reasons are not excuses. Circumstances are not excuses."

"That's a rather harsh view, don't you think?"

"Look around. It's a harsh world."

"Well, it has been for Jude," Maria said.

Comfort stood up. "Objection."

Before the judge could answer, Maria said, "Withdrawn. I have no more questions."

The prosecution's case ended with Anna's testimony, and the judge dismissed the court for the day. The next morning Maria called her witnesses, but they were few. First she called to the stand several students from Jude's school who testified that Jude had never pushed drugs on anyone. They told the jury that they couldn't name anyone Jude had sold to, other than Nick. After the students, she called a psychiatrist who testified to the effects of prolonged domestic abuse in children, trying to reinforce her theory of mitigating circumstances.

Maria kept it short and to the point, and her case

was finished before lunch. Closing arguments took an hour. The trial was done by three o'clock, and the jury was sent out to deliberate.

They took one hour and forty-seven minutes before they filed back into the courtroom to deliver the verdict. The twelve men and women sat down, and the judge asked if they had reached a decision. The forewoman rose from the bench and answered him.

"We have, Your Honor."

She handed over a slip of paper, which the bailiff walked over to the judge.

Jude found that even though he knew the verdict didn't matter, he was still gripping the arms of the chair tightly in suspense.

The judge opened the paper. Then he folded it again very carefully. "Will the defendant please rise. On the count of possession with intent to distribute, how do you find?"

"We the jury find the defendant guilty."

"And on the charge of criminally negligent homicide, how do you find?"

The forewoman looked at Jude, her chin lifted defiantly, and she said, "We find the defendant guilty."

Jude felt Maria's hand search for his under the table. Her soft, dry palm closed around his.

THE COURT RECONVENED for sentencing at ten the next morning, and when the judge emerged from his chambers, Jude noted that he looked older and more tired than at any time during the trial. Jude found himself wondering how old he actually was. Right then he looked like he could be eighty.

The judge lowered himself into his chair and rapped the gavel twice. The room quieted immediately, but he still paused a moment before he spoke. He looked at Jude and smiled. It was a sad, kindly smile.

Then the judge looked back out across the court-room, and his face fell again into tired, sorrowful folds as he addressed the people. "I would like to start off by saying I commend the prosecution for pursuing justice with ardor and determination. I also want to thank the jury for their service and their judgment. They chose to follow the lead of the prosecution, and I think they made a statement about the need for severity and high standards of behavior."

His gaze scanned the room, searching for something that he didn't seem to find. His eyes rested on Jude last, for one fleeting moment, and he nodded as if deciding something.

"However, I believe that sometimes mandatory minimum sentences are excessively harsh, and this is one of those times. In a case like the one we have before us today, considering the age and situation of the defendant, I find it hard to take any satisfaction or to feel like I am doing something that is beneficial to society.

"I think that while we have a need for severity, we have as much of a need for forgiveness. So, in the hope of leaving this troubled young man a chance for a life after his due punishment, I have decided to be as lenient as the law allows. The charge of criminally negligent homicide carries a minimum sentence of five years. The drug charge also carries a mandatory minimum sentence of five years without possibility of parole. These will be served concurrently. I hereby sentence the defendant to a total of five years without possibility of parole."

The courtroom sat in stunned silence while the judge handed down the sentence. Once he struck his gavel, the room erupted. Comfort stood so abruptly his chair fell over, and Jude could hear the voices behind him, which sounded as if everyone in the room was speaking at the same time.

Jude leaned over and asked Maria what the fuss was about.

"Don't you know?"

Jude shook his head.

"That man," she said, nodding at the judge, "has done a very brave thing. They wanted a bloodletting, and he spoiled the party."

"But I got five years," Jude said. It would have seemed long enough to him if he had actually had to serve it.

She looked at him in amazement. "You really don't get it. I was sure that you were going to get at least ten. With any other judge you certainly would have. You don't have many in his position that believe in forgiveness. I just wonder if they'll be able to forgive *him* for it."

Part III

24

WHEN JUDE FIRST arrived at North Central in mid-October, the first thing he noticed was the wall. It was as if all the invisible barriers in his life had taken form in this solid piece of steel-reinforced concrete, four feet thick and thirty-two feet tall. He found out later his experience was not unusual—whenever convicts talked about their first day in prison, they always mentioned the wall, and the feeling they had when the bus rolled through the gate, and they knew they weren't going to leave again for years.

As Jude exited the bus, he had to concentrate on the peculiar, shambling steps that the leg shackles required. The guard escorted him down the path and through a nearby doorway. They were buzzed through the door and into the receiving area, and his guard greeted the man behind the desk.

"Hey, Grosso."

"Hey, Terry. What you got there? Only one?"

"Well, this one's sort of long distance. I don't know how he got assigned here."

"Oh yeah," Grosso cut in. "Yeah, I heard about him. Come all the way from the other side of the state."

"Why on earth did they send him all the way over here?" Jude's escort said.

Jude could have told them if they had asked him. It was one final favor Maria had negotiated: to give him a dummy file and send him where no one would know him—to a prison where his mother hadn't put away half of the criminals inside.

"Well, he's all yours now, Grosso," the guard said. "I got to get back." He bent to unlock the chains from Jude's wrists and ankles.

"Thanks, Terry. See you," Grosso said, smiling.

Then Terry headed to the entrance, and Grosso turned toward Jude. His smile vanished immediately.

"What are you looking at, asshole?" Grosso looked at Jude with a glance that took him in and dismissed him with the flicker of his lids.

No one had looked at Jude like that in almost two years. He may have been a failure as a student, a disappointment to his mother, and even a convicted drug dealer, but for the last two years everyone had known that he was the DA's son, and that translated into being somebody. In those two years he hadn't simply adjusted, he had begun to take it for granted. He wondered how he could have forgotten what it was like to be just himself. On his own he was nothing. It was an unpleasant homecoming, and Jude shifted his gaze to a spot somewhere just beyond the man's shoulder.

"That's better. Now, step right over through there," Grosso said. The unassuming doorway opened into a room with concrete walls, showerheads on one side and crude drains cut in the floor.

"All right, strip down," the man ordered.

Jude slowly peeled off his clothes, folding them as he went and stacking them in a neat pile on the floor.

Grosso waited until he was done, then stooped to gather them up. He crossed the room to the wall, which was lined with empty cardboard boxes waiting to be filled with the discarded lives of men. Grosso tossed Jude's carefully folded pile into the box on the end.

Jude was subjected to a search and a delousing shampoo. The guard threw him a towel, and he was allowed to wrap it around his waist before Grosso led him out of the shower room and up a flight of stairs. They stopped at a doorway. Inside the room Jude could see rows of metal shelves reaching to the ceiling, filled with piles of blue fabric.

"Freckles, you in here?" Grosso shouted.

A man appeared around the corner of one of the aisles. Jude saw immediately the cruel joke in his name; three dark birthmarks spread across his face in uneven blotches.

"Right here, sir."

"How you feeling today, Freckles? Arthritis acting up again?"

"It's a little better. Clear skies today?"

"Not a cloud," the guard affirmed.

"Yes sir, my bones always know."

Jude looked around and saw that there were no windows in the room. All the light came from the flickering fluorescent tubes. It was late afternoon, and the man had not been outside yet that day.

"So what can I do you for?" Freckles asked. "This a new one?"

"Yeah, he needs a whole set."

The old man looked Jude up and down.

"What do you say?" the guard asked.

Freckles smacked his lips. "Size forty-two jacket, sixteen collar, waist thirty-four, leg thirty-two, and"—he glanced again at Jude's feet—"size ten and a half shoe."

"Well? Is he right?" the guard addressed Jude.

Jude nodded.

"Don't know how you do it, Freckles," Grosso said. "But get hopping. I haven't got all day."

The old man disappeared back into the stacks and returned a few minutes later, his arms full. Jude received two pairs of blue pants, two blue shirts, three T-shirts, three pairs of boxers, three pairs of socks, a blue winter coat, a blue summer jacket, two towels, and a pair of brown shoes.

Jude was allowed to dress from his small stock. Then he was told to grab a bundle of bedding, and the guard escorted him down the hall to the records room and left him there. "See you when you get out," Grosso said in parting. "If you get out," he added.

Jude was photographed and printed, and though he tried to wash his hands, his fingers left dark smudges on his bedding when he shouldered it.

A guard was assigned to escort Jude to his cell to drop off his new belongings, then take him along to the cafeteria to catch the tail end of dinner. They left the records room and came to a door with another guard behind a Plexiglas booth to one side. Jude's guard raised his hand to the man, and they were buzzed through to a wide corridor.

"I'm Mike Reilley," the man said. "But the inmates call me Mama because I try to help out the new kids. How old are you?"

"Seventeen," Jude said. He had celebrated his birthday in juvenile detention.

"You're a pretty good size for your age," Reilley observed—Jude now topped six one. "And," Reilley continued, "if you can believe it, you're not the youngest I've seen. We had one kid was fifteen when he came here. Personally, I think that sending a fifteen-year-old here is criminal, but I don't make the laws, so . . ." He grimaced. "Anyway, since you're here, I'll give you the grand tour. This is the security corridor that runs between administration and your cellblock. All the buildings are connected by corridors like this, and at the ends of them they all have sally ports."

As he was speaking, they reached another Plexiglas guard booth by a wide doorway—the entrance to Cellblock B. They were buzzed through, and Jude looked around at the place he would call home for at least a few weeks. It was a cavernous rectangular room with two tiers of cells, which had old-fashioned sliding doors and fat two-inch steel bars.

"This way," Reilley said, indicating the opposite side of the room. They threaded their way through metal tables and benches, and Reilley stopped outside the cell marked A17.

"You live right on Broadway," he said, waving his arm at the open recreation area, "a good address."

"Why's that?" Jude said, sensing something behind the remark.

"It means you have a better chance of not breaking something from a fall," Reilley replied, glancing up at the balcony meaningfully.

"Does that happen often?" Jude tried to make his voice merely conversational.

"Often enough," Reilley acknowledged. "You'd better hurry or you'll miss dinner. You can leave your things on the top bunk. Your cellmate, Old Man River, has the bottom bunk, and don't try to switch with him. He hasn't been able to climb into a top bunk for more than a decade."

"All right," Jude agreed. He stepped into the tiny six-by-twelve cubicle and glanced around. The walls glowed a sickly green in the fluorescent light; there was a sink against one wall, with built-in metal shelves above it, a dirty seatless toilet in the corner, and a double bunk along the other wall.

He left his things on the top bunk and followed Reilley to the cafeteria. The room reminded Jude of the cafeteria at Hartford High. It had the same long, low ceiling and the same cinder-block walls, but as soon as Jude had picked out the similarities, he also noted the differences. The school was the roughest in the city, but the tables and benches hadn't been bolted to the floor, and there hadn't been any bars between the students and the people who served the food.

"Trays and stuff are over there," Reilley said. "You'd better hurry. You've got less than ten minutes."

Already the men at the tables closest had noticed him and were nudging one another. Jude started down the side of the room toward the trays, but he felt the silence gathering at his back, like the front of a storm. As he progressed along the line, pointing at the foods he wanted, the silence followed him. By the time he turned with his tray heavy under the load, it had engulfed the room. All the faces on the benches were turned toward him.

Jude walked through the narrow aisles between the tables. Spotting a seat at the end of one of the benches, he headed for it, half expecting to get tripped up or have his tray upended before he reached it, but nothing happened. He sank down at the end of the bench, ignoring the staring men around him. Then, as if by signal, the silence was broken and conversations started up again.

Jude bent his head over his food to try to hide the pulse beating at the base of his throat. Mechanically he forked up food and chewed.

A shrill bell rang above his head. "Three minutes," someone called through a loudspeaker.

Jude started to eat more quickly. He wasn't hungry, but he knew he would be later if he didn't eat, and there would be no opportunity for a midnight snack here.

Around him men started to rise, taking their trays with them. Jude remained hunched over his food until a guard tapped him on the shoulder with his baton.

"All right, you. Get going."

Jude stood, picked up his tray, and followed the last few men through the open doors at the end of the cafeteria. He bused his tray and followed the stragglers into the corridor.

It was a different place now that it was filled with men. Sound bounced off the hard concrete walls. Before coming to the prison, Jude had prepared himself for violence, for the constant surveillance, for the loss of independence, but he had not been expecting the assault to his ears. It was the first time he had the vague sensation that the small, unexpected details would prove the hardest to endure.

When he got back to the cellblock, he headed straight for his cell. Picking up the things he had deposited on his bed, he separated the clothes from the bedding. The pile of clothes he placed on a metal shelf over by the toilet. The bedding he spread over the inch-thin mattress. Then he swung himself lightly up into the top bunk and lay down on his back. He made sure to lie so that he was facing the doorway.

A few minutes later an old black man, bent into the shape of a question mark under the weight of his years, shambled into the cell. He brought with him an overpowering version of the faint scent Jude had detected in the cell—sweat and aftershave and cigarettes and that indefinable smell of old age.

This, he thought, must be his cellmate, Old Man River.

The old man started to speak but interrupted himself with a hacking cough that bent him even farther over his knees. "Excuse me," he said, banging on his chest with a loose fist. "Goddamned smokes. Those tobacco companies, they're all murdering bastards. They're the ones that should be in here." He shook a cigarette out of the packet and lit it.

"So why don't you quit?" Jude suggested.

His cellmate spoke with the cigarette still pinched between his lips. "It's the damn nicotine they put in 'em. That's how they get you. We didn't know about that shit when I started."

"You know about it now," Jude pointed out.

The old man looked at him. "Do your own time, brother," he said.

Jude had a sudden, overpowering memory—he was thirteen years old again, hanging out with R. J. and the gang near the benches where the ex-cons spent much of their time. Most of them didn't have jobs, so when the weather was good, they came out to smoke or play cards. Jude and his friends made a game of how close they could drift up to the benches and how long they could lurk there before the men scattered them with a spit of curses. They had picked up the men's words and phrases and made them part of their playground talk. R. J.'s favorite had been, "Do your own time."

Jude held up his hands in apology, and the man seemed to accept it readily enough.

"So, how long you out of the world?" the old man asked him. "What they give you?"

"Five," Jude said.

"Walk in the park."

"What about you?" Jude asked.

"I'm doin' all day."

So the old guy was a lifer. Jude was both horrified and fascinated. "How long you been here?" he asked.

"I been inside going on fifty years, but I tell you, I remember that first day like it was yesterday—the first time I saw that wall. She's scary at first, but now I swear she like my mama—strong, solid, and real protective." He must have read something from Jude's face, because he said, "You'll learn to love her like a mama too, if you're smart."

Jude was glad he wouldn't have to twist himself into love. He doubted if he could.

"Well, we'll just see how you do."

"I'll do all right," Jude assured him. He told

himself that he could manage a few weeks. Surely he could do that.

"Maybe. Maybe," his cellmate said dubiously, shaking his head. "My last bunkie didn't make it six months."

The old man was clearly waiting to tell the story. "What happened to him?" Jude asked.

"Some inmate found out from a badge that he was a chester."

"A chester?" Jude repeated. It was a word he didn't know.

"Yeah, you know, a baby-sitter. Got caught foolin' with an eight-year-old. Fellas around here don't take kindly to that. So they thought that they'd give him a taste of his own medicine. Well, he bit the pillow for about two weeks before he ratted on them. He left here in a body bag. You know what they say—there are no secrets in the penitentiary."

Jude hoped that the higher-ups would keep his secret. He didn't want to think about the punishment for being a DA's son.

"You done time before?" the old man asked.

Jude shook his head, glad for once of his height. It made him look old enough for his cellmate to think he might have done time before.

"Damn. They always stick me with the new fish. Think I got nothing better to do than school some wet-behind-the-ears peckerwood. Well, I guess I know enough for two of us. By the way, I'm Old Man River."

"I'm . . ." Jude hesitated, blanking on the name they had given him for his dummy file, and before he could complete his introduction, the old man jumped in.

"You don't have no name here in North Central. Not till someone give you one."

"Give me a name? Who's gonna do that?"

"Depends. Whoever comes up with the one that sticks."

"Does everyone have a name?" Jude asked.

"Sure—every convict, that is. Some of the guards have nicknames too. If you're smart, you won't use them, but I don't imagine you're too quick."

"How do you figure that?"

The old man grinned, showing a wide expanse of gums, and he said with obvious satisfaction, "Well, you're in here, aren't you?"

25

THE NEXT DAY was Sunday, and as they were filing back into the cellblock after breakfast Old Man River asked Jude if he wanted to attend the morning service.

"No thanks," Jude declined politely.

"All denominations welcome," River said. "There's something for everyone. We even have a moment of silence for a Quaker in the congregation."

"A Quaker?" Jude repeated.

"You got something against Quakers?"

"No, I just didn't expect to find any in prison."

River clucked his tongue. "You got to rid your mind of those chains, boy. Look around you. We don't discriminate at North Central. Everyone can find a place here." He looked slyly at Jude. "Even you." Then he turned and followed the last of the men out the door.

With the departure of the religious, there weren't many left in the cellblock. Jude smiled cynically at all those men faithfully attending service every Sunday, like all true gamblers, hedging their bets, but after about ten minutes of lounging in his cell Jude realized maybe they went just because it was something to do.

Most of the men who stayed behind remained in

their cells. There were a couple of scattered groups at the metal tables. Two men were playing chess, another three had cards. Someone on the third tier was picking out a tune on a guitar.

Then he saw them—three men sitting at a table. They had no cards, no chessboard. They were just sitting there . . . staring at Jude. They were big men, their sleeves rolled up to show their bunched muscles and their stretched and faded tattoos. Two had cigarettes dangling from loose mouths, and they watched him with the intense but empty stare of wolves watching a rabbit. The third one, younger than the others, waved at Jude, fluttering his fingers coyly, and when he smiled, Jude could see that he was missing all four of his front teeth.

Jude looked away. He knew that wasn't a good sign.

He was right. Later they trailed him on the way to lunch and ousted other inmates to sit at the table just behind him. They followed close on his heels on the way back as well. They made no secret of their intentions; they were out to get him. The question was, what did they want him for? Jude tallied up how many days were left until the election. Sixteen days. All he had to do was survive for another sixteen days.

Jude spent most of that afternoon at the table closest to the guard's station. He didn't go into his cell. He didn't use the bathroom. He just sat and watched the ebb and flow of the inmates as they milled around the floor—and of course he kept a close eye on the three men. They were sitting at a table playing cards, and they were loud enough with the insults and threats they tossed back and forth that Jude was able to learn their names and the general hierarchy of their group. They were called Lefty, Slim Slam, and the Professor. The Professor was the biggest and the stupidest, Lefty was the most aggressive, and Slim Slam—the one with the leering, gap-toothed smile—was the leader.

Jude hovered around the guard station until lockdown, and he didn't relax until the door clanged shut behind him. The sound that just twenty-four hours before had been so chilling now sounded like salvation.

He let the old man putter around, piss, brush his teeth, fold his prison uniform, and climb into the bottom bunk. When he smelled the smoke from the old man's cigarette, Jude climbed down from his upper berth. He saw that the old man had fallen asleep with the cigarette still tucked between two swollen knuckles. The woolen blanket he had drawn up to his chest was covered with little round burns, and Jude wondered as he plucked the butt from between the old man's fingers if he would die in a fire in his sleep instead of being beaten to death before the two weeks were out. He extinguished the butt and—knowing its value—balanced it on the shelf alongside River's clothes and toiletries.

Jude brushed his teeth, washed his face, and climbed into his own bunk, but just because the lights were off didn't mean the noise stopped. The sound of caged animals, he thought. He didn't include himself in his assessment; he knew he didn't belong there. All the other inmates would know it too—in sixteen days. Fifteen, he corrected himself. Only fifteen now.

26

THE NEXT DAY Jude was given his work assignment. He had no high school diploma, so there was no cushy office job for him. He was going to work in the prison kitchen, though the truth was that he didn't care where he worked, as long as it wasn't with Lefty, Slim Slam, or the Professor. He watched carefully as the inmates separated out into their crews, and he breathed easier when he saw that none of the three was assigned to his group.

In the kitchen Jude was given his work station. He was responsible for washing all the pots and pans. He was also given a partner—a grizzled older man somewhere between forty and fifty with shoulders the size of a mountain and the heavy, misshapen face of a fighter.

Jude started washing, but his partner pulled a book from his back pocket and started reading. When Jude was halfway through the huge stack of pans left over from the day before, the inmate supervisor walked by, stopped, and spoke to Jude's partner.

"Hey, Mack, what are you doing, takin' vacation?"

"The kid said he'd do it," Mack replied.

"Oh yeah?" The man looked at Jude.

Jude shrugged.

"Nice of you," the supervisor said. "What a generous guy." He walked away, chuckling.

There was nothing else to do but wash—and Jude washed for eight hours, with only a half-hour break for lunch. His partner read and smoked while Jude worked, and Jude didn't say a word. Not that day, or the next or the next. He just bit his lip and played the coward. He figured he could stand it for fifteen days.

And it was all right—for the first few days. It was all right until he started getting looks from the other inmates—sidelong glances that noted his hovering around the guard station, narrowed stares that took in his anxious trot at the heels of the guards. After three days of his evading Lefty, Slim Slam, and the Professor, the other prisoners started letting Jude know what they thought of cowards.

The first incident occurred in the cafeteria. Jude was standing on the chow line when the inmate waiting behind stepped forward and stood beside him. Then Jude felt rather than saw the whole line shift three feet to the right, and Jude was adrift beside the line rather than a part of it.

He stuffed his hands, balled tightly into fists, in his pockets, and stood while the line moved past him. When the last man stepped up to the counter, Jude uncurled his fists and picked up a tray. He got his food and sat alone at the end of one of the tables, but he found he had very little time to eat. For safety's sake he needed to be one of the first finished. When he cleared his tray, he scraped half his food into the garbage.

It happened again at the next meal, and after that he simply waited off to the side, head down, while all the other inmates got their food. In some prisons, Jude later discovered, cutting a man in line was punished by no less than a month in solitary. The reasoning behind the strict sentence was that cutting was a mark of disrespect, and men had been killed for less.

But Jude did nothing.

Two days later Jude was shoveling his food down as fast as he could when he sensed someone approaching. He waited, fork clutched in his fist. He felt someone stop just behind him and lean over his shoulder. Then he heard the hawking noise, and the spit landed in the middle of his beans.

A shout of laughter went up around the hall. A rough hand clapped him on the shoulder and a voice said, "Eat up, now."

Jude stared at the puddle of phlegm sitting in his food, listened to the laughter around him, and bent his head so they wouldn't be able to see his flaming face.

After that he was fair game. He had to be careful where he walked because whenever possible an inmate would stick out a sly foot or deliver a jarring shove that sent Jude sprawling out on the cold concrete. When he became adept at keeping his feet, they reached out with stiffened thumb and forefinger to pinch whatever part of his body was closest. The pain was sharp, surprising. At night, when he got undressed, Jude could count his bruises from the day.

And Jude said nothing.

He told himself it was a part he was playing, but he was a little quicker than he needed to be in scuttling after the guards, and when he wilted under the glares of the inmates, it was maybe more convincing than it should have been. There was something—a splinter of true feeling—that made the pretending real.

Jude had lived most of his life not knowing when the next blow was going to land. He had faced down the barrel of a gun, with his father sprawled on the floor beside him. He had let himself be collared and put away for something he didn't do. He had been afraid, but he had always been able to maintain his composure. The fear hadn't affected him this way before. Something was different, but he didn't know what.

He figured it out while lying awake one night, long after the noise of the prison had quieted to a murmur. Jude realized that it wasn't fear that had broken him. He had learned to live with that long ago.

For as long as Jude could remember, he had dreamed of showing his mother that he was worth something. He had promised himself that he would do something to make her say, "Thank God for Jude. What would I have done without him?" He would give up anything, even his pride, to hear her say that.

Now, finally, he thought that he might be close. And Jude discovered that hope was more powerful than fear. You could break a man with hope.

27

SIX DAYS LEFT. Then five. Then four. Jude spent the nights imagining the inmates on the day that he was released: their consternation, their anger, their envy. Then it wouldn't matter how much of a coward he was—at least, that's what he told himself.

Jude made it through the weekend, though he suspected that his survival was due mostly to the fact that Slim Slam was enjoying the spectacle a little too much to want it to end. But Jude didn't care how he made it. All he cared about was that it was Monday, November 3, and he had only two more days to wait.

He had no idea of how Anna was doing in the polls because the televisions were on a closed circuit, controlled by the prison. They didn't show any news programs—only soap operas, talk shows, and sitcoms. A horrible thought occurred to him: What if she didn't win? What then? It was going to be a tough election, that much he knew. Anna was up against an incumbent. Even worse, too many people shared Deberry's idea that women just shouldn't be in politics. Someone had jokingly remarked that Deberry and his constituents still hadn't gotten over the fact that women had the vote. Jude remembered Harry talking about how the only way for Anna to have a real chance was if she stirred things up and brought more people out to vote. If Anna won, it would be because of Jude's sacrifice—and she would win, he decided. It was impossible to think that he might have gone through so much only to have her lose.

Tuesday morning Jude didn't get through as many pots as usual. The supervisor yelled at him, but he barely noticed. Jude didn't care because he was thinking of Anna. He wondered where she was at that moment. He wondered what she was thinking. He wondered if she knew.

Tuesday came . . . and went.

Jude hadn't expected to hear from Anna, but he was still somehow disappointed when the last count of the night was called and they shut down the lights. *Tomorrow,* Jude thought. *Tomorrow for sure.*

He was right. Two guards came for him the next morning.

She was waiting for him in one of the private visiting rooms. When he entered, she was standing in the corner by the barred window, looking out. The guard unlocked the cuffs and left the room, and only when the door had closed behind him did Anna turn. Then Jude could see that her face was tight and hard.

He hadn't meant to speak first, but it burst out of him.

"You lost," he said. He knew it the moment he looked at her. "I'm sorry. I know how much you wanted to beat Deberry."

She looked at him with an expression he couldn't quite read.

"I won the election," she said.

"What?" He wasn't sure he had heard her right.

"Deberry's out. I'm in."

She said it with such grimness, with so little pleasure, that Jude didn't know how to respond.

She went on. "I told myself that the day after the election I would come here and get some answers." She moved to the table and sat down. Then she motioned to the seat across from her. It was like the day they met in the police station interrogation room, a table between them, the real chasm so much wider.

What had gone wrong?

"I want to know why. Forget about the drugs. That was bad, but . . ." She waved her hand. "Let's forget about that. Why didn't you take the plea bargain? That's what I want to know."

She was supposed to thank him. She was supposed to tell him how grateful she was. She wasn't supposed to second-guess the plan after it had worked.

"But it won you the election," he said.

"So that's your excuse. I've wondered for the past seven months what your excuse would be, but I didn't think of that one—turning it around so that protecting your drug-dealer friends somehow won me the election. It's so twisted I can't imagine someone thinking of it, but you keep on surprising me, Jude. And I thought as DA I'd seen it all."

He was suddenly confused. He started to say, "Didn't Harry . . . ," but trailed off before he finished.

"Didn't Harry what?" she said. "Harry stood up for you as long as he could, but even he gave up on you when you didn't take the plea. He said he did everything but get down on his knees, and he couldn't budge you. I was still hoping that you would have some sort of explanation—something, anything—but I see now I was as stupid and blind as all the parents that come through my office. All of them hoping that there was some sort of misunderstanding and that their child couldn't possibly have meant to do these things they so obviously and willfully did."

"I didn't," Jude said.

"Didn't what?" she demanded.

"I didn't sell drugs to anyone. I didn't take the plea bargain because Harry told me not to. He said if we went to trial, it would give you a chance to show the city that you were exactly the kind of person they needed." He glanced at her and couldn't detect any encouragement, but he went on anyway. "It was Harry's idea for me to pretend to sell the drugs. He arranged for the phone call to come just when you were getting home. It was his idea that I should let the answering machine take it so you would hear. And it was Harry who told me I couldn't take the plea bargain. It was all Harry's plan and it worked."

He braved another look and felt that traitor—

hope—spring up again. She was frowning, but not in displeasure. In concentration. She hadn't automatically discounted it.

"But what about the policemen's testimony?" she said. "And those boys from your school?"

"See, I did take Nick to where he could buy drugs, but I never sold them. It's why I agreed . . ." He was about to explain that that was why he had originally agreed to Harry's scheme—to stop his actions from wrecking her career—but when he saw the growing disbelief, the deepening disgust, the words faded before he could say them.

"I see you've learned the art of thinking fast and talking faster," she said. "You'll have an answer for anything I think up, won't you?"

"The truth," he said. "Only the truth."

"When things like this happen, there's proof. Do you have any of that?"

Proof. She was right, there had to be proof.

"The kid who called me," Jude said. "Did you ever get that phone number?"

She shook her head. "Phone booth."

"Whose idea was it to go back to the house just then?" Jude pressed.

"Mine. I had forgotten something that I needed for the evening."

Jude had never known how Harry had worked that. Desperately he said, "Did you ever find anyone who actually said I sold them drugs?"

"So maybe you filtered them through Nick. Everyone knew you sold to him," she said.

"Harry knows," he said. "Harry has the proof."

"Harry would never have done this."

"He did it to help you," Jude said. "He did it so you would get elected. He knew how much you wanted it."

"I never wanted my only child convicted of selling drugs."

"But I did it for you," he repeated helplessly. "Harry said—"

"Oh, stop it. Harry didn't have anything to do with it. You know how I know that? If nothing else, Harry would never have left you in here."

Jude didn't know how to argue with that. He would have said the same. Jude had trusted that belief so firmly he had staked five years of his life on it.

As if she could hear his thoughts, Anna said, "Five years, Jude. Did you hear the judge? There's no possibility of parole."

He tried one last, desperate question. "Then why wouldn't I have taken a plea bargain? If I'm not telling the truth?"

She looked at him a long moment. "That's what I came here to ask you. I admit I had hoped for some sort of explanation, but now I see that was expecting too much. I will tell you one thing, though. I don't see how we can have any relationship if you don't give up this ridiculous story about Harry setting you up. You need to admit what you've done."

Jude thought that he would do anything for her. He thought there were no limits to what he would sacrifice. This was just one more lie on top of a dozen others. But this was a different kind of lie; it was the kind without eventual vindication—without a hero's reward at the end. If he admitted that he had done it, he would be giving up the hope of ever convincing her otherwise.

Even so, he meant to tell her what she wanted to hear. He meant to say, "I did it." But when he opened his mouth, instead of "I did it," he said, "I didn't. I told you the truth."

"I guess there's nothing more to say." Anna stood up to leave, but then she paused—and she did say something else. She said, "What did I ever do to deserve a son like you?"

He didn't watch her as she left the room. He spread his palms out on the table to push himself up, but he ended up just looking at the backs of his hands and the tiny lines that crisscrossed, like all the possible paths in his life not taken.

A moment later Jude heard the door open again. He expected the guards, come to take him to the cellblock, but there was only silence behind him. He twisted around to look.

Harry stood there, just inside the door.

Jude stared at him, his hands still flat on the table, as if glued there.

Harry circled around and sat in the chair that Anna had occupied.

"Harry?" Jude said it uncertainly, as if making sure that the man in front of him was the same one he had known for two years—the Harry he knew had always been understanding and supportive. It was true that sometimes Jude thought he sensed a distance—a sort of reserve—but Harry had always tried to act as a bridge between Anna and Jude. Maybe, he thought, grasping at straws, it was still part of the plan. Maybe something had happened that made it necessary for Harry to keep things secret for a little longer.

"Jude," Harry replied, and his tone killed the maybes.

"So it's true? You're not going to tell her?"

Harry just looked at him.

"How can you do this? How can you do this to me?"

Harry still didn't speak.

"You *know* I didn't have anything to do with it. How can you leave me here, when you know I'm innocent?"

Harry shook his head. "You're hardly innocent, Jude."

"What?"

"You were the one who made it possible for Nick to get the drugs that he OD'd on."

"But you don't get five years for showing someone where to buy drugs," Jude said. "You get it for selling, and you know I didn't."

"I don't know that. I know that police officers saw

you in the projects with him several times. I know all the kids at your school thought you were getting him drugs. I know that you understood it would destroy your mother if it ever came out that you had anything to do with drugs. I know that you lie when it suits you. That's all I know." Harry spoke quietly, as if reasoning with him.

"Harry," Jude pleaded. "What's going on? I don't . . . I thought you were . . ." Jude stopped, unsure of what exactly he thought Harry had been. He said, "I thought you were my friend." Surely he had been that, at least.

"Why did you think that?"

"Because . . . because you always tried to work things out between me and Anna. You stood up for me. You told her you thought I had potential. . . ."

"I did that for Anna. Most of the time she was nearly out of her mind with guilt and worry about you. So I tried to make her feel better about things. I tried to keep her going. She didn't want to hear the truth from me. The truth would have killed her. Hell, it nearly did."

"The truth?" Jude said. The conversation seemed straight from a familiar nightmare.

"That you're not worth it," Harry said. "You were given every possible opportunity to turn yourself around—and what did you do? You got yourself mixed up in drugs when you knew that it would ruin your mother's career. The career that was more important to her than anything. But maybe that was the problem."

Jude felt the words fall into his heart like stones dropping in a well.

"I've done everything for her," Harry said, for the first time showing some emotion. "The last seventeen years of my life I've been trying to make her happy, to give her what she wanted. Maybe it makes up a little bit for having a kid like you."

"But I did help," Jude protested. "I know I made a mistake, but I tried to fix it, and I did—she won. I kept my word to you," Jude said, desperate now. "Without that, I wouldn't be looking at five years. Five years, for God's sake."

"There's that other matter," Harry said. "Did you think I'd forget?"

Jude shook his head, not to contradict, but in confusion.

Harry's voice dropped to a whisper. "Your father. What you did to your father."

Jude had forgotten that he'd let Harry believe he was involved in his father's death. He said desperately, "Harry, listen to me. I didn't have anything to do with that. I just let you believe it because I wanted the questions to stop, and I thought you could stop them. Listen, if I could prove to you that I didn't have anything to do with my father's murder, would you help me get out?"

"And how would I do that?" Harry said.

"With that plan you had that would overturn . . ."

Jude let the sentence fade away. "There was no plan."

"No," Harry said. "Of course not."

"Never any plan," Jude said, finally beginning to understand.

"My first concern was Anna. She's gone through hell with this thing." Harry got up, the chair grinding as it slid back across the floor. "And if I have anything to say about it, you won't have the chance to hurt her again. Ever."

Jude lost all his hope then, and in the space where it had been was a terrifying emptiness.

Harry stalked past him. Jude heard the door open and shut. Harry had left.

A moment later the two guards returned. Jude stood—almost without knowing what he was doing—while the guards put the chains around his wrists and led him out of the room.

They escorted him to the corridor that led to his cellblock, but instead of taking him all the way back, they unlocked the cuffs just inside the last sally port.

"You're on your own now, kid. Good luck," one said, and with that they closed the door behind them, leaving him alone.

He stood there for a minute, his mind a blank. Then he turned and started down the hall. There was a jog in the corridor, and as he rounded the bend, he saw them. Standing there, waiting. Lefty, Slim Slam, and the Professor.

They stood, grouped in a loose triangle, blocking

the corridor. Lefty smirked at him. "Nowhere to run to, Chicken Man. End of the line."

Jude looked at their faces, twisted and ugly with triumph, and it was as if a jolt of electricity ran through him. One second he was numb and empty, and the next he was filled with mindless rage.

Jude had been angry before—but he had never felt anything like this. It burned his brain clean of any thought or feeling except for heat and a dull pounding in his ears. He started walking toward them slowly.

"Watch out, boys, don't let him scamper between your legs," Slim Slam taunted, and he stepped forward to meet Jude halfway.

28

JUDE WOKE IN the infirmary, woozy from the drugs pumped into his system. His moments of consciousness were scattered, and it was hard to keep track of the time. He didn't know if it had been only a few days or if it had been weeks. He tried to tell them he didn't want any more shots, but the orderlies—all prison inmates with good records—didn't listen. One man told him he wasn't going to risk his cushy job without a little persuasion. Did Jude have an extra pack of cigarettes tucked away somewhere? But Jude didn't have anything, so he got the shot and floated away again.

One day he came to as an orderly was unhooking his IV. "Good," the orderly said, noticing that Jude's eyes were slit open. "Enough jackin' rec for you. You're awake just in time."

"In time for what?" His mind was still muzzy from the drugs.

"You're being moved. Can you get up?"

Jude propped himself on his elbows.

"You're gonna need to do better than that," the orderly said.

"I'm working on it. Give me a minute."

"If I were you, I wouldn't keep the badge waiting. He can get mighty impatient, and he may decide to give you a reason to stay in the infirmary a while longer."

Jude managed to sit all the way up and swing his legs over the side of the bed. He waited a moment for the dizziness to subside. When he stood, his legs were weak and his side gave a twinge, but the drugs hadn't completely worn off yet, so he felt only a tightness and a slight ache.

"Ready," he said.

"Yeah, I see that," the orderly said with something like a grudging admiration. "Follow me."

"So where am I going?" Jude asked.

"You're headed for seg."

"Seg?"

"You know. The hole."

"What for?"

The orderly laughed. "I'll give you three reasons: Slim Slam, the Professor, and Lefty. That enough for you?"

"But they jumped me," Jude protested.

"Yeah, the stupid motherfuckers. Two of them are still in the infirmary—different wing." And that was all the orderly had time to say before they reached the door and encountered the guard waiting for Jude in the hall beyond. "He's all yours, boss."

"This way," the guard said roughly.

Jude followed the man down the hall.

The guard, as he walked with Jude, kept sneaking little glances at him along the way. Eventually the man spoke. "So you're the one they were calling Chicken Man."

"I guess," he said.

"They don't call you that anymore."

Jude didn't care one way or another what they called him now. Didn't care much about anything at all.

"I saw the men," the guard continued after a moment.

"Oh?"

"You're pretty lucky. You crushed the Professor's windpipe. He might have kicked it."

"But he didn't," Jude guessed.

"Damn lucky for you. Until the doctor got a tube in, he couldn't get much air down. They're not sure if his brain was affected. Hard to tell, since there wasn't that much there to begin with. How the hell did you do that to them?"

Jude shrugged. He didn't want to admit that he didn't remember much. He remembered the pounding in his head and the sound of someone grunting in exertion or pain—it might even have been himself. Also, he remembered the feeling of recognition at the first punch he'd thrown; for more than a year he had been using boxing gloves, and with gloves you couldn't tell the difference between hitting a bag and hitting a person. Fighting with bare knuckles was different—there was nothing like the feeling of flesh connecting with flesh.

The guard went on talking over Jude's thoughts. "I was the one that found you. Well, I found the other three first. I don't know if I would have believed it if I hadn't seen it. You musta spun out. You took those dogs apart. They were all still in the hallway, but you dragged your ass all the way out to the yard. Remember? You were sitting on the bleachers, cool as a cucumber, with that nice little hole in your gut."

Jude put a hand to his side, feeling the dimple there.

The guard noticed. "You'll have a pretty good scar, I'd say. But you know, it's not a bad trade—a scar and a couple of bruises for a new name. It's real hard to change people's opinions in here, but I guess you did it."

They came to another door with a sally port just before it. The man tapped on the Plexiglas with his baton, and they were buzzed through into the disciplinary unit.

Jude noticed as they stepped across the threshold that the air temperature in this wing was at least ten degrees lower than what it had been in the corridor. He followed the guard to the third cell, where the door was already open. The cell was similar to the other he had occupied with Old Man River, but this one was significantly smaller. It barely had space beside the bunk to stand. There was a mattress on the bunk, but no blankets and no pillow, and instead of being lit by a single bulb, there were two fluorescent tubes recessed into the ceiling and protected by a metal grille.

"After you." The guard motioned toward the door.

Jude stepped through and the guard swung the door closed.

"Welcome to your new home, Duck."

"That the new name?" Jude remarked, but without much interest.

"That's it. You went from Chicken to Duck."

"Not so different," he observed.

"You've got the wrong idea. It's not Duck as in 'quack.' It's Duck as in, when they see you coming, they'd better friggin' duck. But you're not all stitched up yet. Lefty wants to turn you out. You didn't take him down hard enough, and he wants some back. He's calling for a gladiator fight. They're already laying bets."

"Oh yeah?" Jude said, leaning against the wall for support. He wasn't used to standing, and his knees had started to tremble and his head was spinning.

"You best rest up while you can. Lefty will be waiting for you when you get out."

29

JUDE REMAINED IN solitary for a month. He did as much exercise as his cell allowed him, and he kept moving during the one hour a day he was allowed out. He learned to ignore the cold, despite the thin clothes and lack of a blanket, but the light bothered him. He came to hate those two fluorescent tubes behind their steel cage. They remained burning day and night. After two weeks Jude felt as though the light seared his eyelids when he lay down to sleep. There was no blanket to pull over his head, and it got so bad by the end that he would take off his shirt and tie it around his eyes in spite of the chill.

There was no escaping the hours in that perennially bright, cold light. Jude had no library privileges, much less a radio or a television. The only thing he had to distract him from his thoughts were the voices of the men in the cells surrounding him. The guards let the inmates hold conversations between cells, and they talked, it seemed to Jude, nearly twenty-four hours a day. Jude's neighbors discovered early that he didn't respond to any overtures, whether they were friendly or challenging or offensive.

Occasionally someone would ask about him. After a day or two in the hole new guys would say, "So is Duck in here?" Then they'd try to get Jude to talk. Usually they kept it up only for an hour or two. By the time he was released from seg, they had given it up altogether. Any inquiries about Duck would bring the short answer, "Yeah, he's here, but don't bother trying to talk to him. That peckerwood only talks with his fists."

Exactly thirty days after he was led into solitary, the same guard who had escorted him in came to escort him out again. When they entered Cellblock B, it was recreation period, and most of the men had opted to stay inside, out of the freezing wind that whistled through the two guard towers and down into the yard below. Nearly all the men that lived in Cellblock B were milling around the long, rectangular room that stretched beneath the tiers. Some played cards or chess, but most stood idly in groups. Few noticed Jude at first. They glanced up casually, but when they caught sight of him, they stared and nudged their neighbors.

Recognition rippled through the crowd, and everyone turned to look. It was like the first day in the cafeteria, but there was a difference. Because this time there was no silence. Instead the noise of the place swelled. He heard his name, at first muttered, then shouted and followed by laughter. "Duck," they cried, laughing at the simultaneous name and command. "Duck."

Jude ignored it all. He turned to the guard who had escorted him. "Could I go outside in the yard?"

"You want to get it over with? Well, it's as good a place as any—if you want to freeze your ass off. There's a blind on your left as you go out. They can't see in there too good from the guard towers, and there's no video, either."

"Thanks." Jude turned to go.

It was cold outside. The wind whistled around his ears and numbed his hands. Most of the men in the yard stayed near the doorway to be close to the warmth of the building. Jude slipped past them and walked out into the open.

By the time he reached the opposite wall, the number of men in the yard had doubled. Many of the inmates who were filtering out came, as he did, without jacket or hat. They glanced over in his direction but clustered with the others, close to the entrance. The crowd around the door thickened, and finally the man who Jude had been waiting for arrived. The others fell back to make a path for Lefty.

Lefty walked toward him and halted a few feet away. "Last time I saw you, you were gushing like a geyser," he jeered.

Jude didn't reply. In fact, he barely heard him. He was breathing through his mouth, drawing in anger with every breath.

One of the men from the group by the door called out, "Hurry it up, will ya, we're freezing our asses off over here."

Lefty obeyed. Jude caught a glimpse of the knife

in his left hand, and just as he brought his hand up to stab, Jude twisted out of the way. As the knife flashed past, the point piercing the fabric of his shirt, Jude caught Lefty's wrist and pulled. With his momentum already moving in that direction, the man sprawled forward, his hands stretching out to break his fall. When he hit the dirt, Jude was there, stomping firmly on the knife arm. The small bones in Lefty's wrist snapped, and Jude bent down and plucked the weapon from his fingers.

Lefty rolled over and tried to get up, but he was slow. Jude kicked the supporting hand, and Lefty fell heavily, landing on the broken wrist. That tore a yelp from him, and it looked like he was going to stay down.

"Get up," Jude said. When Lefty curled himself protectively around his wrist, Jude kicked him. "Get up," he demanded, and when Lefty only folded tighter, he kicked him again and again. He would have kept on, but the other men reached him then, hands grabbing his arms, wrapping around his waist, pulling him away. He hadn't even heard them approach.

"Get off of me," he panted, trying to shake himself free. He dropped the knife and heaved. About half of the weight dropped away, and when that happened, the others let go. As if from far away, he heard them yelling, "He's firma, man. He ain't gettin' up. You won. Back off, you won."

The whole fight from beginning to end had lasted less than a minute.

Jude stood there panting, the cold air searing his lungs and puffing out in heavy clouds. Someone tried to touch him, to lay an arm across his shoulders, and Jude shrugged him off violently. Another offered him a coat, but he knocked the hand away and turned from him. He walked to the far end of the yard, until he reached the fence.

He heard noise behind him, and he swung around, ready to go again. Wanting it.

"Hold on there, I don't want to fight you." The inmate who spoke to him was small and thin, with a crooked nose and a cocky swagger. "I just came over to let you know I got something of yours." He held out the knife, flat in his palm. "Spoils of war."

Jude reached out to retrieve it. Hefting the blade, he turned it, inspecting the steel. Then he pitched it up and over both fences.

"Christ." The curse came like an explosion. "Why the hell did you waste a perfectly good banger like that? It's worth at least five packs in here."

"I don't smoke," Jude said.

"Jesus." The man rolled his eyes. "You're too much. Okay, so you didn't want the knife. Will you take some advice?"

"I might," Jude said.

"You shouldn't stand out here by the fence alone.

The men up in the towers have mighty itchy trigger fingers."

"Thanks," Jude said, and started toward the building.

"Loners always stick out," the little man said. "You might want some company."

Jude didn't respond, but he did slow his pace a little, and the man fell in beside him. They walked together toward the door.

Jude glanced over and saw that Lefty was still lying there on the ground.

"Stretcher brigade will be here in a minute," the man said. "Nothing we can do for him, and nobody wants to get caught standing over the body. Let's go inside."

"I'll wait," Jude said.

"Okay. Well, I might as well freeze with you. By the way, I'm Fats."

"Fats?" Jude repeated, looking at the skinny little man in front of him.

"They say there are two kinds of prisons," Fats said. "There's the kind where I'd be called Fats, and then there's the kind where I'd be called Slim. I'll introduce you to Slim later; he clocks in at about three twenty. If you ever get shipped out to a prison where you meet a guy named Slim and he is, then you're in some hot water. Those kinds of prisons make this place look like playschool. You read?"

Jude smiled slowly. "Yeah."

The ambulance service—with a staff nurse in the lead, an inmate pushing a gurney, another carrying an emergency medical kit, and a third with oxygen—trundled out through the door.

"Okay, they're here," Fats said. "You coming back in now?"

Jude followed him, but the guards were waiting for Jude just inside the door. They slammed him roughly against the wall and yanked his hands behind his back to cuff him.

The inmates around them hissed and shouted, but the guards bundled him away anyway, and Jude found himself back in the same solitary cell he had left less than an hour before.

30

THE NEXT YEAR Jude spent in and out of lockup and the infirmary, with only brief stays in the regular prison population. As soon as he was out, he would fight, and it would be the same cycle all over again. It seemed that everyone wanted a piece of him. At one point there were so many they set up a waiting list. Whenever he got out, the next on the list would have a shot at him, and Jude was happy to oblige.

It was all he thought about—the next fight. Mostly because it kept him from feeling the knot of emptiness lodged in his heart and protected him from remembering his life before prison. There was no past and no future outside the next battle. He barely even remembered the faces of the men he fought—only the feel of his fists connecting, and the corresponding burst of pain when one of his opponents scored a hit. In the midst of his rage their blows somehow reminded him of love.

The first two fights were quick because his opponents had expected easy prey and were unprepared for any sort of attack, much less the ferocity Jude unleashed. As time went on, not only did they know what to expect, but only the ones who thought they had a real chance were willing to face him. However, no matter how quick or strong or skilled his opponents, they were never quite prepared for Jude's savage delight in the event. Nothing short of unconsciousness would end the fight for him. It almost came to that a few times, but somehow he always hung on to win.

As the fights got progressively harder, the injuries added up. Over the course of the next twelve months he suffered a concussion, five broken fingers and three broken ribs, and the loss of much of his hearing in one ear. He spent a month in the infirmary and the other eleven in solitary.

Jude won so many fights that for an inmate to lose to him was no disgrace. A man's reputation was made if he simply scored on Jude. The inmate who cost him his hearing was practically a celebrity for a couple of months, but with each fight that Jude won, the waiting list shrank. There were fewer and fewer who wanted to face him, and the ones who already had didn't want a repeat performance.

They didn't realize that Jude was getting ripe to lose. Some of his fingers didn't heal properly, and he couldn't make a solid fist with his right hand. The ear that had been damaged also caused him a bit of trouble with his balance, so that sometimes simply walking or even standing brought on a rush of dizziness so strong he staggered under it. Increasingly he had trouble sleeping. Most nights in solitary he lay awake, staring up at the thin, greenish light. It was the same kind of light that was in the kitchen of the last apartment he had shared with his father.

Jude's weeks of lying flat on his back in the infirmary ate away at his muscles, and he got tired of trying to keep in shape in the hole. He did a few sit-ups, some push-ups, and that was it. Whenever it came time to fight, the strength came from somewhere else altogether.

After a year passed, the waiting list shrank to nothing. No one else wanted to fight him, and the inmates wondered what would happen when he got out.

But then a new fish arrived in Cellblock B.

His name was Benito, and he had been sent up on a double murder charge. He was a big guy, six three and lungs to fit. He came in with none of the timidity that usually accompanied a new arrival. Benito was used to being feared, but when he got to North Central and he said, "I ain't afraid of nothin' or nobody . . . 'cept my mama," the inmates there didn't nod and laugh and agree like everyone had in his old neighborhood. Instead they said, "Oh yeah? Wait till you meet Duck. He's a bug—a goddamned crazy man." Or, "You want to see tough, you wait till Duck gets out. He's a case." Or, "You think so? Duck would make your mama look like mercy itself."

Every time he heard one of these responses, Benito's scowl deepened. Finally he said, "I can't wait to meet this Duck person. Think someone can arrange an introduction?"

And the fight was considered on.

There had been other newcomers who said they

wanted a chance against Jude—but there had always been a waiting list, and they were able to see Jude in action before getting a chance at him. All but the real fighters had an opportunity to back out, but when Benito issued his challenge, there was no one else waiting to fight. The slot was his.

Three weeks after Benito arrived, Jude was released from solitary. He was thin and pale and moved slowly, as if he had just recovered from a long sickness, and Benito laughed when he saw him. "This is the famous Duck?" he scoffed. "This is the guy who's so tough?"

He said it loud enough for Jude to hear as he was passing by.

Jude stopped and looked Benito up and down. "Who's this?" he said, and his voice was rough with disuse.

"He's just drove up, Duck," Old Man River said. "Thinks he can take you."

Several men standing nearby chuckled at that.

"I know I can," Benito retorted, annoyed.

"Seriously, who's next?" Jude said, turning away from Benito. He usually heard something about his challengers while still in solitary, and he liked imagining the fights. This time he had heard nothing.

"He's it," Old Man River said.

Jude shook his head. "No, really."

"What, you scared?" Benito taunted. "The mighty Duck is scared to face me? You know what I say to the mighty Duck?" He was getting revved up. "I say fuck the Duck. That's what I say. Fuck the fucking Duck."

Jude looked at him again, and for the first time Benito had a stirring of unease. There was something in Jude's gaze that unsettled him. The eyes that looked at him were flat, dead eyes. He felt as if he was being inspected like a side of beef.

"Well, if this is the best you can do . . . ," Jude said.

"I'm the best there is," Benito shot back.

Then Benito saw a spark kindle. "That right?" Jude drawled. "Well, I guess we'll see."

"I guess you will," he promised.

"When?" The eyes that looked at Benito weren't dead anymore.

"Tomorrow," Benito said, ignoring the flutter of fear. "After the work shift."

THE NEXT NIGHT was a beautiful evening. The air felt cool after the heat of the day, but the asphalt still felt warm to the touch. There was a light breeze that riffled the hair of the inmates as they stood waiting for the two fighters to arrive. The guards, as always, had a piece of the action so they wouldn't arrive until it was all conveniently over.

Jude got there first. He stood a little apart, his hands in his pockets, a strange, faraway look on his face.

Benito arrived a few minutes later with a confident grin; he had purchased a piece of insurance to make sure he would win.

When Jude took his hands out of his pockets, Benito felt the crowd step back.

Benito dropped to a crouch, his hand going to his waistband, where he had a short length of pipe tucked away as a little surprise, but the thin, sickly-looking kid in front of him just stood. Benito feinted forward and the kid didn't even flinch.

"Come on, pussy. You want me? You want me?" Benito taunted. He feinted forward again and threw a clumsy uppercut.

Jude actually staggered a little before the punch even landed. He had seen the punch coming, but when he was about to duck out of the way, he felt the ground lurch beneath his feet, his inner ear betraying him, and Benito's fist glanced off his chin.

The crowd let out a hiss of surprise, and Benito danced back again, out of the reach of Jude's fists. If he had just pressed his advantage, Benito might have had him then, but Jude righted himself and shook his head clear. The pain from the blow sharpened his mind, and he shifted his weight to the balls of his feet and curled his hands into fists.

The easy punch charged Benito with confidence; he discarded his early caution and lunged forward, intending to use his weight advantage by grabbing Jude in a wrestler's hold and throwing him to the ground. But before Benito could get his arms around his opponent, Jude's fist had buried itself in the high, soft part of his gut, and he was the one on his knees, struggling to draw a breath. He clambered to his feet, but no sooner was he up than Jude hit him again, a blow to the side of his head that sent him staggering.

Benito backed away, and the ring of men around him bulged to give him more room. He heard a low murmur from the crowd. Well, he'd show this punk, he thought, and he pulled the pipe out.

The murmur changed to cheers and laughter. Someone called out, "Now, that's a bone crusher."

Suddenly rediscovering his confidence, Benito passed the pipe from one hand to the other. He suspected that Jude might have something as well—a club or more probably a knife—so Benito was watching for him to retrieve a weapon. That was the reason he didn't see the look on Jude's face. If he had, he might have had more warning.

Jude was just coming off a three-month stint in the infirmary and solitary—the longest yet. The need to fight had built in him like an addict's craving. Jude felt himself slipping, giving in to the rage. Later he wasn't even sure how it had happened. Abruptly he found himself with the pipe in his fist, the man sprawled on the ground in front of him, and he was swinging it like John Henry with his hammer. Each blow landed with a dull *thud*.

Once again Jude raised the pipe high above his head, but suddenly he froze there, arm uplifted. All around him was a deep, terrible silence. The men were staring at him. Jude blinked and looked at the broken figure on the ground. Benito didn't stir. In fact, he hadn't even moved under the last few blows. Jude's fingers loosened and the pipe dropped, ringing hollow on the pavement.

Fats stepped up, stooped to retrieve the pipe, and passed it to another man in the crowd. A few others squatted by Benito and rolled him over. The crowd closed in so Jude couldn't see, and he let Fats lead him back inside.

Five minutes later Jude found himself back in the cellblock, sitting at a table with Fats. Fats had the cards out and was dealing. "Pick them up," Fats hissed.

"Was he dead?" Jude said.

"I don't know. Pick up the goddamned cards."

"Why bother?" Jude said. "They know I was the one fighting."

"They might know," Fats whispered, "but they don't have any proof. That might be real important. Am I your stickman or what? Don't I look out for you? Just trust me on this one."

The guards came for him ten minutes later. There were two of them, and they arranged themselves one on either side of Jude's chair.

"All right," the one on his right said. "Let's go."

Fats spoke up. "Go where?"

They didn't look at Fats when they answered; they kept their eyes on Jude and their hands on their batons. They knew that there had been some trouble in the past. Twice guards had tried to take Jude back to solitary when he was still keyed up from the fight, and he had not gone quietly.

"You know where, Fats. He's headed right back to solitary."

"What for?" Fats persisted. "He hasn't done anything."

"Yeah, right. Come on, now."

"How 'bout you let me finish this game?" Jude said.

"Wish we could." One of the guards tried to drop a hand on Jude's shoulder, but Jude shrugged it off sharply and stood.

"Easy there," the other guard said as both men took a step back. Almost, Jude thought, as if they were afraid.

31

BENITO WAS ALIVE, but barely. Reports from the infirmary said it was touch and go whether he would hang on. If Benito died, Jude could get a life sentence.

Jude lay on his bunk in solitary, staring at the overhead lights and thinking about the men who were lifers. They had a look to them, a smell, the air of men who were beyond the rest of them somehow. Everyone else counted down to the next parole hearing or watched their date of release crawl closer. The lifers clung to a sort of hope too. They still poured over trial transcripts and law books to find the hole in the case that could get them an appeal, but deep down they, and everyone else, knew that there was only one date for them to count down to, and that was a different kind of release.

Jude couldn't sleep—couldn't even close his eyes because whenever he did, his eyelids provided the screen for images he didn't want to face. He saw his father carefully packing the dime bags at the kitchen table. He saw Anna's face as it had looked when she took the stand in court. He saw his father's body on the kitchen floor. He saw Harry's face when he had told Jude that he wasn't worth it.

There were times when Jude thought he must have fallen asleep with his eyes open. At least, he hoped he had fallen asleep, because it was either that or he was losing his mind. He imagined he saw his father standing over him, and his father held a pipe high over his head, about to bring it down on him. Something shifted and it was Jude standing there with the pipe and Benito on the ground, but in his dream Benito opened his eyes and said, "You're just like your father." Then Benito's face turned into his mother's and she cringed away from him, crying, "No, Anthony. Please." He would shout at her, "I'm not Anthony," but she still cowered away from him and didn't seem to hear.

On the third day a guard came to the door of his cell in the middle of the afternoon.

Jude raised himself on his hands, and he felt his arms tremble under his weight.

"Hey," the guard said. "Benito's gonna make it. Thought you might like to know." He turned and walked back down the hallway. Jude let himself slowly back down onto the mattress.

His neighbor in the next cell said, "Hey, great news."

"What? What news?" the men down the range called out.

"Dig this out, Jude got paid. He drew a free pass on this one."

The block of cells was boisterous that night. The men were buoyed by the feeling that one of their own had gotten away with something in a place where the smallest triumphs were precious. In the midst of the celebration, when the noise hit one of those strange, sudden lulls, the man in the cell next to Jude's thought he heard something. The first time he heard it, he frowned and crossed to the door of his cell.

In the next lull he heard it again. It was a low noise—barely audible—but it raised the hairs on the backs of his arms. It was the sound of someone crying.

32

"YOU'RE LUCKY—JUST goddamned lucky you're not serving Buck Rogers time," Fats said to Jude.

They were sitting outside in the yard, up against the wall in the shade, but the shade didn't offer much relief—it was still close to ninety with the blacktop and the bricks holding heat like an oven.

It had been a long two months in solitary—the longest two months of Jude's life. When he got out, he saw the other inmates noting the difference in him. He had dropped at least ten pounds, and his prison shirt hung on his shoulders as on a hanger. He shuffled when he walked, like an old man or a lifer.

And he didn't ask about the next fight.

He waited for someone to bring it up, but no one mentioned anything. In fact, no one spoke to him much at all. Instead they sent Fats over to talk to him.

"I heard it was touch and go," Fats said. "Flip of a coin. If it had come down tails, you'd be here for the big bitch and not this little five-year walk in the park. You hear me?"

Jude nodded.

"There's something else, too. Nobody wants to fight you no more. That's it, Duck," Fats said. "You're done."

Jude closed his eyes. "Yeah. I know."

To his surprise, Fats said, "Thank God for that. They elected me to tell you. I was kinda worried how you'd take it."

Jude opened his eyes. His friend's narrow face was creased with a huge smile of relief.

"What did you think I would do?" Jude asked him.

"What do you think?" Fats said. "I thought you'd beat the shit out of me."

"I guess I deserve that," Jude said, sounding very tired.

"I didn't mean—"

"Don't worry about it." Jude waved off the apology he sensed coming. "You're probably right."

They sat in the shade of the building, the sweat meandering down their foreheads and dripping into their eyes. The shadows shortened as the sun reached higher. Their toes were in the sun. Then their feet. When it reached their knees, Jude said, "In solitary I didn't think I was going to make it."

"What do you mean by 'not make it'?" Fats asked.

"I was thinking about cutting up. I was checking the cell for places high enough to tie a sheet," Jude said.

"Damn. Was that when you thought Benito was gonna kick it?"

"No, it was after I found out he was gonna be okay."

"After? That don't make no sense at all."

"Before all I was thinkin' about was whether he was gonna make it or not, but after I found out . . . I had to face up to a whole lot of other shit."

"I can see how facing a lifetime here at the Graybar Hotel would make you want to waste yourself, but what was so bad that you wanted to string yourself up when you just got your friggin' life back?"

"Me," Jude said. "Me."

Fats didn't say anything.

"It's like I woke up from a bad dream and realized that it was all true. My worst nightmare come true."

"What's that?"

"That I would end up like my father. It's the one thing I said I would never do. Anything, as long as I wasn't like him."

"What did he do that was so bad? Was he an ex-con? Did he kill somebody?"

"No," Jude said. "Nothing like that."

"So what did he do?"

"He hit me. Before that, he hit my mother."

"So? You never hit your wife or your kid. You just beat up on some assholes that would have done the same to you if they got the chance. I don't see how it's the same thing at all."

"I don't know if I can explain how it's the same thing, but it is."

"Try me."

"Okay," Jude agreed. "But you can't laugh."

Fats said, "Cross my heart and hope to die."

"All right. I know I'm just like my pops because I understand him. I never did before, but now I know why he hit my mother and why he hit me. I can see how he came to that. I don't just see it, I feel it. I know it. I know what it felt like to be my father."

"What does it feel like?"

"Oh God." Jude gave a laugh that was half sob. "It feels like you've got enough rage to fill the entire world, and it's too much. After a while you can't hold it all in, and when it spills out, you hurt someone. My father spent his whole life angry. I'd rather die than live like that."

"But you didn't try it, did you?" Fats said. "If you'd tried and they caught you, you'd be in that other wing now. You'd be a cat like all the other Looney Tunes."

"No, I didn't. You know why?"

"Don't tell me you got religion?"

"No." Jude smiled. "No, that's not it. It's just I started thinking."

"Dangerous," Fats observed.

"I started thinking—I only ever wanted two things in my life. One was to be as different from my father as it was possible to be. You know how well I've done with that."

"So what's this other thing?"

"I wanted to show my mother I was worth something. I wanted to make her proud."

"How the hell are you gonna do that?"

Jude had spent most of the last two months trying to answer that question. He told Fats what he had decided on. "I'm gonna be a lawyer."

"Bullshit."

"You asked," Jude said.

"You can't be a lawyer when you're a ex-con, can you? There must be some sort of law against it."

"I looked into that. Turns out anybody can go to law school," Jude said. "And there's no law against convicted felons becoming lawyers. Hell, there was a guy who was a cop killer who got permission to take the bar. You just have to get approved by this committee, called the Character and Fitness Committee. All you have to do is convince them that you've reformed—that you've become an upstanding citizen."

"Oh, well, I guess that's no problem. We'll just ignore the fact that you're in prison. Just put that aside for a minute, do you even have your GED?"

"No," Jude admitted. "But I'll get it."

"You need a college degree, too, you know."

"I know."

"This is crazy. It'll take years."

"Years I have," Jude pointed out.

"More years than you have in here," Fats said. "I don't know that you can become a lawyer in prison. That seems like it might be kinda difficult."

"So I'll do the law school thing after. I'm gonna do it, Fats."

"All right, you're gonna do it, but let me ask you one more question."

"Yeah?"

"After you become this hotshot lawyer, how much will you charge old friends who saved your ass?"

Jude grinned. "Double. At least."

33

JUDE DIDN'T EXPECT it to be easy—there wasn't much in his life that *had* been easy—but he didn't expect it to be quite so hard, either. He'd heard of kids who managed to graduate high school without knowing how to read, and he thought that he was experiencing something of what they felt. How had he gotten so far and learned so little? If all he had wanted was his GED, he could have managed to scrape by without too much effort, but Jude was looking at college as well, and he knew he'd need better-than-average grades to get into a law school after that. He found the difference between learning enough to get by and learning enough to understand was like the gulf between thought and action. He had been a junior in high school when he was arrested, but he found he had to go all the way back to seventh-grade level in most subjects and work up from there.

It wasn't just the schoolwork, or the fact that every day he felt more stupid than the last. There was also the anger. It didn't just go away because he'd decided he didn't want to feel it. It was there every time he had to ask permission to use the bathroom, every time he opened a book and discovered that it hadn't gotten any easier since the last time he closed it, every time any inmate got released or admitted, every time the door of his cell shut at night, every time he thought of Harry.

The urge to fight hadn't magically left him either. It was as if his battles in prison had opened a new window into his soul, and what had been a sport had turned into an addiction. As with most addictions, he didn't discover the strength of it until he had to give it up. Even with the Benito scare the craving didn't just go away. He found the need remained, like an alcoholic's thirst. The smallest things could trigger it—the wrong word, a suspicious glance, the accidental knock of shoulders in a crowded hallway. Jude kept his fists stuffed deep in his pockets and his head down, but the energy needed to come out somewhere. He tried lifting at the weight pile, but that only seemed to make it worse. He always seemed to come off a workout itching to fight.

He stopped lifting, but he knew he needed to find something else. Then he discovered running. He loved feeling the pain bursting in his lungs and the exhaustion in his legs. He loved feeling it and plowing through anyway. It reminded him of the struggle in a really good fight, when you felt the only thing that kept you going was stubbornness.

For the first year Jude felt that sheer stubbornness was the only thing that kept him going with the studying as well. On weekends he had help from volunteers who taught classes at the prison, but during the week he studied on his own, and that was hard—he wasn't sure if he could have made it through without Mack.

Mack was his dishwashing partner. With all the time he'd spent in the infirmary and in seg, Jude had worked only a few days, but when he returned, he was back in his old spot, and Mack retrieved a thick book from his back pocket and started reading. Jude was fresh off of Benito at the time, and he didn't want to start a fight, so he washed without complaining. He put up with it for three days before he asked Fats if he knew anything about his work partner.

"Poor bastard," Fats said. "It wouldn't hurt to give him a couple weeks' rest."

"What's his story?"

"He's been on dishwashing duty for God knows how long. Years."

"Shouldn't he have moved up to loading and unloading the machines at least?"

"It's a crime he's in the kitchen at all. He's got a Ph.D. in science or some crazy shit. He don't look like a Ph.D., does he? Big as a damn truck."

"Is that how he got his name?" Jude wondered.

"I don't know. Maybe. That or Mack's just his name. Anyway, the story is that he pissed off the warden, and the warden said he wasn't no better than any other convict. That all his brains and degrees didn't make a damn bit of difference here, and he could just spend the rest of his sentence washing dishes."

"How long is his sentence?"

Fats made a face. "He's a lifer. And the whole

time you've been in seg, they didn't assign him anyone else to take your place."

Over the next week Jude washed in silence and let Mack read. It was a big book, and Jude tried to catch a glimpse of the title, but Mack always kept it folded open. Finally Jude worked up the courage to say, "Hey, if I'm going to do all the dishes, at least you could help break the monotony."

"I'm reading," Mack said, not looking up.

"I'm not saying you shouldn't. Why don't you read a couple pages out loud?"

"You wouldn't like it."

"Try me."

To Jude's surprise, Mack did. And he was right, Jude didn't like it. Or rather, he didn't understand it, but when Mack stopped after a few pages and said, "Well?" Jude said, "Beats just standing here."

As Mack kept reading, Jude was able to follow a bit better, and by the end of the day Jude was engrossed in the story. When Mack closed the book, Jude said, "Hey, that's not too bad. What is it?"

"*Moby Dick.*"

Jude recognized the name. "I heard of that."

Mack smiled, and Jude knew that it was a stupid thing to say.

"I thought you were a scientist or something," Jude went on quickly.

"I used to teach science, but I minored in English as an undergrad," Mack said.

"I'm gonna get my degree," Jude told him.

"Are you thinking of majoring in English?"

"Maybe. I don't know yet."

The next day Mack opened the book and asked, "Do you want me to go on?"

"Yeah. Sure."

The guys in the kitchen started calling their sink the book club. It took several months and a score of books before Jude ventured to voice an opinion, but by the end of the first year Mack had become Jude's unofficial teacher.

With a lot of hard work he was able to pass his GED in under a year, and one of the weekend volunteers recommended him for a job in the prison office, but Jude turned it down to stay with Mack. He began a correspondence program to earn his college degree, and he told Mack he wanted to major in English lit. Six months later he was offered another position, and this time Mack got wind of it before Jude had a chance to turn it down.

"Take the damn job," Mack said. "We can still work in the evenings, and when you get out, you don't want the prison kitchen to be the only job you ever had. You may be a hotshot honors student now, but you still need work experience—something better than washing dishes."

So Jude went to work in the prison offices, though he often told Mack that washing dishes with him beat the hell out of filing and learning to type.

Prison time, usually hard to fill, was no problem for Jude. He studied every chance he got and actually had to reserve time for cards with Fats and Old Man River. But Jude still had his bad nights—they were the nights that he thought of Harry.

IN THE WINTER of Jude's fourth year Old Man River caught a cold. Instead of clearing up, it hung on with a stubbornness equal to River's own and ultimately turned into pneumonia. He was moved into the infirmary, and Jude knew the old man wasn't coming back when they assigned Jude a new roommate.

River knew it too. They had given him one of the few private rooms, and that was always a sure sign. He complained about it to Jude.

"Damn people, they stick you in a tiny cell you're supposed to share with another man, make sure you never have a moment alone to yourself for fifty goddamned years—not even to go to the bathroom—and as soon as you start to get used to it, they stick you in a room alone to die. Now, I ask you, does that make any sense?"

"No," Jude said.

"Aren't you going to tell me I'm not going to die? That I still have a good bit of life left in these old bones?"

"No," Jude said.

"Goddamned unfeeling bastard," River said with satisfaction. "You were never one for bullshit, I'll give you that, and you were the only cellmate I ever had who didn't stink to high heaven."

"Okay, what do you want, River?" Jude said. Over the years he had come to realize that River gave out his doubtful attempts at praise only when he wanted something.

"Nothing," the old man snapped irritably. "Why do you assume I want something?"

Jude waited.

"And what if I do want something? Isn't a dying man allowed a last request?"

"Sure. Of course. What is it?"

"I want you to hear my confession," River said.

"You're kidding, right?"

"Do I look like I have time to kid?"

"All right, let's get this over with," Jude said.

River pulled a cigarette from the packet on his bedside table, lit it, and took a deep drag. Exhaling, he said, "I never told you the story of what I did to end up here, did I?"

"Armed robbery, wasn't it?"

"Armed robbery," the old man chuckled. "That makes it sound so serious. I went into a drugstore with a lousy Derringer—at least thirty years old—that I stole from my grandfather's dresser, and you know what the take was, that is if I had gotten away with it? Grand total of twenty-four dollars and thirty-three cents." He laughed, his mouth opening wide enough for Jude to see the fillings in his back teeth. "Armed robbery. Oh yeah. Oh yeah.

"It was all because I wanted to take my girl out that weekend and show her a good time, and I needed some cash. It was the only way to get enough. Tell you the truth, I'd done it a couple of times before without a hitch. They always handed over the money without a peep. I was smart and I always went for the places that wouldn't have a whole lot lying around. I thought, who's gonna make a fuss about a few bucks?

"And I was right. I kept myself in cash and no one got hurt, but then there was this guy, this fucking guy," and River's voice thickened with anger. "You know, it was partly my fault. I should've known. He was one of those foreigners, from one of those Arab countries or something. A brother wouldn't have been so tightfisted, and a white man would have been smarter, but this guy, this guy, he says that he's not going to give me a dime. I got hot under the collar, and I started waving the gun around. He caved in and opened the register, supposedly to get the money, and what do you think? The guy came up with a piece. It was pure instinct. I pulled the trigger and the damn bullet hit him, I swear, right between the eyes.

"A woman came running out of the back screaming her head off, and I fired at her. She went down, and I leaned over the counter to get the cash out of the register. I was so pissed off I cleaned it out. That was my first mistake. Usually I just went for the bills and left the change, but this time I didn't want to leave them with a penny. All told, it was eighteen dollars in bills and six dollars and thirty-three cents in change.

"And just as I was leaving this couple walks into the store. I mean, it was two in the morning and they stroll in like it's the middle of the afternoon. If it wasn't for them, I still could have gotten away clean. I shot them on my way out, and that was my second mistake. I was worried about being identified, but taking the time to shoot them slowed me down enough that the police were able to get me just a couple of blocks away.

"I was just a stupid kid. I was so jazzed I hadn't thought to get rid of the gun, but I don't suppose that would have made much difference anyway because I had blood on my clothes and my shoes, and my fin-gerprints were all over the cash register.

"So the way I figure it, that was pretty much the last day of my life. Since then I just been doing what other men told me to do—sleeping when they told me to sleep, eating when they told me to eat. That robbery was the last real act of my life, and all because—"

He broke off abruptly and sat there, the cigarette still burning between his fingers. It had burned itself almost to the filter, but he took a short drag to smoke it to the nub.

"I been here a long time. Fifty-six years, I think.

Maybe it's fifty-five or fifty-seven. I'm starting to lose track, but that's a long time to go between the last day of your life and your reward in heaven. I been waiting a long time—a real long time—and I don't guess I need to tell you that to make it through that kind of time, you need something. Something to hold on to."

Jude nodded. He knew.

"Well, this is what I never told anybody. The thing I held on to was that one shot. God help me, I'm proud of that shot. My first try, *bang,* through the forehead." He went to take another drag, but he found that the cigarette had gone out. He flicked it to the floor.

"My lawyer told me the reason I didn't get the chair was that I only managed to kill the one guy. The other three pulled through. I might not even have gotten life if the guy hadn't died." River paused, and when he spoke next, he looked Jude straight in the eye.

"I been going to service for near fifty years now, and for fifty years I've been hearing about forgiveness. You've got to forgive, and if you don't, you won't be forgiven your sins. I didn't try too hard. I always thought it would just come with time, but it hasn't. I spent so much time being proud of that shot, and now it's too late. I can't forgive him."

"Him?" Jude said.

"The only reason I'm here and he's dead is that he

was so greedy he couldn't spare me twenty-four dollars and thirty-three cents. So I'm proud of that goddamned shot. Right between the eyes. I couldn't have lived through the last fifty years without it, and now I can't give it up. I can't give it up."

"That's okay. You're trying. I think that makes a difference."

"You think so?" River asked hopefully.

Jude had no idea, but he wanted to say anything he could to comfort his friend. "I'm sure it does."

"I don't know when it happened," River said. "I don't know when it turned into something that I needed to keep going."

"It doesn't matter."

"Do you ever look around at all the men here, look at yourself, and think, God, what a waste? What a shameless waste? I think that's what did it for me. I saw the waste of my life and I thought, there's got to be a reason. It's got to be somebody's fault, and I figured I was bearing the punishment, I didn't have to carry the blame, too. That's just too much."

Jude thought of Nick and his death—how no one wanted to blame him. He had died, so he couldn't bear the burden of guilt as well. Then Jude thought of Harry. But it really *was* Harry's fault he was here, he told himself.

"You tell me," River said. "Tell me the truth, now. Whose fault do you think it was?"

He couldn't quite bring himself to say, "It was

your fault. Of course it was your fault." Instead he said, "Why can't you share it?"

"Share it?" the old man repeated. "Share it? That don't solve anything. That just makes it worse."

"How does it make it worse?" Jude asked.

The old man explained, and his answer made more sense than anything Jude had heard before. He said, "If we share it, then I need to forgive two people instead of just one, and if I can't forgive him, how the hell can I forgive myself?"

34

JUDE WAS AT the end of his fourth year, he had three quarters of the credits he needed to graduate from college, he'd gone through two roommates since River and almost all the decent books in the prison library, but he had never gotten a visitor since the day Anna and Harry came. It had been more than two hundred Sundays without his name showing up once on the list. Until that particular Sunday.

Jude was playing poker with Fats and Hammerhead and Mack as the guard read out the list of inmates.

"Hey," Fats said, "didn't they just call your name?"

"You're stalling," Jude accused him. "Bite the bullet and call the bet. Unless you want to fold?"

"Screw you, I'm taking you for all you're worth."

But before they could finish the hand, a guard walked up to them. "What are you, deaf? Get your ass up there."

Jude looked up. "What?"

"If you want to see your visitor, I'd suggest you move it."

"I told you," Fats crowed. "It's a forfeit."

But Jude didn't even hear him. *A visitor,* he thought. He had a visitor. He fought off a wave of nausea. It was Anna. Who else could it be?

Since he'd been in jail, she'd won a second two-year term, and she would be up for a third this coming fall. However, he hadn't heard this from her; he'd discovered this through old copies of the newspaper in the prison library. He also found out from the paper that she and Harry had gotten married during her second term. Since reading about her marriage, he'd stopped expecting to hear from her. He knew that Harry would do his best to keep them apart, but Jude decided that was fine. He could wait until he really had something to show her—like a letter of acceptance to law school.

Now that she was here, he didn't know whether to be excited or disappointed. He didn't want their reunion to be like this, here, when he didn't even have his college degree yet, but he also couldn't just leave her sitting there.

He stood, let the guard cuff him, and followed the others through the hallways to the visiting rooms. He tried to look calm, but he could feel the muscles of his legs trembling as if he had just finished one of his long runs. The guard opened the door, let him in, and closed it behind him.

It wasn't Anna. Or even Harry. It was a complete stranger.

He was a young man, blond with model-perfect features behind horn-rimmed glasses.

"I think you've made a mistake," Jude said.

The young man shook his head. "I haven't made

a mistake. But I guess you don't remember me, Jude."

Jude. He had called him Jude. No one was supposed to know he was Jude here. His dummy prison file was supposed to protect his identity. "Should I?" Jude managed to ask.

"I guess there's no real reason you would." The young man smiled ruefully. "I'm Davis Marshall."

"Davis Marshall," Jude repeated, and the name was familiar.

"I was in your class—at Benton. Once I asked you for an interview for the school paper."

"I never did an interview for the school paper," he said.

"That's 'cause you told me to get lost."

"Oh."

"But I did an article on your trial. I cut school and tried to sneak in. The first day it was packed and they wouldn't let me through. The next day, though, I got there really early, and I got a seat. I remember you just sat there like you didn't have a care in the world, and I figured you didn't. I was sure it would all come out in the defense."

Jude wanted to ask what Davis had thought would come out in the defense, but he didn't dare. Instead he said, "How did you find me?"

Davis grinned. "Trade secrets. Can't reveal the sources, but the truth is, it wasn't that difficult. Other people could have found you if they wanted to, but I guess they just never tried hard enough. No reason, I suppose. Old news."

"So why did you?" Jude asked.

"Well, after I graduated from Benton, I went to Northwestern, and I'm majoring in journalism. For the last two summers I've been interning at the *Courant,* and they've already offered me a job for when I get out, but they told me that you've got to have some years under your belt before they put you on the news desk—that or a big story."

Now Jude knew why Davis was there. "And I'm supposed to be your big story?" Jude said. "Listen, I hate to disappoint you, but you said it yourself. I'm old news."

Davis leaned forward. "You don't think it will make headlines when I break the story that you were set up?"

If Davis expected a reaction, he was disappointed. Jude had been in prison four years—he knew how to keep his reactions to himself. But if Davis could have seen inside Jude's head, he would have been more than satisfied because, inside, Jude was gasping.

"I was at the same school as you, remember? Even then I knew I was going to be an investigative reporter. You think I didn't know absolutely everything there was to know about you? I knew that you showed Nick where to get his drugs, but I also know that you never sold them."

Davis leaned back and waited for Jude's response.

But Jude didn't say anything.

"I figure they planted that heroin on you and they used some sort of trick to get you out into the park that afternoon, and the kids at school who were involved, they were so scared they practically shit in their pants. They were ready to tell the cops anything they wanted, even if it wasn't true. They were perfectly happy for you to take the rap. As for the cops that testified, well, that's easy. They saw you when you were taking that friend of yours to the neighborhood to buy. The only thing that doesn't fit is your mother's testimony about that phone call. I figure either it wasn't exactly what she remembered, and it was another setup, or she was in on it. Either way, it's a hell of a story, don't you think?"

"I think you don't have a shred of proof," Jude said.

"Not yet, but if we work together, we can crack it. We'll be just like Woodward and Bernstein. You'll just have a less active role being in here, but it's the same kind of thing. Corruption at the highest levels of city government and a travesty of justice."

Davis was so young, Jude thought. Had he ever been that young? But of course, by the calendar at least, they were nearly the same age. Somehow the thought made Jude sadder than he had been in a long time. Davis was smiling at him with a bright, open grin. Jude wondered what it was about that look that made him feel so strange. Then he realized—Davis was looking at him as if he was innocent, and the belief shining out of that handsome face was like a glimpse of the man he might have been.

The desire that swept over him was as fierce as it was sudden. For the last two years he had concentrated on studying and getting good grades so when he got out, he could get into a law school. Then he could go back to his mother and show her the letter of acceptance and tell her, "I'm going to be a lawyer." He had substituted that dream for the other one—the one where he convinced her of the truth about what had happened. Davis resurrected the old dream and held it up in front of him, and for a moment Jude was tempted to tell him, "Yes, you're right. You're absolutely right and here's how it happened." But as soon as he imagined the words in his mind, he knew he couldn't say them. He could see the headlines now—MAYOR'S SON CLAIMS IT WAS ALL A PLOT TO GET HER ELECTED. It would be ridiculous. It wouldn't convince her. It would disgrace her. Sure, the kid would get his headline, but Jude would be left with nothing.

So he said, "There's only one problem with your plan."

"What's that?"

"We won't be working together."

"Why not?" Davis cried.

"Because you're wrong," Jude lied. As he said it, he stood and turned away to the door. It was hard to speak, knowing his words would wipe that belief from the kid's face, but he had been through worse.

"I can't be wrong," Davis said.

Jude was already knocking at the door.

"I know I can't be wrong. I can get you out of here. What are you afraid of?"

The guard opened the door.

"Wait," Davis said. "Wait."

But Jude was gone.

Part IV

35

JUDE HAD TO take clothes from the charity bin at the prison. The best he could find was a pair of blue pants—remarkably like the ones he had been wearing for five years—and a wrinkled white button-down shirt, frayed and gray at the collar and cuffs.

The clothes that he had worn the day he entered the prison were returned to him, but they had barely fit even when he was seventeen. He simply dumped those in the bin when he took the new ones. The guard at the door warned him that it was cold out, and he searched through to find a jacket. The only jacket he could find was an enormous brown corduroy. He didn't need a mirror to know that it made him look like a bum. He almost put it back before he caught himself, and he had to smile. It was pure vanity that nearly made him return it to the bin, and he hadn't thought there was even a spark of vanity left in him. He had just over a thousand dollars in his pocket, but he would need at least half of that to pay for his law school applications. It was cold out, and he needed the coat more than he needed his pride. It was as simple as that. He threaded his arms through the sleeves, then crossed to the door and waited for the guard to buzz him through.

"You take care out there," the guard said to Jude.

"Thanks. I will."

"'Cause I don't want to see you back here in six months like that loser Shorty Dog."

"Or Tank or Junior," Jude added. "They just got to come home."

"If anyone's gonna be different, I think it's gonna be you. You'll make it out there."

"Thanks, I hope so."

"You ready?" the guard asked, with his finger on the buzzer.

"I'm ready," Jude said patiently. He had been ready five minutes ago. He had been ready five years ago, but he had learned to wait.

"Okay then," and the guard pressed.

The door buzzed and Jude pushed it open. The air was shockingly cold, and he buttoned up the tattered jacket before continuing down the driveway toward the gate.

He saw the car when he was about halfway to the gate. It was a silver BMW, idling just beyond the entrance—the same make that Anna had had when he went in. Jude kept his steady pace down the pitted asphalt.

When he reached the front gate, the guard stepped out of the guardhouse into the cold to shake Jude's hand and wish him well. The man swung back the gate with a flourish and Jude walked through.

For a moment Jude forgot about the car in front of him, forgot about the low, hulking misery of the prison behind him, and just looked up at the sky. It

was the first time in five years he'd had an unob-
structed view, without the corner of a gate or wall or
barbed wire or prison tower slashing across the blue.

A gust of wind rattled the trees and cut right
through the thin corduroy. He shoved his hands deeper
into his pockets and looked at the car. The windows
were tinted, so he couldn't see who was behind the
wheel, but just then he saw the driver's door open.

It wasn't Anna.

It was Dolores. Jude immediately recognized the
housekeeper who had sharpened her tongue on him
more than once in the year and a half they had shared
Anna's house.

"Jude," Dolores said.

Hearing that name called in a familiar voice
brought back all the old confusion and hurt. Five
years ago he hadn't known how to deal with them.
Now he said, "Hello, Dolores." He stood, shoulders
hunched against the cold, waiting.

"Get in, I'll drive you wherever you're going."

She spoke in the same short, snapping style, in
which everything sounded like a command. Maybe it
was the fact that with his damaged hearing, her voice
wasn't as sharp or as loud as it used to be, but now all
he heard was embarrassment and emotion in her
abrupt words, and it came to him that embarrassment and awkward emotion were probably what had
always been behind her prickly speech. She cared—
she just didn't know how to show it.

"I don't know how good it would be for me to show up at the halfway house in a BMW," he said, smiling.

"Oh. Well, get in anyway. I want to talk to you, and it's warmer in the car." Dolores got back inside and leaned across to push open the passenger door.

Jude looked down at his cracked shoes and baggy pants. The wind pushed at his back and numbed his ears. He stepped forward and lowered himself into the car.

It was like entering another universe. The deep bucket seats were a cream leather, and the heater was on high, making the car nice and warm. He had almost forgotten that people lived like this—he had been gone from the world for so long.

Dolores was looking at him with a strange expression. "You've changed," she said.

That made Jude smile. He could barely remember the angry, hopeful kid he had been when he last saw her.

"I forgot that you're not a boy anymore."

"I'm twenty-two," he said.

"Still young," she assured him.

He felt more like eighty-two sometimes, but he didn't contradict her. "So you're the welcome party?"

Dolores looked uncomfortable. "Harry arranged that your release was kept a secret so you wouldn't be swamped with cameras and TV crews and microphones."

"So are you still with Anna, then?" Jude asked politely.

"I don't clean anymore, but she keeps me on to run the house. She's got less time now, so I take care of bills and the new housekeeper and the shopping. She says I'm good at it. Three years ago she gave me this car, as a Christmas present."

So it *was* Anna's old car. "That was nice," he said.

"Yes, very."

There was another awkward silence, and Dolores asked again if she could drive him anywhere.

"No, thank you. I'll take the bus."

"All right," she said.

"So how did you end up having to come meet me?" Jude asked. "Did you draw the short straw?"

"I said I'd come."

"Brave of you," Jude observed.

"No," she corrected him sharply. "If I had been brave, I would have said what I thought. I would have told Anna that I thought she should be the one. She's your mother."

"That's okay. It's more my fault than hers."

"She's your mother," Dolores said again, as if this refuted everything.

He didn't know how to answer this, so he said, "Well, it was nice of you to come. Thanks."

"If you need anything . . ."

He nodded and started to open the door.

"Oh, wait a second, I almost forgot. This is for

you." She fumbled in her bag and brought out a thick envelope. Jude's hands were steady as he took it and opened it. It was filled with hundred-dollar bills—he could tell there was at least three or four thousand dollars inside. He held it in his lap a moment before folding the flap back over and tucking it closed. The money would make things easier, but he knew he couldn't take it. He wanted to do this on his own, with no help, even from his mother. He laid it on the armrest between them.

"I'd better go. I think the bus might not stop if I'm not out there." He opened the car door and felt the wind rush in and swirl around him, as if to claim him back from luxury.

"Don't forget this." Dolores held up the envelope with the money.

"I didn't," Jude said, making no effort to claim it as he got out and shut the door gently behind him.

IT WAS LATE when Jude arrived at the halfway house. All the stores in the area were shut tight for the evening, their metal grilles pulled down over the doorways and windows. The only light came from the streetlights and from the bright fluorescents radiating through the windows of a Burger King at the end of the street.

Jude rang the bell of the halfway house and was buzzed in a minute later. He filled out the forms they had for him and was assigned to room four on the second floor.

"Don't I need a key?" he asked.

"Seeing as there are no locks, I don't think so," the man behind the counter said.

Jude understood when he reached number four. The room had two bunk beds along each wall, dorm style. There were clothes and towels and shoes strewn over the floor and hanging over the iron railings of the beds, but the room was deserted.

He returned to the hall and heard the sound of voices. He peeked into rooms one, two, and three. They looked identical to his, crammed with bunks and smelling faintly of sweat and smoke. He followed the sound to the end of the hall and found the rec room. It had a TV in the corner switched to a sitcom, but no one was watching. The focus of the room was a table with six men sitting around it, huddled over a deck of cards, with several more on chairs pulled up behind watching the game. All had cigarettes, and the air in the room was thick with smoke.

Jude had a sudden, dizzying moment of vertigo, and he put his hand out to the doorway to steady himself. The gathering was identical to the games that had gone on every night in North Central. For a second he thought he was back there and that his release had just been another version of the dream of freedom that every convict shared—the dream that made sleep so inviting and waking so difficult. But in the center of the table there was a crumpled pile of money instead of the heap of cigarettes that prisoners always played for, and he noticed again the low ceiling of the room, so different from the cavern of Cellblock B, and the windows that looked out on the harsh brilliance of the streetlights. These men—all ex-cons—had simply transferred the life they'd had in the prison to this room.

Once he had recovered, the sight made him smile, if a little bleakly. There were so many thousands of prisoners right now burning, dreaming, and despairing over nothing more than a chance at freedom. These men had certainly lain awake nights thinking of the fantastic things they would do when they got out, and here they were, doing exactly what they had done on the inside.

They heard him or sensed his presence, and they looked up and stared at him coldly. "What the fuck are you grinning at, you stupid peckerwood?" one man said.

And here was the prison attitude all over again. He hadn't had it directed at him for almost five years, but he had seen it just last week when the latest new fish walked into the cellblock.

"Nothing at all." Jude turned away and left them to their game.

That night Jude ate at the Burger King. It was the only place in sight that wasn't closed for the night, and it was too cold to venture farther on foot. He sat at a booth in the back, looking out on the wasteland of brightly lit plastic chairs and tables. He had often imagined his first night out—he had envisioned a clean, soft bed, a dimly lit restaurant, and a wild, soul-filling joy. Never in all those night imaginings had he envisioned a sordid top bunk or an empty Burger King, but the joy was there, and he found the rest didn't matter.

JUDE SLEPT IN his clothes and in the morning just splashed water on his face before heading out into the bright sunshine. Most ex-cons had mandatory appointments with their parole officers, but under the condition of the sentence Jude had served his full time. No parole, no parole officer. However, they didn't just send him out into the world without a helping hand. He had an appointment with the social services agency that helped ex-cons find employment.

Jude found the office building and sat for three quarters of an hour before Mr. Travis came out to the waiting room to fetch him. He turned out to be a large, beefy man who looked more like a construction worker than a social worker.

"Call me Mike," he said to Jude. "Come on, follow me. I always have to come get my new cases because you'd never find your way through this maze."

He led the way along narrow pathways through cubicles and finally reached his office.

"After you," and he motioned Jude inside.

Mike followed and took the seat behind his desk. He had a file open in front of him, and he glanced down at it. "I took a look at your file this morning, then had a peek at our openings. It might not be exactly what you had in mind. . . ." He hesitated.

"That's okay," Jude said. "I don't mind starting at the bottom and working my way up."

Mike looked away for a moment, as if embarrassed. "That's good. That's the kind of attitude you need, but you see, it's not so much a matter of moving up as much as just waiting for the right opportunity somewhere else."

"I understand," Jude said. He knew what Mike was getting at. He braced himself and asked, "What's the job?"

"It says here that you've worked in the prison kitchen for a while, and there's an opening in the kitchen staff at a good restaurant not too far from here. They're very open minded. They're willing to hire even violent offenders."

Jude thought of his work in the prison kitchen. He didn't remember greasy pots as much as *The Great Gatsby, For Whom the Bell Tolls, A Tale of Two Cities,* and all the other books they had read over the deep metal sink. Jude said, "For the last two I've been working in the warden's office. By the time I left, I was pretty much running things. I got my GED and a college degree. With honors," he added.

"I know, I read that in your file, and you should be

damn proud of what you've done. This is always the hardest part for me, when I get a candidate like you. The problem is, there just aren't all that many firms that are willing to hire ex-cons, no matter how qualified. We have a few, but they don't have any spots open at the moment. Believe me, I checked. On the other hand, you never know when something's gonna pop up. So I thought you could take this, to tide you over and show that you're willing to work."

"There's nothing else?"

"I'm sorry. There isn't. Your best bet might be if you have any contacts—anyone who could pull some strings for you somewhere. I hate to say it, but that's the way the world works these days. So is there anyone . . ."

He obviously didn't have everything in that file in front of him, Jude realized with relief. The man didn't know who he was, or rather, who his mother was.

"No," he said. "No one." He didn't want his mother's help. Not now. And once he got into law school, he wouldn't need it. He could probably get a job in the school library or something. In the meantime he could do this. He'd just gotten through five years at North Central—washing dishes for a few months was nothing. "It's okay. I'll take this for now."

"And I promise, I'll keep an eye out for you."

"I'd appreciate it," Jude said.

"It's minimum wage, but you can get extra shifts if you want them. Here's the information." Mike handed a sheet of paper across the desk, and Jude reached out and took it.

"When can I start?"

"Tomorrow. They need people for the morning shift, and that starts at six."

Jude wondered what kind of restaurant had a morning shift that started at six. He glanced down at the sheet and it answered his question. He was going to be working at the Sunshine Diner.

It didn't matter. It might even be easier to work on his applications with this early shift. "That's fine," he said. "No problem."

"You're staying at the halfway house, right? I think that's great. It helps to have people around who you can relate to."

Other criminals, Jude interpreted.

The man must have realized how it sounded, because he said, "I mean other people who are going through the same thing. I always worry about the men who go right into a place of their own. The best, of course, is when you can stay with family, but if that's not an option, the halfway house is a good place. Have you met Marvin yet? He's another one of mine. Oh, and if you meet him, tell him I want to see him. He missed our last appointment."

Jude thought that the last thing he would do if he met Marvin would be to tell him to go see his social worker.

"Give me a call and let me know how it's going,

and if you move, give me your new number so if anything comes up . . ."

"Yes, I will."

"Great. Well, good luck." Mike stood and offered his hand.

Jude shook Mike's hand and found his own way out.

THE NEXT MORNING at six Jude entered through the back of the Sunshine Diner and made his way into the kitchen. He found it warm and bustling with people and immediately picked out the man in charge—a skill honed from years of obeying orders.

"Who are you?" the man demanded when Jude approached.

"I'm supposed to start work this morning, my name is—"

"Oh, you're the new jailbird, huh? Hope you work out better than the last guy. He was here three days. A record, I think. So we'll shoot for a week, okay? You work the sinks. How 'bout a pop quiz to see if you're qualified? Do the taps turn clockwise or counter-clockwise?" He waited. "No? I thought you were some sort of dishwashing expert. Can't trust anybody to tell the truth these days. Everybody's an expert, but I've got a soft heart, so I'll let you give it a try. You wash. Pots, pans, some silverware, except for the knives. We got to take our precautions." He smirked.

Jude knew the man was trying to provoke him, but after North Central he was immune to these types of insults. He had perfected his poker face when he was a kid, but it was only in prison that he had managed to match it with an inner calm, and it was mostly due to his studies. When he started, his only thought had been to become a lawyer to impress his mother, but he found the work helped him in ways he hadn't imagined.

So Jude was back to washing dishes, but he didn't let it bother him. It was only a temporary setback. He woke before the sun came up, rode the empty bus through the predawn streets to the diner, and washed dishes from six till three, when he emerged into the cold fall afternoon. Most of the kitchen staff in the back spoke Spanish, and they chattered on around him as if he didn't exist. He tried a couple of short phrases—*buenos días, cómo estás*—but their eyes skidded over him, their lips curled, and they turned away.

The real day started after he finished work. He went straight from the diner to the library. The first week he spent researching the law schools in the area. He picked ten to apply to. At fifty bucks a pop it was all he could afford, but he thought that ten would cover it. He chose two that would be a stretch, and the rest he picked from schools he thought he should have a good shot at. His grades were way above their average, and he had scored in the top ninety-fifth percentile on the LSATs. Once he had decided on the schools, he spent an afternoon calling to request the applications. Some of them, he discovered, he could download from the Internet using the library's computer. He was able to start on those immediately while he waited for the others to arrive in the mail.

Within three weeks Jude had sent off all ten applications, and then he had only to wait for their replies. He had rented a post office box for the purpose, and since most of the schools had rolling admissions, he wouldn't have to wait until spring to find out where he would be attending in the fall. Maybe he would even be able to take some early classes in the summer.

The first response came back in less than a month. It was from one of two dream schools. His hands shook as he tore open the envelope. He read, "Thank you very much for your application, but we regret to inform you . . ." He didn't need to read any more.

It had been a reach anyway, he told himself. He'd had to try, but it wasn't exactly a surprise that he hadn't gotten in. There were still nine schools to go.

He didn't start to get nervous until he had heard back from six, all very politely turning him down. Then it was seven. Eight. Nine.

Still Jude didn't give up hope. The tenth school—his last chance—was also his best. It was what he thought of as his safety—the one he would surely get into. An acceptance letter from this last school wouldn't be as impressive, but what the hell. He would still be a lawyer, and that would surely be enough for Anna.

It was three agonizing weeks before he got the last letter. He tore it open, but all he had to see were the first two words, "We're sorry . . ."

36

ONCE THAT DREAM had died, Jude decided to resurrect another; the next afternoon he arranged to meet Davis across the street from the offices of the *Hartford Courant.*

Jude spotted Davis the moment he walked out with a bag slung over his shoulder, his head bare to the wind. The pale blond hair was impossible to miss.

"Jude." Davis clasped his hand. "My God, you're out."

"Can we talk somewhere?" Jude said.

"Sure. Absolutely. There's a place around the corner."

Jude followed him, and they were soon settled at a table in a restaurant so fancy Jude wouldn't have dared to enter alone. He took one look at the menu and closed it. The meal would cost him almost as much as he earned in a day. The waiter came around to ask them if they wanted drinks. Davis ordered a beer and a steak. "The filets are great here," he told Jude.

"I just ate," Jude said, though it had been almost eight hours since he'd had lunch at the diner. "Nothing for me, thanks."

The waiter looked at him over his pad and said, "Nothing?" in a tone that seemed to suggest he saw through Jude's claim, though thankfully Davis seemed oblivious.

"A cup of tea, if you have it."

"You drink tea?" Davis said after the waiter left.

"Why wouldn't I?"

"I don't know." He seemed embarrassed. "No reason, I guess."

Jude knew why Davis was surprised. He decided to have a little fun. He told Davis, with a perfectly straight face, "Everybody drinks it inside the pen. Especially the herbal ones."

"You're kidding. I would never have . . ." Then Davis stopped. "Oh, of course you *are* kidding. I'm such a sucker."

"Sorry, I couldn't resist." Jude paused, then plunged in. "Listen, you have to promise me you will never print anything about me—not even that I've gotten out—unless I say you can, and I should warn you that I hope that I'll never tell you to." Jude was anxious about Davis's answer. How could he ask a journalist to help him—without even the promise of a story? But what choice did he have?

"You're telling me you're not going to let me publish anything?"

"Pretty much," Jude said.

"That's insane," Davis said. "And it will probably drive me crazy not being able to write this up, but"—and he grinned—"you know what? I don't care. I promise."

"Really?"

Davis laid one hand on his heart and raised the other in the air. "Scout's honor."

So Jude told Davis everything. He thought it would be difficult, but the only difficult thing was how to get the words out fast enough. He started with his father's murder and took Davis all the way through to the confrontation with Harry in the prison. However, he skipped over most of the last five years, mentioning only that he had gotten his GED and college degree and that he had been planning on going to law school.

Davis sat quietly listening to the story, but when Jude was done, he burst out, "I can't believe what you gave up. Five years of your life—and what did you say you're doing now? Washing dishes in the greasiest diner in town? If you hadn't agreed to be set up, your mother would never have gotten elected as mayor. Maybe Harry was right and she would have lost her job as DA, too. So what? She'd be in private practice now, pulling in half a million or so a year in a cushy partnership. You would have finished at Benton, gone to college, and you could be doing anything right now. You could be in the law school of your choice."

For a moment Jude imagined it—imagined that he had gone right from Benton to college to law school. Looking at it like that, he would already be in his first year. Then he remembered—he hadn't even decided he wanted to go to law school until after Benito, and the way he'd been going at Benton, he might not have even graduated, much less gotten into college. Maybe, he thought, he had needed something as bad as Benito to get him to work as hard as he had. Maybe nothing else would have been enough. He had probably gotten further, at least with his education, than he would have if he hadn't gone to prison.

The thought made it easier for him to say, "Well, it's done and there's nothing we can do about it."

"You know what we can do? We can get your reputation back. Get your record cleared. We'll get the proof, and I'll write the story—"

"First of all, there isn't any proof," Jude interrupted. "Not anything concrete, at least. If there ever was any proof, you can be sure that in the last five years Harry has taken care of it. It doesn't matter, though. You wouldn't be printing the story even if we had the proof. You'll never print the story. Remember?"

"I remember," Davis assured him. "And I'll keep my word, but for heaven's sake, why?"

Because of Benito, Jude thought. *Because of Old Man River.* Aloud he said, "I don't want revenge. I don't want to ruin Harry and Anna, and if the story came out, I'm pretty sure it would. I just want a bit of my own back. I just want her to know the truth. That's it."

"So how do we do that? How do we convince her of the truth if there's no proof?"

"The only way is if Harry tells her."

"How do we get Harry to tell her?"

"That," Jude said, "is the fun part."

37

A WEEK LATER Jude stood by the curb under the light of the bright red-and-yellow Burger King sign, while the headlights of the cars caught him in their beams and swept past. Davis had offered to pick him up where he was staying, but Jude didn't want Davis to see the halfway house—didn't want him to walk into the dirty entryway with the iron grille over the reception desk and the cigarette butts that littered the floor—so Jude had named the Burger King as a more convenient meeting place.

Davis and Jude had met twice in the last week, both times downtown near the offices of the paper. They discussed what to do about Harry. Strategizing, Davis called it.

"Okay," Jude had said. "To get Harry to do what we want, we need to find something to use as leverage."

"You mean we blackmail him into telling her?"

"Now all we need to do is find something to blackmail him with."

"What if there's nothing to find?" Davis said.

"There's what he did to me—though I doubt if we'll find any trace of that. But there'll be something else. I mean, think about the odds. We all have something—some little secret that could ruin us. Hell, I have one. You . . . well . . ."

"No, you're right." Davis grinned. "At heart we're all scoundrels."

Jude looked at him, and he thought that Davis looked about as far from a scoundrel as possible. People who passed him on the street often turned to take another look. Women smiled at him in hopes of catching his eye. Everyone seemed to want to please him, and Jude had seen him ask just one or two questions of a waiter or a coat girl and get practically their whole life story. It wasn't until Jude had seen this happen twice that he realized he had done the same thing. He had told Davis everything, or almost everything. Davis would be a great reporter; it was only a matter of time, and Jude had told him so. "Oh, I know," Davis had agreed, but when he said it, it didn't sound conceited. It sounded honest. "But I don't want to wait that long, and just sitting back and waiting for it to come—well, that's not what I think of as a reporter. I want to be the kind that goes after the story. The kind that makes things happen. I don't want to coast. I want to . . . to blaze." Then he had laughed at his melodrama, but it was a good word. He did blaze.

"You're hardly a scoundrel," Jude said. "Besides, I didn't mean that. I just think everyone has something that they're ashamed of. I just hope we can find what Harry's ashamed of."

"If it's there, we'll find it. We just need to figure out where to start looking."

They had talked a long time and finally decided that Jude would use his connections and see where they might lead. That's how they came to visit Mr. Levy.

A CAR PULLED into the Burger King, and instead of turning toward the drive-through, it pulled up behind Jude. When he looked over his shoulder, the headlights blinded him, but he then heard Davis's voice call out, "You coming?"

Jude rounded the car and climbed in the passenger side.

"Are we set?"

Jude held up a piece of paper in answer. "I've got the directions, and we have an appointment for tonight."

"How on earth did you arrange it?"

"The same way anyone gets in to see important people. I pulled some strings and a friend sent a letter of introduction."

"Friend? How exactly did you meet this friend?"

The inmates that Jude had fought in that first year of his sentence later turned into good friends. It was one of these who had provided his connection to Levy.

"I beat him to a pulp," Jude said.

"Half the time I don't know what you're talking about," Davis complained.

"Don't worry about it. Let's just find the place, okay?"

The place was a restaurant—housed in a narrow brick building with Christmas lights strung up around the plate-glass windows. They parked the car, and Jude led the way inside. They were met by a short, fat man with a folio in the crook of his arm. The man glanced at Jude, then his eyes slid to Davis, standing half a step behind. He chose to ignore Jude and spoke instead to Davis. He said, "I'm sorry, sir, but do you have a reservation? We're quite full this evening."

Davis hesitated and started to say, "No, but—"

Jude interrupted. "Is there anything under the name of Duck?"

The short man reacted suitably. He stood up straighter and took another look at Jude. "Right this way, *sir*," the man said, ignoring Davis now and dipping his head to Jude. As he led them through the restaurant, they passed through the outer room, then a smaller back room, and finally through a swinging door into the kitchen. The kitchen was like a sauna, heat rising from the huge stove that ran the length of one wall. The temperature was increased by the swarm of bodies that tended the pots and ovens, bent over the sinks, and stood along the long chrome table where they carefully arranged the plates of food. The man snaked his way through the chaos, and Jude and Davis followed as best they could. When they caught up to the maître d', he was standing by a narrow table covered with a white tablecloth and pushed against the back wall. There were three chairs pulled up, and one of them was occupied by Mr. Levy.

He looked like what he usually pretended to be: a very wealthy elderly businessman. He was carefully dressed in a charcoal suit with a white shirt and a red tie. He had a white linen napkin laid across his lap, and on the table in front of him were the remains of a meal. It was an incongruous picture—set as it was in the midst of the chaos of the crowded, sweaty kitchen. Jude suspected that Mr. Levy had chosen this place deliberately but wasn't sure of the reason. If he had chosen it specifically to talk with Jude, then it was to emphasize how far he was stooping to meet with him. If he used this as his regular meeting place, then it would mean something else altogether, but Jude didn't get a chance to ask him.

The man who led them there pulled a chair out for Jude. Davis claimed the other one.

"So . . . you're Duck?" Levy said, inspecting Jude. He had the accents of privilege, though Jude had heard rumors that he'd come from nothing and any privileges he had were ones he had won for himself.

"Yes," Jude replied.

Davis must have shot Jude a bewildered look, and Mr. Levy's sharp eyes caught it.

"And who's this?"

Jude answered before Davis could speak. "This is Davis Marshall. He's a reporter for the *Hartford Courant*, but he won't write anything about you, sir."

"Of course he won't," the old man said. "Not if he wants to keep his job. What has he to do with you?"

"He's helping me," Jude said. "He's a friend."

"But a friend who doesn't, I think, know about your nickname. Why is that, I wonder?"

Jude didn't answer. It had taken all of thirty seconds for the old man to uncover what Jude was most ashamed of. It was no wonder, he thought, that this old man had the power that he did.

Mr. Levy spoke to Davis.

"In prison every inmate gets a nickname. Your friend's was Duck. That's what he's been called for the last five years. What do you think of that?"

Davis assumed that the name referred to the bird and that it was meant to be unflattering. "I think they probably named him early and learned pretty soon what a stupid mistake they made," Davis declared.

"Your loyalty is touching, but misplaced." Mr. Levy looked at Jude but continued speaking to Davis. "Your friend here was too modest to tell you himself, so I will."

"No, not too modest," Jude said, breaking in, unable to let that remark pass. "It's not something I'm proud of, and I've done nothing to earn it for almost four years."

Mr. Levy cocked his head. "I see. So that's how it goes with you. Your mother's son after all," and he laughed at the expression on both their faces. "You didn't think I would let you in to see me without doing my homework, did you? I think I can still sniff out a fake prison file, even if I am getting old. That's the real reason I agreed to meet with you—not because some convict asked me. I wanted to see you for myself, and I was curious about what you wanted. But to finish the story," he said, turning back to Davis, "the name Duck carried something of a different meaning than you first imagined. It was part of a little saying. If you see him coming, you'd better duck. In his last fight he beat a man almost to death with a pipe."

It was just as well Davis knew the truth, Jude thought. It served him right for not telling Davis in the beginning.

"But you didn't come here to listen to stories about yourself. Tell me, what is it you came to me for?"

"I have heard," Jude said carefully, "that you have the police department in your pocket."

"Half," Levy said, laughing. "Only half the police department, but since that's all I really need, I try not to be greedy."

"And I was told that you would be able to tell me if a cop had done anything . . . that he shouldn't have."

"Yes, I could tell you that. You begin to interest me. Go on."

"Harry Wichowski," Jude said. "I want to know about Harry Wichowski."

Mr. Levy considered. "You want to know about Harry?"

"Yes."

"So you're going that route? Yes, that's clever. That would certainly hurt her."

It took Jude a moment to realize what the old man meant. He thought that Jude wanted to know about Harry in order to hurt Anna.

Jude was willing to let Mr. Levy think whatever he wanted, but Davis broke out, "You've got it all wrong. That's not why he——"

"Shut up, Davis," Jude said, but it was too late.

"That's not it, then? The plot thickens. I find you *very* interesting," Mr. Levy said to Jude. "Very interesting. And I would like to help you; there aren't many cops out there that haven't slipped up at least once on the job. I'm not saying that Harry Wichowski hasn't, but he is either unusually honest or unusually careful, because unfortunately I have nothing on him. There were some rumors at one time, several years ago—but I was never able to find anything concrete. Unfortunately for us both. It has proved rather inconvenient to me recently. I'm sorry I can't help you, but is there anyone else?"

Jude was about to shake his head no, but on a whim he said, "Anthony Arvelo. What about him?"

"Your father? He was honest, if that's what you want to know. He wasn't crooked. He was a cop's cop, but he had his one slipup—though I happen to admire him for it. He did a favor for an old friend from the neighborhood who also happens to be a colleague of mine."

An old friend. The words triggered something deep in Jude's brain, and he remembered a voice saying, "We grew up together. We're not exactly friends, but when you go that far back with someone, that means you do something for them if you're in a position to." He remembered the man who talked to him over the body of his father and left him alive.

"What was the man's name?" Jude asked, trying to keep his voice casual.

"Joseph Palazzo," Mr. Levy said. "He needed somebody like your father around a few years ago. He's serving at the federal prison down in Danbury. Before you get your hopes up, I want to assure you that Harry wasn't in on your father's favor. That was before they were partners. Harry probably knew about it, but he didn't have any part of it."

Jude nodded as if that answered the question he had meant to ask.

"But I haven't helped at all, have I? Is there anything else I can do for you?"

"No, thank you," Jude said politely. "Nothing that I can think of."

"Well, you come back whenever you think of anything, and I'll try to do better. In the meantime, maybe I can do something for your friend here. You said he was a reporter for the *Hartford Courant*?"

"Yes."

"Is he any good? Oh, I suppose it doesn't much matter. There's someone who hasn't been cooperative of late. I've been meaning to settle accounts but haven't gotten around to it. Now I think I will. I'll have some information sent to your friend at the *Hartford Courant* in the next few days. I'll include some names to verify the information, and your friend can go ahead and print that story. It's amusing. I'm sure you'll enjoy it. You sure there's nothing else? No? Then I hope you won't mind if I ask that you show yourselves out."

Davis kept quiet as they trooped out of the kitchen and wended their way through the tightly packed tables to the front door. When they emerged onto the sidewalk, Davis couldn't hold it in anymore. "That was incredible. What about when he said that he could—"

"Save it for the car," Jude snapped.

"Oh, yeah, sorry," Davis said, but he burst out as soon as they were inside the car.

"Do you really think he's going to send me a story? Something good?"

"Yes," Jude said. "He'll send it."

"This is exactly what I've been waiting for. I can hardly believe it, and it's all because of you."

"Don't mention it," Jude said, staring out the passenger window, bracing himself for what he sensed was going to follow.

Davis subsided and remained quiet as he drove the unfamiliar part of the route, retracing their turns until he hit a main road that would lead them most of the way back to Jude's neighborhood. Then it came, as Jude had known it would.

Davis's voice was uncharacteristically hesitant when he spoke next. "Don't worry about what Mr. Levy said about you. You already told me that you did some things in prison. You know it doesn't change anything."

Jude didn't turn from his study of the buildings flashing by. "Thanks."

There was an awkward pause. Davis was the one who broke it. "We didn't get anything on Harry," he said.

"No," Jude agreed grimly.

"But he did say there were some rumors."

"If Mr. Levy couldn't find out what it was, I don't think we'll be able to," Jude said.

"So what do we do next?"

"I'll have to think about it."

The Burger King came up on the left and Davis pulled in.

"You're sure I can't take you farther?"

"No thanks." Jude opened the door and started to get out.

"Hey, wait a second," Davis protested. "When will we get together again?"

Jude pulled his leg back in but didn't shut the door.

"I was thinking maybe you could come over for dinner," Davis said. "I'll get my sister to cook. I can barely boil water, but my sister's a whiz."

Muscles Jude hadn't realized were tensed suddenly relaxed. Things really *hadn't* changed, despite what Davis had heard. They couldn't have if Davis was inviting him over to his house. He smiled and said, "Okay."

"How does next week sound? How about Wednesday?"

"Yeah, that's fine."

"Let me give you my address." Davis pulled out a notebook and jotted down his address and directions. "Seven okay for you?"

"Works for me."

As Jude rode the bus out to Davis's house, he watched the street signs for his stop. When he got off and the bus roared away, Jude was left on an empty road with a guardrail along either side and trees beyond. Davis's directions took him off the road into a dark, narrow lane bordered by fences and tall shrubbery. The houses—all set back from the road—were invisible.

Jude followed the numbers on the mailboxes and located number twelve. There was a gate across the driveway, but he found a door off to one side. He started up the driveway and soon got a glimpse of the house. It was a sprawling old Tudor, dark and fortresslike. He knew the houses in this part of West Hartford were big, but he hadn't quite expected this.

Davis answered the door with a dish towel thrown over his shoulder and a huge grin.

"You came," he said. "Thank God. Otherwise I don't know what we would have done with all this food. Come on in. We're still getting things together in the kitchen. Hey, did you see the article yesterday?"

"What article?"

"The one with the scoop from your friend Mr. Levy. It came last week, right after we saw him. I checked everything and wrote it up, and it ran yesterday. Front page. I'll show it to you later, after dinner."

Jude followed him through the hallway, catching glimpses of the rooms they passed.

"Nice place," Jude said.

"I have Lizzie to thank for that. She's the one who keeps it from turning into a pigsty. I'm a terrible slob."

"Lizzie?" Jude said, making it a question.

"My sister. Didn't I tell you that she agreed to cook for us tonight? If I have to fend for myself, it's pretty much a choice between takeout and cereal."

"Your sister cleans your house?"

"Well, yes, but it's her house too. We both live here. After my parents died, instead of selling, we decided to keep the house and live in it. I just agreed because I knew I could get her to cook," and with that he led Jude into the kitchen, where Lizzie stood with her back to them, bent over a pot on the stove. "And here she is. Lizzie, this is Jude. Jude, Lizzie," he performed the introductions.

Lizzie turned around, a slotted spoon held loosely in one hand, the other palm cupped beneath to guard against drips. She looked a lot like her brother, but less dauntingly perfect. Where Davis's hair was golden, hers was dirty blond. Where his features were perfectly regular, hers were just a little off, and she showed her gums when she grinned at Jude. She said, "Hi. Hope you like chicken."

"Who doesn't like chicken?" Davis said, rolling his eyes at Jude.

"Vegetarians don't," she said.

Jude smiled. "She's got you there."

"But you're not a vegetarian. You can't very well be a vegetarian in—" He broke off abruptly, then finished rather lamely, "Well, where you've been for the last few years."

"He's been very mysterious about you," Lizzie told Jude. "He keeps starting sentences, leaving off in the middle, and letting me fill in with my wild imagination. Now you're here, maybe you can tell me yourself. Where have you been that you couldn't easily be a vegetarian?"

"Lizzie!" Davis protested.

"It's all right," Jude said to Davis. Then he answered her. "I've been in prison."

There was only the slightest of hesitations before

she said, "Well, thank God. I was afraid you were going to say that you'd been somewhere dreadful."

"Like?" Jude said, wondering what she would come up with.

"Oh, like working in the peace corps in Burma or someplace. Then we'd have to sit and listen to your stories about the native customs for hours and pretend to be fascinated and awed by the simple beauty of the people, when all we'd really want to talk about is the last movie we saw."

"You can rest easy with your near escape," Jude said.

"You're not kidding. You should see some of the horrific people that Davis brings home to dinner with him. He does it just to charm them with his nice house and his plain sister who happens to be able to cook. Whenever he brings someone home, I know he wants something from them, and I just thought it sporting to warn you."

Jude remembered how touched he had been at the invitation. *So much for that,* he thought wryly.

When they had dinner, Jude discovered why Davis had so importantly announced that Lizzie was cooking. It was better than any dinner he had been able to afford since he got out, and it bore no resemblance to what they had been served in the prison cafeteria. That made it the best meal he'd had in years. When Jude helped himself to thirds, Lizzie said, "This is the first guest you've brought home who really knows how to compliment a cook," though he hadn't said a word.

During dinner Jude let Lizzie and Davis do most of the talking. He found out that the two were twins, though Davis was the elder by about ten minutes. "He was always the pushy one," Lizzie said. After college they decided to share their parents' house, though they hadn't lived together since they were thirteen. Lizzie admitted that she had been sent away to a boarding school. "I was going through a tough time, and the old parentals didn't know what to do with me. They kept Davis because he knew how to fool them into thinking he was an angel, when he was actually worse than I ever was," she said, laughing.

"I wish. I remember desperately wanting to be a rebel in school but failing miserably. You know, Jude was my hero in high school," Davis said. "He was everything I wanted to be. He was so cool."

"Jude went to Benton?" Lizzie said. "But . . . ," and she broke off there.

Jude knew what she had been about to say. She had been about to wonder about his ending up in prison. He had almost forgotten that she knew he was an ex-con. There weren't many students who attended Benton and ended up serving a prison sentence. He saw her making the connections. "Jude . . . Grady?" she said.

"I don't go by that name now," he replied.

She nodded as if it was no big deal, and simply

went on with her story. Jude found out that Lizzie worked at a bank as a lending officer. He let his surprise show, and she explained easily, "I like numbers, and you don't have to be political to get ahead. You just have to do good work. I'm not so hot at the political stuff. I leave that stuff to Davis. He got the looks and the charm, and I got the brains."

Davis clutched his chest. "Oh, a hit."

They joked and laughed, and Jude thought about how his life might have been different if he'd had a sister. Especially a sister like Lizzie. Their banter touched that empty spot in his heart.

"What am I going to do when you abandon me?" Davis said to his sister.

"Oh, hire a maid and a cook, I suppose," she replied.

"Seriously, Lizzie, the food was fantastic."

"My cue." Lizzie winked at Jude and stood, starting to clear the table.

Jude stood too and started gathering up dishes.

"Lizzie will take care of that," Davis said.

"Really, I can take care of this," she agreed.

"Didn't Davis tell you I'm an expert at dishes?" he said, and despite both their protests, he helped clear the table and load the dishwasher, and then he tackled the pots. Lizzie dried and Davis returned them to the cabinets. When the kitchen was clean, Lizzie turned to Jude and said, "You can have a job here anytime."

Out of the corner of his eye he saw Davis make a

sharp negative movement at Lizzie from just behind him. If he hadn't learned to see from the corners of his vision when he was very young, he wouldn't have caught it.

"What? What did I say this time?" she asked.

"Never mind," Jude said.

"That means it was terrible, wasn't it? But you'll forgive me."

"Of course," Jude assured her.

"And to prove it, you'll come over again. How about next Friday?"

Jude's refusal was automatic. "I'd like to, but I can't," he said. "Another time."

"Okay. When?"

Jude hesitated and glanced at Davis.

"Tell him he has to say yes," Lizzie commanded her brother.

"You might as well just give in," Davis conceded. "She's used to getting what she wants. Spoiled brat."

"Only if you let me help you cook," Jude said. "Maybe I can pick up a few of your secrets."

"God, I love this man," she said. "So when are you free?"

"You can figure out the details later," Davis interjected. "Right now I need Jude all to myself."

"Fine. Go work on your story."

"It's not for a story," Davis said.

"Oh right." She turned to Jude, rolling her eyes in disbelief. "Davis is *always* working on some story.

Sometimes I think it's all he cares about. When he's writing, he even forgets to eat. But don't *you* forget that I've got a rain check for dinner."

Davis led Jude into the den, and they settled down in two armchairs. "I can get you out of the dinner if you want," Davis said.

"Only if you'd prefer it."

"No," Davis said quickly. "Not at all. I'm glad you came tonight. Lizzie really liked you. She's never invited my friends back. She usually disapproves of them, but she likes you."

"I like her, too," Jude said. "Now, about our plans."

"Did you come up with something?"

"Yes, I had an idea."

"Shoot. What is it?"

"After we struck out with Mr. Levy, I was trying to think who else might know—and have proof—of whatever it was that Harry might have done."

"And?"

"And I thought of somebody who certainly knows."

"Who?"

"Harry," Jude said. "Harry knows what he did."

"Yeah, sure, but I don't think he's going to tell us."

"No, he won't. At least not voluntarily, but we might be able to find out from him anyway. I was thinking there might be something in his papers. It could be as simple as tax evasion. Hell, that's how they got Al Capone. Plus Harry was always a fanatic about his records. He was always getting after Anna about keeping better files. He's the kind who never throws anything out."

"It's a bit of a long shot."

"Yeah, I know," Jude admitted. "But it's the only thing I can think of to do."

"Okay. So how are we going to get at his papers?"

Jude coughed. "Well," he said, "I've got this friend who's good at locks, and he owes me a favor."

38

IT TOOK JUDE two days to track down his old friend Thumbs. He was living with his mother in an apartment not too far from the halfway house. Jude arranged to meet him. When Jude arrived, Thumbs was waiting out on the sidewalk in front of his building, rubbing his hands and jumping up and down to keep warm. "My ma doesn't like visitors too much," he explained.

"I'll take you out for a whiskey," Jude said, and the man's eyes lit up.

It turned out to be several whiskeys. Jude explained what he wanted Thumbs to do. "You just let us in, and you can take off," Jude finished.

"But I've gone straight. I've got a job now. A pretty good one," Thumbs protested.

Jude convinced him in the end. Then he only had to work up his own courage for the next step—a trip to his mother's new house. The one she shared with Harry.

HE AND DAVIS made plans to drive down with Thumbs to scout the house, but Jude knew he needed to be alone on the first visit.

He took the bus as close as he could get and walked the rest of the way. The house was set back from the road, with a decorative iron fence along the border of the property. It would be easy to climb, but first Jude strolled past, keeping an eye out for guards or dogs. When he saw neither, he doubled back and climbed over the fence.

Jude kept to the bushes as he circled nearer the house; he approached just near enough so he could see into the lit rooms. He saw the living room and library, and circling around the side, he discovered a window into the kitchen.

That's when he saw her. He took a step back into the shrubs, glad there was no one with him to observe his reactions.

She was sitting at the counter in the kitchen with a newspaper spread out on the table in front of her and a bag of potato chips open beside it. It was the first time Jude had seen his mother in five years.

He stayed for a quarter of an hour, watching her read. She didn't even look up when she reached for the chips. He was waiting for her to raise her head so he could see her face, but when she finally glanced up from the paper, she didn't look toward the window, but away from it. She swiveled abruptly, as if something had startled her.

Jude looked as well and saw what had captured her attention.

Harry walked in, crossed to the counter, and dropped a kiss on her cheek. Jude could see her face now. She was smiling and saying something. She held up the paper. Harry nodded, started rubbing her shoulders while she talked.

The kitchen looked bright and warm, and suddenly Jude was aware of the residue from an earlier rain clinging to the leaves of the bush he was using for cover and the numbness of his fingers and the tip of his nose. Just then Harry laughed at something she said. Jude could see him tilt his head back and open his mouth, and he could hear the faint echo of his laugh as it traveled through the glass and across the lawn to where Jude hid in the shadows.

It seemed as if Harry were laughing at him.

And Jude knew that what he had done to Benito hadn't been just a fluke. The old anger was back, and he was afraid.

39

THROUGH HIS JOB at the paper Davis found out about a fund-raiser at which the mayor was scheduled to speak. He made a few calls and discovered that Harry was on the guest list as well. He and Jude put that together with the discovery that Anna had no live-in help, and the night was set.

Davis picked Jude up in his car—he had taken to calling it the getaway car—and they were on their way to pick up Thumbs when Davis said, "So how good is this guy?"

Jude glanced at him, hearing the underlying note of anxiety in his voice. "Pretty good."

"How good is pretty good?"

"Pretty good," Jude repeated. "He did end up in jail, after all. The best don't get caught."

"Great, I guess there goes my career," Davis tried to laugh.

"You don't have to do this," Jude said reasonably. "Why don't you wait out in the car?"

"No way. I'm always playing it safe. Lizzie says so, and Lizzie is always right about those kinds of things."

"Oh?" Jude said. Then he had to tell Davis where to turn, and when they rounded the corner they both spotted the lone figure standing in the glow of a streetlight.

Davis pulled up alongside and Thumbs got in the backseat.

"Fucking cold," he said. "Point those vents back here."

"Thumbs, this is Davis," Jude said.

Thumbs grunted.

"So, you feeling good?" Davis asked over his shoulder as he drove.

"Feel like shit," Thumbs grumbled.

"You want something? I have aspirin in the glove compartment."

"Yeah, I want something, but it ain't aspirin. Pull up over here," Thumbs commanded.

Davis pulled over and Thumbs hopped out. He crossed in front of the headlights and disappeared into a store across the street.

"Jude, he's gone into the liquor store," Davis hissed. "When he gets back in, don't you think that you should tell him not to drink before? After, sure, but not before."

"I can't tell him how to do his job," Jude said.

"Maybe he just wants it for after," Davis consoled himself. "For a little celebration."

Jude had smelled the alcohol on him when Thumbs first climbed in, but he didn't mention that to Davis.

Thumbs reappeared with a bag, recrossed the street, climbed in the backseat, and slammed the door.

"Jesus," Davis whispered under his breath, and pulled away from the curb.

They both heard the rustling from the backseat, and Davis shot Jude an agonized look.

"Hey," Davis said when they both heard the sound of Thumbs taking a pull off the bottle. "Do you think that's a good idea?"

"Yes," Thumbs said, and offered the bottle to Jude in the front seat. Jude took a slug without looking at the label. He, in turn, held it out to Davis. Davis grabbed it and took a huge gulp, then another, and handed it back.

"So you know all about alarm systems and stuff?" Davis asked a couple minutes later.

"No, what are those?" Thumbs said.

"A regular comedian," Davis said, but he didn't sound amused.

"Can you get this guy to shut up?" Thumbs demanded of Jude.

They didn't speak again for the rest of the ride.

They parked the car in a spot they had chosen earlier in the week, and they walked the distance to the house slowly, in single file, as close to the trees as they could manage. They hopped over the fence, one at a time, and made their way to the house. It was lit up on both the first and second stories.

"Shit, they stayed home," Davis whispered, and Jude and Thumbs said, "Shhh," at the same time.

They circled, looking for movements in the rooms. They waited for fifteen minutes, then they made another circle.

"All you," Jude said to Thumbs.

Thumbs stepped out of the bushes and walked up to the front door—looking for all the world as if he belonged there. He rang the bell and waited patiently to see if anyone would answer. When no one came, he reached into his pocket, took out his tools, and bent over the lock. He had it open in less than a minute and disappeared inside.

Jude and Davis held their breath, waiting for Thumbs to come running out if he wasn't able to disarm the system. Nothing happened. There was no wailing siren, and no police cars squealed into the driveway. Eventually the front door opened again and Thumbs beckoned to them.

They moved quickly, slipping inside and closing the door behind them. Jude led the way through the hall, checking rooms as they went. Davis was the one who found the study with the two tall filing cabinets against one wall.

"It could be Anna's office," Jude said.

But Davis discovered that the drawers of the desk contained Harry's stationery.

"This is it," Jude agreed, and crossed to the window to close the curtains.

The filing cabinet was locked, but that didn't take Thumbs more than a few seconds.

"Desk too," Jude said, and Thumbs tackled that as well, then retreated to a corner to wait.

Jude and Davis went to work. They had brought two handheld scanners that Davis had borrowed from the newspaper. The scanners could copy a page in seconds and they held more than three thousand pages of text.

Jude opened the first drawer and verified that it held Harry's papers, and they went to work.

At first they took whatever came to hand, but as the first hour drew to a close, and Thumbs snored in the corner, Jude started being more selective. He had Davis working exclusively on taxes and bank statements, while he took the phone bills and credit cards.

Harry was insanely neat, and that made it easier to put things back exactly as he had found them. When the third hour was almost gone and Davis had nearly finished the financial files, Jude checked his watch.

"Time to go," he said. "Can't risk any longer."

They gathered their things, woke Thumbs, and beat a retreat. Once they reached the road, Jude watched for a car to come down the road and turn into the gated drive. The urgency with which they had left gave the illusion that Anna and Harry were fast approaching, but the street remained dark and silent, and no one came.

Thumbs fell asleep again in the backseat on the

way home. Jude had to wake him up when they reached his apartment building.

"'Night," Jude said.

Thumbs grunted in answer and opened the door. They watched him trudge over to the dark doorway, drop his keys, and stoop slowly to retrieve them.

"So, are you going to give him some money? Do you need to borrow some?" Davis asked.

"He did it as a favor to me," Jude said.

"Yeah, I know, but you'll give him something, won't you?"

"It was a *favor*," Jude repeated.

"But he risked getting sent back to prison. He deserves to get something for that, don't you think?"

"Is that the only reason you can think of for doing something? Do you expect me to offer *you* money?"

"No, of course not. I just thought that since he doesn't seem to have much . . ."

"He has more than you know," Jude replied.

"What, he's got a cache stored away from some big job he did?" Davis joked.

Jude didn't reply. He hadn't been talking about money.

"Though, come to think of it," Davis said, "it wasn't so much of a favor as it could have been. If he'd really wanted to do something for you, he could have stayed sober, for one thing."

Jude couldn't let this slight go by without correcting it. "He was sober—for him. Usually by that time of night Thumbs can barely stand. I can't even imagine the effort it took him to stay that sober, so I would bet that neither can you."

"Okay, okay. I didn't realize he was so very precious to you."

"Well, now you know." Jude answered the scathing remark seriously.

They drove in silence until Davis reached the Burger King.

"Um, when will I see you tomorrow?" Davis asked. The remark was a tentative peace offering, and Jude chided himself for snapping. He couldn't expect Davis to understand.

"I can get out early," Davis went on. "Should I pick you up when you get off work?"

"Sure," Jude agreed.

"I think it would be easiest to have everything printed out. I'll do that at work tomorrow, but to go through the documents, we'll need somewhere to spread out. We could do it at your place, or if you want, we could do it at my house. I never use the study—I'm always at the office. We could set up in there at the big table."

As they certainly couldn't work at the halfway house, Jude accepted gratefully.

"Tomorrow at three, then?" Davis said.

"Tomorrow at three."

"I think we have something. I swear I have this feeling that we've got him."

"We'll see," Jude replied cautiously. He wanted it too much to talk lightly about the possibility that the answer to his dreams lay in the backseat.

DAVIS MET JUDE in front of the diner at three, and he chattered away in excitement as they drove back to his house. "I didn't realize how much stuff we got. I spent the entire day printing it out. I've got three cardboard boxes' worth in the trunk."

When they reached the house, they carried the boxes upstairs to the study and heaved them up on the table. They exchanged a look of barely repressed excitement, and, in concert, they each lifted a stack of paper out.

In the car they had agreed that the best course would be for them to sort all the papers before starting their search. Jude had thought this task would certainly take the afternoon, but he was pleasantly surprised to find it took less than two hours. It turned out that Harry was as scrupulous with his papers as he was with his other belongings. Everything had been divided into categories and filed by date. Not only that, but they were exhilarated to find that Harry had been a pack rat. He appeared to be one of those people who never threw anything away—he had records going back almost thirty years. Thirty years of bank statements. Thirty years of tax returns. Only twenty years of credit card bills. Twenty years of mortgage payments and phone bills.

They plunged in, with Davis expecting and Jude hoping to stumble across "it." Whatever "it" was. But the only thing they discovered in the first few hours was that there would be no early dramatic discovery. It was their first taste of the reality of detective work—and they found it slow, monotonous, and dreary.

Lizzie found them there, arguing over whether one sheet of paper belonged in the tax folder or the correspondence folder. It was a letter to his accountant that referred to his taxes but had other information as well. They didn't even notice her in the doorway until she said, "What on earth is all this?"

She stepped inside and picked up a sheet as if to read it, but Davis practically leaped out of his chair and snatched it from her.

"You can't look at this stuff, Lizzie."

"Okay, but what are you doing with this Wichowski's phone bill—" She stopped abruptly as she put two and two together. They could see the connections firing: Harry to Anna to Jude.

"You can't talk to anybody about this," Davis commanded. "Not anybody."

"What do you take me for? But how did you get—"

"And don't ask us how we got them," Davis cut her off.

"For God's sake, Davis. What have you been doing?"

"It's my fault," Jude said.

"I wanted to," Davis protested, as if Jude were stealing glory instead of taking the blame.

She sat down, propped her elbows on two piles, settled her chin in her hands, and said, "Sounds fascinating. Tell me all."

"I can't, sis. Not this time."

"You know I can keep a secret. Better than you, certainly."

"It's not my secret to tell."

She looked at Jude. "Oh. Right." She recovered quickly. "Oh well. I'll just have to suffer agonies of curiosity, I guess. Will you two come down and have some dinner if I make something?"

"Make something? What's the special occasion?"

"Well, what else would you eat?"

"Oh, we'd order pizza or something."

"I think we can feed Jude something a little better than pizza," she said. "I'll call you when everything is ready. Don't worry, nothing fancy tonight. I can't very well anyway because I think all we have in the house is canned tuna and cheese."

So they worked until Lizzie called them. They broke thankfully for dinner, then went back to work until eleven, when Davis said, "I can't take any more. That's it for me."

"It's late," Jude agreed. "We both need to sleep."

"More tomorrow?" Davis said, not quite as enthusiastically as the night before.

"Sure."

"I can't get off early again, but I'll give you the key and you can come over after work if you want. I'll be back around seven."

THEY FELL INTO a pattern. Jude would come straight to the house when he finished at the diner and set to work. Davis joined him in the evening around seven. Lizzie usually got home between seven and seven thirty, and she took care of dinner. Jude could tell that she wanted to know what they were working on, but she had too much pride to ask. Instead she just said that she wanted to help, and if the only way she could do that was to make dinner, then that's what she'd do. Davis and Jude would go back to work after dinner, and around eleven Jude would tuck a file or two into a bag so he could continue poring over the papers on the bus ride home.

One night, over dinner, Lizzie said to Davis, "Don't you think it's a little silly that Jude takes the bus to work, then out here, then back home again, and does it all over again in the morning, while we have three spare bedrooms sitting empty? I mean, he spends all his time here anyway. He can't possibly do anything but go back and sleep. Doesn't it make sense that he just sleep here instead? At least while you're working so hard."

There was only the slightest hesitation before Davis knocked his head with his palm and said, "I don't know why I didn't think of that. My sister the genius. How about it, Jude?"

"I couldn't."

"And why couldn't you?" Lizzie demanded.

"You need your privacy."

"It's not as if we don't spend all our time together anyway," Davis said. "I usually go straight to bed after you leave."

"I barely see you guys. And the back bedroom has its own bathroom attached, so that's no problem," Lizzie added.

"But . . ."

"But what?" Lizzie prompted.

Jude had nothing to say.

"Then it's settled. You'll bring your things tomorrow."

Jude knew he should say no. But he didn't.

The next afternoon Jude brought his things, and that night he slept in a soft, clean bed in a room by himself. For a long time he lay awake listening to the silence. For the first time in years he couldn't hear the sounds of other men's dreams.

He woke up feeling better than he had in ages, and the longer he stayed with Davis and Lizzie, the more the sense of well-being grew. It almost felt like he was part of a family. Unfortunately, none of Jude's newfound contentment helped with his progress on Harry's files. They refused to be anything but ordinary files. Davis and Jude found out that Harry spent too much money on his suits, but that he hadn't taken a real vacation in eight years. When he went out to eat, he always went to one of two favorite restaurants. They saw that he gave a big check every year to the Police Benevolent Association and a smaller check to the local Fresh Air Fund, which took underprivileged kids out of the city for a week in the summertime.

They tried calling the numbers that appeared most frequently on Harry's phone bills and discovered nothing. Jude spent a whole afternoon blacking out the name on every document in the tax file, and Davis took it to his accountant and asked him to go through it and tell him if there was anything out of place. When the accountant called back, he said the only thing that was strange was that the guy was such a stickler and didn't try to get around anything. "Is he a politician or something?" the accountant joked. Davis laughed dutifully and swore when he hung up.

"This guy is the straightest, the most virtuous, most tedious bastard I've ever seen," Davis exclaimed after more than three weeks of poring over the pages. "There's nothing here. He pays his taxes so honestly you'd think he was trying to get a job at the IRS. He doesn't spend more than he makes. He doesn't seem to get any money that's not from his salary. He doesn't have any friends that aren't cops or politicians. Jude, I'm starting to think—"

"Don't say it," Jude said. "You can't be giving up already."

"It's been three weeks. We should at least start thinking about what else we might do."

"Let's give this another week. One more week before we start looking at other things." He said it calmly, but he felt desperate. He knew he was running out of ideas, and worse, Davis was running out of patience. Davis had been fine when they were visiting criminals and breaking into houses, but the monotonous labor of sifting through papers was draining his resolve.

"Okay, one more week," Davis said. "But I can't work tomorrow night. I've got a dinner thing, so it'll be just you and Lizzie."

Jude worked the next afternoon in the study—the same as always. And Lizzie made dinner when she got home, just like she had every night for the last three weeks. But dinner itself was different. It was the first time they'd spent together without Davis around, and Jude found himself telling Lizzie the whole story. Later he wondered why he hadn't done it earlier. It was long overdue. They had dinner, and a bottle of wine, while he told her about growing up with his father and how he came to live with his mother. He got through the point where Anna announced she was running for mayor, and they moved to the living room with a second bottle of wine. At first he sat on the couch while she curled up in a nearby armchair, but soon Lizzie moved over to sit next to him. By the time he told her about Harry's visit to the prison, she had reached out for his hand. He loved the feel of her hand in his, but he knew it was about to be withdrawn, because he wasn't going to make the same mistake with her as he had with Davis; he was about to tell her about Benito.

Jude described the first fight against the welcome committee. He explained how Lefty challenged him and how the fights just seemed to continue after that. Finally he told her about Benito. He didn't soften it at all in the telling, but though she listened intently, he couldn't sense any trace of revulsion.

When he finished, they sat a moment in silence. Finally Lizzie said, "It's amazing how, at the same time, you can be so much better a person than I am—I could never have done what you did for your mother—while you also have done something worse than I could ever imagine. The best and the worst. What does that make you?" she wondered.

"Human, I think," he answered, and she laughed.

40

NOW THAT SHE knew the story, Lizzie announced that she could finally help Jude and Davis sort through the papers. The next day she left work early, and she came straight to the study, where Jude was flipping through the pages of a folder for what felt like the thousandth time.

"Okay, I'm ready to work," she said, taking off her suit jacket and slinging it over the back of a chair.

"Lizzie, I'm starting to think this is just a wild-goose chase," he said. "We've gone over this stuff a million times. I don't think you'll find anything."

"Your faith in me is touching."

"You know what I mean. I'm just not sure there's anything here to find."

"Give me a chance at least. Maybe all you need is a new set of eyes. Now, show me all the different folders you have."

He went through them with her.

"Well, I might as well start with my strength," she said. "Hand over the bank statements, please, and go get us something to drink. I'm dry as a bone."

By the time he got back with two beers, she was already deep into the bank file. He placed a beer in front of her on the table. She said, "Thanks," and reached for it without even looking up.

For the next half an hour they worked in silence. Lizzie plunged in with a concentration and seriousness he would never have guessed at. She spoke only once, to ask him if they had the cancelled checks anywhere.

"We have the registers," Jude said. "And some of the oldest checks, but it would have taken all night to scan all the cancelled checks he had."

"Can I see what you have?"

It was twenty minutes later before she spoke again. He was paging through Harry's credit card bills, lingering over the purchases of jewelry. One, Jude was sure, must have been the engagement ring. Another must have been the wedding rings. He could trace the other purchases by anniversaries.

"I think I've found something," Lizzie said.

Her voice was so calm, so matter-of-fact, that it took Jude a moment to realize what she had said. "You found something," he repeated.

"Come over here and take a look."

THAT'S WHERE DAVIS found them an hour later—in the study, bent over the papers.

"What is she doing in here?" Davis demanded. "She's not supposed to be in here."

Lizzie and Jude looked up.

"Lizzie found it," Jude said simply. "She found what we've been looking for."

Davis opened his mouth to say something, and it stayed open, but nothing came out.

"Take a look at this," Lizzie said. "You've just been searching for the wrong thing. You've been looking for deposits and expenditures—for money that he shouldn't have had—but I stare at these things all day, and I was just looking for anything strange, and this is what I found." She laid out thirteen bank statements in front of him and pointed. "Here and here and here and here, see these? These are all checks for between fifteen hundred and three or four thousand. They don't exactly stick out here because he has car insurance every year that's a thousand, and a bunch of other expenses that go up to twenty-five hundred. It was the three and four thousand that caught my attention, and when I looked at the check register, look what I found." She shuffled through and found a page and pointed. "There." She flipped through to another page. "There." Then another page. "There. They correlate to those thirteen checks. All of them made out to Cash. There doesn't seem to be any regularity that I can find. The first one is the biggest, and it's a lot of money, especially for back then. It was, God, more than twenty years ago. The next one comes six months later. The third, eight months after that. Then fourteen months. Then nine. There doesn't seem to be any real pattern. Between the eighth and the ninth there was only a two-month lapse, and this here"— Lizzie found the sheet and indicated the check—"that's the last. Thirteen years after the first, they stop. There's not a single other check written to Cash since. That's almost ten years without another check written to Cash. I tallied them up. Altogether they add up to forty-two thousand dollars. That's a lot of money for a policeman, even spread out over thirteen years. Now, what I want to know is—what were those thirteen checks for?"

In his excitement Davis seemed to forget the concern about Lizzie's knowing the story. "That's it. That's it." He swept Lizzie up in a great hug and then, to Jude's astonishment, did the same to him. "So how do we find out what they were for?"

"That's the hard part," Lizzie admitted. "But this is what we've come up with so far. We can make a chart and put down the different dates of the thirteen checks and the amounts, and then we'll try to match it up with other things in his life—cases, friends, phone calls. We'll have to go back over all the material again with an eye to those dates."

"All right. Let's do it." Davis slapped his palm down on the table. "Jude, let's get to work."

"What about me?" Lizzie said. "I'm the one who found it. You can't just get rid of me now."

Lizzie went out and bought a piece of poster board. On it she made a grid with the dates of the checks and the amounts in big black letters that they all could see as they worked.

Then they each took a file. They checked the obvious places first, but Harry hadn't declared the payments as any tax deduction on his returns, and they couldn't see that there was any one phone number that correlated specifically with the dates.

They made an outline of Harry's career and promotions. He'd had only one partner after Jude's father, and they weren't partners for long. The exposure Harry got from heading up the investigation into Anthony's disappearance seemed to jump-start his career. In less than six months Harry got his promotion to sergeant, then lieutenant, captain, all the way up to deputy commissioner, but they couldn't connect the checks to his promotions.

Jude went back—alone this time—to Mr. Levy, but he returned empty-handed. Davis tried calling the one partner Harry had after Anthony, explaining that he was looking into doing a piece on the commissioner. The man talked to him but disclosed nothing useful.

There were times that Jude despaired of connecting the checks to anything—the pattern seemed so random—but Lizzie insisted that there was some sort of correlation behind the apparent disorder, they just hadn't found it yet. That was how it worked—whenever anyone got discouraged, one of the other two would spur him or her on. For all their frustrations and disappointments, they were a team. They had passionate, cheerful fights over dinner and stayed up so late that, in their exhaustion, they burst into fits of giggles over the quirky things in Harry's files.

Two weeks passed, then three. Everything seemed wonderful . . . until the Saturday Jude decided to call in sick. His schedule at the diner had him working six days a week—every day but Monday. And every day he had to be there by 6 A.M. What with the commute, that meant he had to be up by four thirty.

That Friday night they'd worked on Harry's papers until eleven—then Jude intended to go to sleep, since they'd been up late the night before as well. But both Lizzie and Davis wanted to go out. They coaxed and cajoled and finally convinced him. Before he knew it, it was past two and they were all drunk. They didn't make it home until three, and they all stumbled off to bed. But when his alarm went off, Jude knew he couldn't manage his shift. He called in from the phone in his room and rolled over and fell back asleep.

But Davis and Lizzie didn't know he had stayed in bed. He was always gone by the time they woke up, so they assumed he had gone to work just as always. Otherwise they probably wouldn't have been talking about him—and he certainly wouldn't have overheard their conversation.

He was going to the kitchen to get some breakfast, and he was just outside the door when he heard his name. He stopped instinctively and caught Davis saying, "Sure, I think Jude's a great guy too. But he's not like us."

He could see them sitting at the kitchen table.

Lizzie's back was to him, but Davis was sitting facing the doorway, where Jude stood. The only reason Davis didn't see him was that Lizzie blocked most of his view.

Lizzie's voice was a murmur Jude couldn't make out, but he knew she must have offered some kind of defense, because Davis replied, "I *know* he didn't do it. But you know what? It doesn't matter. Guilty or innocent, nothing will ever change the fact that he did time in a state prison. That never gets erased from his record. Even if he moves to the other side of the country, it's there. He has to put that down every time he goes for a job, when he applies for an apartment, hell, he probably has to put it down if he wants to buy a dog. He's always going to be an ex-con."

Lizzie spoke again, but her voice was even lower this time, and Jude had no chance of hearing the words.

"All I'm saying is that he can't stay here forever," Davis replied. He paused, then said, "I don't want to tell him to leave either, but it's my responsibility. I'll take care of it."

Lizzie's chair squealed against the floor as she shoved it back from the table and went over to the sink. Jude tried to draw back, but the movement caught Davis's attention, and he looked up right into Jude's face. Davis flushed and opened his mouth to speak, but Jude shook his head, laid his finger on his lips, and pointed to Lizzie. Then he backed away from the doorway and retreated to his room.

A few minutes later there was a soft knock on his door. Then Davis opened the door. "Jude?" he said hesitantly. He took a step into the room and said, "What are you doing?"

"What does it look like?" Jude asked, folding another T-shirt and stuffing it into his bag.

Davis stood there a moment, watching Jude pack. Then he said, "I didn't mean for you to hear it that way."

Jude just continued folding clothes.

"You don't have to go right this second."

"I'm going to leave my stuff here for the day, if that's all right," Jude replied. "I'll come back for it tonight, when I've found a place."

"Of course. That's fine. You can take as long as you need. I mean . . ." Davis flushed again. "I mean, if you need a few days . . . ," he faltered, then went on. "Listen, I'm sorry you had to overhear that. It's not the way I wanted this to happen. And I didn't mean for you to leave so abruptly, but . . . maybe it's for the best. You understand, don't you?"

"Completely," Jude replied.

"She doesn't . . . she's naive. She doesn't understand how the world works. I'm afraid she might be getting ideas. But you understand why that would never work—how impossible that is."

"Impossible, or just inconvenient for you?" Jude asked.

"I don't think I deserve that," Davis said. "I've tried to help you. I'll still try to help you—anything

I can do. It's just that . . . I'm sorry, but I want something better for my sister than to see her fall for an ex-con."

"Is that how you think of me?" Jude said.

"It's how the world thinks of you," Davis replied. "And we live in the world."

Jude snapped his suitcase closed. "I'll be back for my stuff later. It might be best if you and Lizzie weren't here."

"But how am I going to explain it to Lizzie if you just disappear?"

"I'll come back tonight to say good-bye," Jude said. "I owe her that much. But after that I'll be out of your hair."

Jude studied the apartment listings on the bus into town. He chose three to go see. They were all small and shabby, but the last one was small and shabby and cheap and available immediately, and he signed the lease.

Then Jude took the bus back to the house. Thankfully, he found it empty. He retrieved his bag from his room and then went to the study and started to collect the folders. He secured them with rubber bands and loaded them into the cardboard boxes. After he was finished packing those, he looked at the grid that Lizzie had done of the checks and the dates. After a moment's consideration, he bent the slippery poster board into a loose tube and secured that also with rubber bands. It was almost evening when he tucked the poster under one arm, shouldered his bag, and carried the stack of boxes to the bus stop. Jude wanted to avoid the spectacle of leaving with all his belongings packed and slung over his back. He especially didn't want Davis to offer to drive him to his new apartment. What if Davis insisted on helping him carry his things up? He would see the dingy studio with the kitchen appliances lined up along one wall and two grimy windows opposite. Davis would pity him. And he didn't want Davis's pity. He didn't need it. Davis would never understand that, for Jude, as cheap and shabby as the room was, it was *his*.

Jude took the bus, walked the five blocks to his apartment, climbed the three flights, and finally dumped the boxes on the floor of his room. He was exhausted and wanted to sit down, but there was nothing to sit on. There wasn't a scrap of furniture in the place—just the boxes and his bag sitting there in the middle of the empty room. He unpacked the folders and lined them up along the wall. Then he unrolled the poster and put folders on either end to help flatten it out again. He took his clothes out of the bag and put them away in the closet, and that was as much unpacking as he could do. Tomorrow he would go shopping.

Jude checked his watch and realized that it was getting late and he should go back to say good-bye. It was past ten when he rang the doorbell. Lizzie must have run to get it, because the door opened almost immediately and she was there.

"Where have you been? Where are your things?" she demanded.

Jude saw Davis appear over her shoulder.

"Invite the man in, Lizzie. Don't keep him standing on the front step."

"Thanks." Jude stepped inside.

"I held dinner for you," she said. "Come on."

"She didn't care that I was starving," Davis said. "I told her that you might not be back tonight, but she insisted that you'd be here."

"And I was right," she said.

Jude followed them into the kitchen, and they sat down in their usual places.

"Where are the files? And all the rest of your stuff?" Lizzie asked again, not making any move to help herself to any food.

"Oh, a friend of mine called and told me about a really good deal on an apartment that just came up. It was too good to pass up, so I decided to take it. But I had to move on it right away."

"That's great," Davis said heartily. "Great luck. Sometimes it can take forever to find something decent. I had a friend who looked for months before he found anything that was even livable."

Jude suspected that what Davis's friend considered livable was substantially different from his own requirements.

Lizzie ignored Davis's response, as if he hadn't spoken. "And you decided all this without me? How could you, Jude? I thought we were a team—and what about the project? Are you just going to abandon that?"

"I've kept you working on this too long. I'll continue on myself, and if I find anything, I'll let you know."

"You'd better," Davis said.

"But do you have any furniture?" Lizzie asked. "What will you sleep on? Do you even have blankets? Surely you'll stay here one last night? You're not going to go running out on us?"

"It's furnished," Jude lied. "And I'd love to stay, but all my things are already there, and I'm anxious to spend my first night in my own place."

"But where is it?" Lizzie asked.

"Over in South End."

"Where?" Lizzie persisted.

"I don't remember the building number," he put her off. "It's on Maple Avenue." Maple Avenue was at least two miles long.

"But you'll call us to give us your number?" Lizzie asked anxiously.

"When I get a phone hooked up," he said.

The dinner was subdued. The spell had been broken, and suddenly no one knew exactly what to say. When dinner was over, Jude said, "I'd better catch my bus."

"When will we see you again?" Lizzie called after him.

"I'll call," he said. But he didn't say when.

41

DESPITE SIX WEEKS of living in Davis and Lizzie's huge house, Jude found that he settled easily into his little room. After all, he had spent five years of his life in a cell not much larger than his bathroom. Compared with that, his new apartment was a palace.

He threw himself into fixing up his new place. He bought a mattress and, in a spurt of indulgence, an expensive set of sheets. He found a nice old kitchen table with a set of four chairs in a secondhand shop, but he delayed delivery until after the next weekend so that he could repaint the apartment. He spent a while lingering over samples at the store and finally chose a color they called Deep Ocean.

As the clerk was ringing it up, he asked Jude what he wanted the paint for, and Jude told him that it was for his apartment. The clerk looked dubious. "I don't know about this for an apartment. It's a little unusual."

"I know. If I hate it, I'll just paint over it." But he didn't hate it. He loved it. It wasn't like any other room he'd ever seen. During the day, when the sunlight shone through the newly cleaned windows, the color looked crisp, and at night it darkened along with the sky.

He bought a bright van Gogh print and tacked it

up above his mattress. Then he put up Lizzie's poster board on the opposite wall. He looked at it, almost took it down, but in the end left it.

One afternoon he noticed a plant that someone had left for dead on the sidewalk, and brought it back up to the apartment. When he cleared away the brown fronds, he found it wasn't as bad as it had appeared. He set it on the sill, and under the bright spring light the plant slowly came back to life. He liked the look of it, and he went out and bought several others—a tall, spiky cactus and a long, trailing ivy.

About a week and a half after moving in Jude returned to his room, opened the door, and knew that it had become a home. But he found himself unable to enjoy it because as soon as his apartment project ended, his mind naturally turned to wondering, *What next?*

It wasn't that life was so awful. Work had gotten better. Somewhere in the last month the other employees in the kitchen had accepted him, and they included him in their conversations now. They joked with him about his gringo Spanish, which he took as a compliment. If it had been truly awful, he knew they wouldn't have kidded him about it. They even invited him out with them to a club in Frog Hollow, though they couldn't get him to dance—even with the incredibly pretty sister of one of the busboys.

But most days he went straight home from work. He spent a lot of his time reading, stretched out on his mattress in a beam of sunlight, the breeze from the open windows carrying the smell of fresh bread from the bakery two buildings over. Nights he had a harder time concentrating on the words, and then he usually ended up listening to the murmur of the televisions in the apartments on either side. The noise around him seemed only to intensify his solitude. That's when he missed Davis and Lizzie most. Or rather, he tried to convince himself that he missed Davis and Lizzie, but it was usually only one name that he thought of. He spent too much of his time sleepless and staring at the wall opposite—at Lizzie's poster of dates.

One night almost three weeks after he moved in, Jude lay on the mattress willing sleep to come, but as the night turned into early morning he remained stubbornly alert. He stared absently at the poster, almost without seeing it.

And then it came to him.

Maybe it was the apartment, similar to the dozens he had lived in with his father, maybe it was having the poster always in front of him, but suddenly he knew what those dates meant.

He knew what the money had been for.

JUDE THOUGHT ABOUT calling Davis and Lizzie right away, but in the end he decided that he would sit on the discovery for a few days and see if he could find some proof to back it up before he called.

He had pored over Harry's files for months, but

now that he knew what he was searching for, the proof took only two days to find. On the evening of the second he found it—in the phone records, a number that he recognized. It appeared only once, but that once was enough.

When Jude finally called Davis and Lizzie's house, Davis answered, which was a relief. At least, he told himself it was a relief.

"Jude," Davis said, surprised. Lizzie must have been in the room, because he heard Davis say a second later, "Yes, it's Jude. Hold on and let me talk to him first." Then, "Sorry, I'm back. How are you? I've been wondering why you haven't called us."

Lizzie's voice broke in, "Yes, I've been wondering that too." She must have picked up another phone.

"Lizzie, I was talking to Jude."

"I called to talk to both of you," Jude headed off the argument. "I wanted to know if you would have time to meet up with me."

"You can come over tonight if you want," Lizzie said. "We're not doing anything, and it would be great to see you."

"Not tonight. I was thinking the day after tomorrow."

"I'm free," Lizzie said.

"Yes, I can make that," Davis agreed. "So we'll see you over here at eight?"

"Since you both work downtown, I thought somewhere around there. It's closer for me."

There was a pause, then Davis said, "Yes, great idea. I know a place—"

"I have a place that I've come to like," Jude interrupted. "It's not fancy, but the food is good and it's within my price range. If that's all right with you."

"Sure, sure," Davis said.

"It's called Tosca. What time works for you guys?"

They decided on seven thirty.

"See you then," Jude said, and hung up before either could ask anything more.

JUDE HADN'T HAD the courage to take Davis and Lizzie to this restaurant before. The places Davis took him all had linen tablecloths and linen napkins and soft jazz music playing in the background. Tosca had plastic red-and-white-checked tablecloths and paper napkins and cheap, rickety wooden chairs, but Tosca wasn't about the decor; it was about the food, and the people who knew about it kept it booked solid seven days a week.

Jude went early, at seven fifteen, intending to be the first, but when he arrived, he found both Davis and Lizzie already there. They stood when he entered, but neither of them knew exactly what to do when he reached the table. Jude solved the problem by nodding and sitting down, and they followed his example.

"I hope you haven't been waiting long," he said.

"No," and, "Not at all," Davis and Lizzie said at once.

"Have you gotten a chance to look at the menu?"

"Just tell me what's good," Davis replied.

"Anything," Lizzie agreed.

So Jude beckoned the waiter over and ordered for all three.

"How's your new place?" Davis asked awkwardly. "Settling in?"

"It feels like home," Jude said.

"Great. Great. Though the house feels empty without you. It took a while to get used to it, didn't it, Lizzie?"

"Yes. It did."

Jude glanced at her, then quickly away. "But you must enjoy getting your lives back," Jude said. "I took up too much of your time."

"It was the most fun I've had in years," Lizzie replied. "I wasn't ready to give up just yet. I think about it a lot, and I still say that we could have gotten somewhere with it."

"We did the best we could," Davis said, as if it were a conversation they'd had before.

"I just can't get it out of my head," Lizzie admitted. "I wish you'd left a few of the files so I could at least work on them on my own. I can't stand the idea that we'll never know."

It was as good an opening as any. "You don't have to," Jude told her. "I figured out what the money was for."

They stared at him.

Then Davis erupted with a whoop.

"I'm dying," Lizzie said. "Don't torture me."

He had forgotten how good it had been. Their spontaneous, jubilant reaction brought it all back, but his joy in it was missing. His discovery seemed to have drained all the happiness from him. It felt like only one thing would make him happy now.

"I pinned the grid up on my wall in the apartment, and I spent a lot of time looking at it," he explained. "One day it just came to me. I was coming at it from the wrong direction. Remember in the first place we were looking for extra money that Harry might have had around, when we should have been looking for anything out of the ordinary? The same thing happened with the dates. I was looking for things in Harry's life to connect to the dates, but it wasn't anything in his life that triggered those checks."

"What was it?" Davis asked.

"My life. Not Harry's life. My life." This time he couldn't keep the emotion from his voice. He heard it, sharp with fury. "Harry wrote the first check three weeks before my father took me. That's just about when I was born. That must be when my father really decided to go through with his plan of taking me. All the other dates coincide pretty much with every time we moved. Harry was sending that money to my father.

"I might have noticed it a long time ago if the checks had stopped when my father was killed, but they stopped two years before. Our last move."

"So if he was sending money to your father, that means . . . you're saying that Harry knew where you were the whole time?" Lizzie whispered.

"Not only that, he knew what my father was planning beforehand, and he helped him," Jude said.

"And now he's married to your mother," she continued, unraveling the implications of the news. "He helped your father steal you, consoled her, and volunteered to head up the investigation, while all the time he knew exactly where you both were. That's . . . that's horrific. I mean, if he had wanted to, he could have gotten you back for her at any time."

"Any time," Jude agreed.

"It's hard to believe. I'm still not sure I do," Davis admitted. "We need more than a random coincidence of dates."

"I know," Jude said. "That's why I went back through the phone records. There's only one there, but one's enough."

"One what?" Lizzie demanded.

"Phone number. My father's phone number, to be exact. It was the one we had just before we moved back here. I wouldn't have recognized it unless I was looking, but . . . I was looking. Harry called us. That proves he knew where we were."

Davis blinked. "Yes. That proves it. Oh my God," he said, getting excited, "that proves it. You've got him."

Jude smiled. "Yes," he said. "I've got him."

"So are we sticking to the same plan? We threaten to publish the story if he doesn't tell Anna what he did, right? I don't see how he could possibly say no. It's bound to work."

"That's the plan," Jude said.

"I wonder how your mother is going to react," Lizzie said.

"She's going to get down on the ground and kiss Jude's feet," Davis declared.

"I wonder," Lizzie said again, thoughtfully. "I hope it's everything you ever dreamed of," she said to Jude. "I really do." But she sounded doubtful.

The food came then, and they all dug in. Lizzie and Davis claimed that it was the best meal they'd had in ages. "It's so much better than the stuffy restaurants that I always go to," Davis said.

They lingered late over coffee, but finally Davis looked at his watch and said, "God, I had no idea how late it was. I'm going to need some sleep if I want to be at my best when I make that call tomorrow. We'd better get the check."

"Already taken care of," Jude said. He had excused himself to visit the bathroom and picked up the check at the same time.

"No way. You have to let us give you something toward dinner," Davis protested.

"Tonight I don't have to do anything. Tonight is mine."

Davis hadn't heard that tone from Jude before.

He was used to having the comfortable upper hand.

"What happened to you in the last three weeks?" Davis tried to say it jokingly, but there was too much truth in the words for it to slip by. "I'll tell you one thing. I'm glad I'm not Harry right now. He doesn't have any idea what he's in for. So what do you want to do now?"

"I want an appointment with Harry."

"Do you think he'll agree to it?" Davis asked.

"Yes, I'm sure of it," Jude said, smiling. "Because you're going to make the appointment. You'll say you want to do a piece on him for the paper. Harry never could resist good publicity."

42

THE NEXT AFTERNOON when Jude finished work, he found Davis waiting for him outside the diner. Jude took a deep breath and crossed to Davis's car. He bent to the passenger window.

"Guess what?" Davis said. "I got the appointment with Harry."

Jude's stomach dived and jumped as if it were on its own roller coaster. "When?"

"This afternoon. You coming?"

"Now? You mean right now?"

"I got him on the phone this morning," Davis explained. "Turned out he had some time free this afternoon, and I figured, the sooner the better."

Jude opened the door and got in without another word.

It didn't take long to reach the house. They got out of the car and walked up the path together, but it was Davis who pressed the doorbell. A moment later they heard the sound of footsteps approaching, the door opened, and Harry stood in front of them on the stoop. He looked first at Davis, and he started to smile. Then his gaze slid past to Jude.

Their eyes met, and Jude felt suddenly breathless with hate. The power of it almost scared him, but he merely said, "Hello, Harry."

Jude caught a flicker of emotion cross Harry's face before it was replaced with a bland smile. "If you wanted to see me, Jude, all you had to do was call," Harry said. "There was no need for this subterfuge about an article in the paper."

"Oh, that part's true enough," Jude said. "Aren't you going to invite us in?" He brushed past Harry without waiting for an answer, and Davis followed close on his heels. "You have somewhere we can talk?"

"Of course." Harry closed the front door, then gestured for them to follow. He led them down the hall and into the room where they had spent hours scanning his files. Jude and Davis sat in the two chairs. Harry moved around the desk and settled himself into the high-backed leather chair.

The last time Jude had faced Harry across a table was in the prison. Jude knew that he was barely recognizable from the child he had been, but Harry had hardly changed at all. He still had the same powerful build, the same easy self-importance. There were probably a few more wrinkles, maybe a little more white in the salt-and-pepper hair, but Jude could almost have believed that it was only weeks that had passed and not years.

Harry must have been thinking along the same lines. He said, "It's funny, you used to be the spitting image of your father, but you don't look much like him anymore."

"I do, actually. I look more like him," Jude corrected him. "This is what he looked like when I knew him. After he spent a lot of years indoors. Just like me." Jude's smile was more like a baring of teeth. The men at North Central Penitentiary would have recognized it from Jude's early days. They would have known that smile meant trouble. Even Harry looked a bit uneasy for a moment before he covered it with his usual confident bluster. "And who's your friend?"

"Let me introduce Davis Marshall." Jude motioned to Davis, who sat quietly beside him. "He was the person who called you, and he *does* write for the *Courant*."

"Good for him," Harry said in a patronizing tone.

"And not so good for you," Jude responded.

Harry leaned back in his chair and laced his hands across his stomach. "Ah yes, this article you mentioned. I imagine that you're trying to get him to publish your ridiculous claim about how you were set up. Seems to me like I've heard that one before. It's not exactly original. Don't you have anything better to write about at the *Courant*?" he said, switching his attention abruptly to Davis.

"There aren't many stories better than this one," Davis replied.

"You think that because you're young. But even if you were right, you'd still have a problem—you need actual proof before you can publish a story. If you don't know that, I'm sure your superiors at the paper will certainly inform you. And I should warn you that if you do, in fact, publish anything of the sort, I *will* take you to court."

"Are you sure there's no proof?" Jude baited him.

Harry's head jerked around.

Jude smiled. "Are you sure that you left nothing to uncover? Are you absolutely positive that there's nothing to back up my story?"

"There can't be proof of something that's not true," Harry said for Davis's benefit. Jude wondered if he would have bothered with the pretense if it had been only the two of them. Harry continued, "Unless you fabricated evidence." Jude could almost see Harry's mind racing, asking himself if there was something he had overlooked. "What is it you think you have?" Harry's tone was derisive, but Jude was used to identifying fear beneath bravado, and he recognized it in Harry.

"Nothing," Jude said nonchalantly.

"I knew it. I knew you were bluffing," Harry said, triumphant in his relief.

"I didn't finish," Jude chided him. "I was going to say nothing . . . yet."

"Bullshit. What is it you're expecting to find? No, wait. Let me guess. You don't want to say."

"I don't mind telling you," Jude said. "You're my proof. You're going to admit everything."

Harry snorted. "Is this a joke?"

"It's no joke," Jude told him.

"Any confession exacted under duress isn't worth anything, you know."

"I know."

Harry shrugged, as if giving up. "I don't understand. You were never particularly bright as a child, and it seems prison hasn't helped. Why on earth would I admit to being responsible for—"

"For my whole life," Jude said ferociously. "My whole life, you son of a bitch."

"I don't know what you think you—"

"I don't think—I know." Jude leaned forward. "I know."

"What is it you think you know?" Harry said, trying to sound indulgent, but Jude could sense the growing fear. Jude fed off that fear. It was like that moment in a fight when he sensed his opponent's weakness—the point at which the scales tipped in his favor and he was able to inflict the most damage.

"I know you ruined my life—I know that you're the reason I didn't grow up to be Michael Grady. When my father stole me, you were the one who made sure we were never found. Did my father have something on you, that you had to help him? Or did you just want us out of the way so you'd have a clear field with my mother?"

Harry rose from his chair, saying, "This is ridiculous. I think it's time for you to leave." Then he stood there, waiting for them to move.

Jude didn't budge.

"Did you hear me? I want you out." Harry pointed ineffectually at the doorway. When Jude simply sat there, Harry's face flushed red with anger. "I'll throw you out myself," he said, starting around the table.

"I wouldn't do that." Jude's words were soft, but the menace in them stopped Harry before he emerged from behind the desk. "Besides, it isn't necessary. We'll leave if that's what you really want. But then you'll be reading about the rest of what we discovered in the paper tomorrow. You see, we have proof enough for this story, even if we don't for the other. Davis, you think you can get the article in for tomorrow, right?" Jude said.

"Absolutely."

"All right, then. Let's go." Jude rose languidly and led the way to the door.

"Wait." Harry stopped them with a word.

Jude paused and looked over his shoulder. "Yes?"

"Come back and sit down. . . ."

Jude didn't move.

"Please," Harry added.

Jude smiled a little at that. Then he nodded and returned to his seat. Davis followed, and once they were both seated, Harry sank back into his chair as well.

"So what is it you want?" Harry asked, his voice rough.

"I told you before. I want you to admit the truth about the drug charge and my trial. If you do that, we won't print this story."

"But then you'll print the other story," Harry pointed out. "I don't see how that's much of a deal."

"We wouldn't print either story."

"Then what's the purpose of my admitting to anything?"

Jude looked at him. "I want you to admit it to Anna. I want you to tell my mother the truth."

There was a small silence.

"I see," Harry said after a moment. "And if I did this, you would agree never to print either?"

"That's right."

"You'll sign a nondisclosure agreement if I draft it?"

"Yes."

Harry chewed on his lower lip. "Before I agree to anything, I want to see evidence of this proof you have. For all I know, you could be bluffing me."

"Of course I'll give you evidence. First there are certain rather large checks that you made out to Cash, which just happen to coincide with every move my father made. I can get you photocopies of the transactions, if you'd like."

"Circumstantial," Harry said. "If that's all you have . . ."

"No. We have better. You got sloppy. You called my father just before our last move. It's on your phone records. Unfortunately I don't have a copy on me, but if you take out your phone bill and flip back to August, nine years ago, I can show it to you."

"How did you get all this information?"

"It doesn't matter how I got it. The only thing

that matters is that you believe I have it. Is it enough evidence for you?"

Harry hesitated, then nodded curtly.

"And what's your decision?"

"Fine," Harry said.

"Fine what? Fine we should go ahead with the story?"

"Fine I'll tell her," Harry growled. "If you sign the agreement drawn up by my lawyer."

"I'll sign . . . after," Jude said.

"What? I'm just supposed to trust you?" Harry sounded outraged.

"It's that or nothing. You can't be surprised if I don't want to trust *you*."

Harry nodded again grudgingly. "All right. If you give me your word you'll stick to the agreement."

"I do."

"If you screw me over . . ."

"You mean like you screwed me?" Jude said. "What will you do? You see, that's the beauty of it. You can't do anything. So you don't really have a choice, do you? You'll just have to pray that I have a little more integrity than you do. Isn't that funny? You the deputy commissioner and me an ex-con."

"It just shows I know how the world works," Harry said. "Well, let's get this over with."

"We have to wait until Anna gets back," Jude pointed out.

"I heard her car about five minutes ago," Harry said.

Jude looked up sharply. Just knowing she was in the house made his stomach lurch. He had been dreaming of making his mother proud of him even before he knew her. The moment he had been waiting for was finally here.

"I'm going to call my lawyer and get him working on those documents," Harry continued. "They'll be ready by the time we're done."

By the time we're done, Jude repeated the words in his head. Then Anna would know the truth.

Jude sat patiently while Harry made the call to his lawyer and explained what he needed, but inside Jude felt anything but calm.

Harry hung up the phone, and rising, he said, "Now, I'll just go prepare her—"

"No," Jude interrupted. "I don't want you to speak to her without me there."

"You think I'm going to go in and say, 'What I'm about to tell you is a pack of lies'? Because you know I could say that after you left just as easily."

"I've learned that it's easier to prevent damage than to repair it."

Harry shrugged. "If you prefer it that way. I have only one condition."

"What is it?" Jude asked warily.

"I want you to promise that you won't disclose the information you have about my involvement with your father."

"I already said that we wouldn't print it."

"I mean to your mother. You have to give your word that you won't tell Anna."

Jude hesitated. If Anna knew about the circumstances around his drug conviction, that was what was important, he told himself. That would be enough. "If I agree to that, you not only need to tell her the truth, you need to convince her. If Anna doesn't believe the story, she'll be reading about your little cover-up in the paper tomorrow. She doesn't believe it, all bets are off."

"But if she believes it?"

"No one else ever knows about it. Including Anna."

"It's a deal," Harry said. "So . . . are you ready?"

Jude took a deep breath and stood up.

Davis stood as well.

"The reporter stays here," Harry said.

"I should be there," Davis whispered to Jude. "I can help. I can back up your story."

"I'm not admitting anything in front of a reporter," Harry said. "But even if I did, how do you think your mother would feel, finding all of this out with a reporter in the room?"

Jude turned to Davis and said, "Wait for us here."

"Hold on," Davis called after him as Jude turned to the door.

Jude stopped, expecting another argument, but Davis stood and took off his blazer. "You can't go in looking like that. You want to look nice for when you see her, don't you?"

Jude looked down. He was wearing his work clothes—a pair of khaki pants, not quite clean, and a long-sleeved T-shirt. The blazer would help. Jude reached out and took the proffered jacket and slipped it on. It was a little tight across the shoulders, but it wasn't too bad.

Davis gave him a thumbs-up.

Jude smiled. "Thanks." Then he turned and followed Harry out of the room.

43

HARRY LED HIM down the hall and stopped in front of a closed door. He rapped lightly. "Anna? It's me."

Jude heard a muffled invitation to come in.

Harry opened the door just wide enough to stick his head in. Jude remained behind in the hall, but he could still hear Anna as she continued, "I would have said hello when I got in, but your door was closed, and it sounded like you had someone in with you, so I thought I wouldn't bother you. Who was it you were meeting with?"

"Actually, I have someone with me now. He wanted to speak with you as well."

"Who is it?"

Harry opened the door wider and motioned Jude through.

At that moment Jude wished he had let Harry speak to Anna beforehand. Then at least it would have been easier to step into that room. If Harry hadn't been standing there holding the door open for him, he would have turned and fled. But he stepped inside, and there she was, sitting in an armchair with the newspaper spread over her lap. She put the newspaper aside, stood up, and smiled pleasantly at him. "Aren't you going to introduce us, Harry?"

She didn't recognize him, Jude realized with a jolt.

Jude said, "It's me." His voice broke and he cleared his throat. "It's Jude. I'm Jude."

Her smile disappeared. "Jude," she repeated. "What are you doing here?" Then she caught herself. "I mean, it's good . . . you look good. How are you?"

He bunched his hands in the pockets of Davis's blazer and said, "I'm good."

She nodded. "Good. I'm glad to hear it."

There was an awkward pause, and Jude was reminded of the fact that, though she was his mother, they were virtual strangers. In his twenty-two years he had known her less than two.

"Um . . ." Anna looked over to Harry for help.

"Come on, let's sit down," Harry suggested.

For the first time Jude took a look around. It was a beautiful room lined with bookshelves, and at the far end there were French doors that opened onto a small brick patio, the green lawn stretching beyond. In the middle of the room there was a small cluster of armchairs, and this was where they headed. They all sat down. There was another long pause.

"So, Jude," Anna began. "It's really good to see you—to see you're okay. I hope you understand why I couldn't be there when you . . . that I haven't . . . I mean, why I haven't been in touch."

"I know," he said. "It's because I wouldn't admit what I'd done. That's what I'm here to talk to you about."

"It's not just that. In general, circumstances have

made it difficult for me. There are always people waiting for me to make a wrong step. So your actions . . . it's just difficult. I'm sure you see that."

"What is it that makes it so difficult? My actions and the fact that you're mayor?" Jude smiled. "That's funny."

She drew back a little in her chair, as if offended. "Funny? How can you think it's funny? It's awful."

He felt like he was fifteen again and he couldn't say anything right. "I meant funny in the sense of ironic," he explained. "And it's ironic because all I was trying to do—the only thing I cared about—was helping you become mayor. I wanted to make you glad I was your son. I thought that helping you win the election would do that. It's why I agreed to go along with Harry's plan—"

"Oh, no. Not this nonsense again," Anna interrupted. "Surely you don't still maintain that you were framed?"

"Yes. I do," he replied evenly.

"Do you even realize how many times I've heard that line? 'I was framed. I'm innocent.' I've had that said to me hundreds—no, thousands of times. It's the convict's litany. And I should tell you, nothing upsets me more." In her building agitation she abruptly stood up and paced over to the window. "It's what's wrong with this whole country. No one is willing to stand up and take responsibility for their actions. It's always someone else's fault. Everyone's a victim."

"Anna," Harry tried to break in.

"No, Harry, let me finish." She turned back to Jude. "In all my years of trying cases, I have to tell you that I don't think there's another case in which someone was so clearly guilty as you were. Do you think if there was even the slightest doubt in my mind, I could have gone through with that trial? You broke my heart. How dare you come here and tell me that you're innocent? I don't understand how you can sit right in front of me, look me in the eye, and lie to me like that. Or, after five years, have you managed to convince yourself that it's the truth?"

"It *is* the truth," Harry said quietly.

She swung around on her heel. "What?" she demanded. "What did you say?"

"It's the truth, Anna. Jude was framed."

"You must be joking. It's not possible. Framed by *who*?"

"By himself. With my help. You'd better sit down, and I'll explain," Harry said.

Anna did as he instructed and sank back into her chair.

"Do you remember that morning, just a couple weeks after the boy died, when I brought in the newspaper? You hadn't seen it yet, and the incumbent mayor's office was making allegations about a cover-up in your office?"

"Of course I remember," she said impatiently. "It was the start of everything. It was only a couple of days later that I found out what Jude had been doing."

"Actually, I discovered it," Harry said.

"You what? No, don't you remember? You found out when I told you. We were in the car, driving back to the office. I had just overheard that conversation, the one where Jude made the date in the park. I was the one who told you."

Harry shook his head. "No. That's just what I let you think. But I had already done some digging. I found out he'd been spotted going back to his old neighborhood with the boy who died."

Anna sat up straighter in her chair and gripped the arms as if she might fall off. "You knew he was selling drugs before I overheard that call, and you didn't tell me?"

"I didn't say that."

"But you just said that you found out that he had been spotted with the boy going back to his old neighborhood. Obviously that was to purchase drugs."

"Yes, that's true," Harry admitted. "But Jude wasn't the one who was selling them. Jude brought the other boy so he could purchase the drugs from someone else. If Jude had been selling them, he would just have done it in his own school, as he was supposedly doing when he was arrested."

"Supposedly? What do you mean, supposedly? I heard the call. And when he was arrested, he had the drugs with him. There was no doubt."

"That's what it was supposed to look like—as if there was no doubt," Harry told her.

"What . . ." She took a deep breath. "What are you trying to say?"

"What Jude already told you—it was all set up, Anna. We set it up. Jude and I. When I found out Jude had been going back to his old neighborhood with the boy who died, I confronted him, and he admitted he had gone—as a sort of protection. But he was adamant that he had never, not once, bought or sold anything."

"Did you believe him?"

"It was supported by the evidence. No one the police questioned ever admitted to having bought drugs from Jude."

"He was selling. He *had* to have been," Anna insisted.

"Think about this," Harry said. "When I arranged the setup, I forgot one important thing. Afterward I was sure someone would notice, point it out, but no one ever did."

"What was that?"

"When the police searched Jude's room, they found the drugs, but they didn't ever find any money, did they? If he had really been selling, where was all the money?"

Jude couldn't believe he hadn't thought of that. In all the years in prison, all the years he'd spent thinking about chinks in the case against him, he'd thought only of evidence, not lack of it. He looked at Anna to see her reaction.

She paused, looking almost frightened. But then something occurred to her. "He hid it," she declared with relief. "Of course he hid it."

Watching her, Jude realized that his mother didn't want to believe what Harry was saying. She *wanted* him to be guilty. He felt suddenly very tired. Not angry. Not surprised. Just tired.

Harry responded to Anna's solution, "You mean he didn't bother to hide the heroin, but he hid the money? And where do you think he hid it—you didn't find it when you moved out, did you? Did he bury it in the backyard?"

"He used it. Spent it," she suggested in desperation.

"Did you ever see anything he bought? Any evidence that he had spent thousands of dollars?"

"No, but . . ."

"You never found the money because it wasn't there," Harry said gently. "And it wasn't there because I forgot to give it to him to put in his room when I gave him the drugs."

"*You* gave him the drugs?" she echoed.

"Yes."

"And the phone call?"

"It was my idea. I set it up."

"So it wasn't an accident that I went in right at that moment? That the answering machine picked up so I could hear everything?"

"It wasn't an accident," Harry confirmed. "In

fact, if you think of it, it's a pretty big coincidence. How often did you go home in the middle of the day? And then what are the chances that he got the call seconds before you walked in the door? Do you think it was coincidence that he was just slow enough in answering the phone that the machine picked up?"

Jude watched belief take hold and spread over his mother's face.

Here it was. Finally. The moment he had been waiting for. The moment when she knew what he had really done. He found himself holding his breath as she turned to him. And what she said was, "How could you?"

"How could I?" Jude repeated stupidly. Of the several thousand different responses he had imagined, this was not one he had foreseen.

"Both of you," Anna amended. "How could you make a decision like that without consulting me?"

While Jude was still speechless, Harry was ready with an answer. "It wasn't your decision to make. It was Jude's. Even if Jude had nothing to do with actual buying or selling, just his accompanying the boy was enough to ruin your political career—especially coupled with the fact that his involvement was hushed up by the police. It was his mess, so it was also his decision whether he wanted to clean it up. As it turned out, he did."

"I did it for you," Jude said.

"How could you think I'd want you to sacrifice five years of your life for my career?"

"Like Harry said, it was my mess. And I *do* believe in taking responsibility for my own actions."

"Oh, Jude. I don't know what to say."

In his mind Jude said, *Say you're proud of me. Say you understand. Say thank you.*

"Five years," she continued. "Five wasted years."

"Not wasted," he said. "Don't say they were wasted."

"How could they be anything but wasted?"

He thought of all that he had learned in prison—and not just from books. He had learned about people. And about himself. He thought of River and Fats and Mack, and he couldn't imagine a life in which he didn't know them. But he couldn't explain all of this to his mother, so he said, "You got elected. So it wasn't a waste."

"That's right. It does seem I have you to thank for it," she said.

Jude wondered why she didn't sound thankful.

His silent question was answered by her next words, "And all these years I thought I'd earned it. It seems you earned it for me. Children aren't supposed to sacrifice for their parents. It's supposed to be the other way around. But then, you never really were a child, were you? Not in the normal sense."

"I wanted to be," he said.

"A normal child would never have done what you did. Five years . . . ," she repeated again.

"It wasn't supposed to be five years," Jude said.

"What did you think would happen?"

Jude looked at Harry.

Harry cleared his throat. "I told him that I would get the charges reversed after the election."

"You what?" Anna said.

"I told him he wouldn't have to serve more than a few months."

"And you left him there? When you knew he hadn't done it?"

It was the first moment of real satisfaction for Jude; Anna was looking at Harry with a dawning horror and revulsion. "How could you?"

"I can explain."

"I can't imagine how you can explain that."

Suddenly Jude remembered. He had forgotten this part of the story. He hadn't even considered that Harry might use this as an excuse.

"I left him in prison because I knew that even if he hadn't done what he was convicted of, he had done something worse."

"What could be worse?"

Harry paused for effect, then said quietly, "He killed his father."

"How do you know that?" Anna demanded.

Harry looked at Jude. There was triumph in that look. "Because he told me."

Anna looked at Jude.

"I didn't," Jude said.

"I swear on my life, Anna, he told me that he did it," Harry vowed.

Anna looked back to Jude.

"I did say that," Jude said, "but only because he told me that if I admitted I had something to do with it, he'd make sure I wasn't questioned anymore. The man who killed my father threatened to kill me as well if I told anyone. Harry said he'd make it go away. So I told him I did it."

"Did you say that to him, Harry? Did you tell him that you'd 'make it go away'?"

"I admit, I pulled some strings so that no one looked into it too closely. I thought it would be best for everyone. Not only for you, but for Jude as well. I thought he should have a chance. Who knows what he went through with his father? I thought, given the opportunity, Jude might turn things around. But then it didn't seem to get better. Do you remember? He was getting in fights and barely passing his classes, and I could see his attitude wasn't improving, and then finally that boy dying . . . it's true, Jude didn't actually sell drugs, but he was the one who made it possible for that poor boy to get them. That, with what he admitted to me about his father—well, I didn't feel too guilty about leaving him in prison. I know it wasn't right under the law, but morally I felt it was justified."

"But what if he's telling the truth, and he wasn't involved?" Anna said, getting more upset. "That's why there needs to be a trial. To give someone the opportunity to defend himself."

"He did it," Harry insisted. "He confessed."

"Haven't you heard of false confessions?" Anna said.

"You believe him?"

She hesitated. There was a long silence, and both Harry and Jude waited for her answer. She finally said, "At this point I don't know what to believe."

"But you understand that I didn't leave him there without cause," Harry said.

Anna frowned and twisted her hands together in her lap. Jude could almost see the battle going on in her head. This was something he hadn't considered. She had been with Harry for two decades. Presumably she loved him. Now she had to face the fact not only that Jude had been framed, but that Harry was the one who did it. So Jude couldn't exactly blame her for looking to excuse Harry, at least a little.

After a moment Anna said to Harry, "I understand that you felt you had cause, but that doesn't make it right. And Jude"—Anna turned to him—"I don't know what happened with your father." He started to speak, but she stopped him with a hand. "It doesn't matter. You served enough time as it is, so I don't see any need to go digging all that up again. As for the trial—I can see you meant the best, but I wish you'd confided in me. I would never have asked you to do that. How could you think that an election would be more important to me than your future? If you'd told me the truth and given me a chance to defend you, I would have given up the race, and I would have been prouder of that than of winning an election."

Jude listened to his mother's speech. She hadn't said thank you, and she hadn't said that she was proud of him, but she *had* said how important he was to her—more important than even her job. That would have been enough to make him happy—if he believed her. It was easy now to say what she would have done six years ago. It was another thing to be faced with the situation and choose. He wished there were some way for him to know. And for once in his life one of Jude's wishes would come true.

44

HARRY AND JUDE returned to the study. Davis was on his cell phone. He hung up quickly and said to Jude, "How did it go?"

"Well, she knows the truth now," he said. Half an hour before, if someone had told him that he was naive, he would have laughed and said there was no way to spend five years in a state penitentiary and come out naive. But he saw now that was the only word for his simple belief that if only his mother knew the truth, she would suddenly turn around and tell Jude what a wonderful son he was and how she didn't know what she would have done without him. Why hadn't he seen that the situation was so much more complicated, and that in order to do that, she would have had to despise her husband and discount what she thought of as her greatest achievement?

As Jude took his seat, Harry crossed to the fax machine, extracted two sheets from the tray, and placed them in front of Jude and Davis.

Jude pulled the sheet toward him. "I need a pen."

Harry rummaged in his desk and tossed a pen to Jude.

Jude reached up and caught it deftly in his fist. He bent over the paper and skimmed the lines. It seemed relatively straightforward, so he signed. His only thought was to get out of that house as fast as he could.

"Thank you," Harry said, whisking away his copy.

Jude turned to Davis and handed him the pen. Davis took it but then put it down on the table. "I'm not signing it."

Both Harry and Jude stared at him.

"We had an agreement," Harry protested.

"Sign the paper," Jude said to Davis. "Harry did what I asked him. And I gave my word."

"But I didn't give mine," Davis pointed out.

"Is this something you two cooked up?" Harry said. "So you could get out of keeping your word?"

"If I'd really wanted to do that, Harry, I wouldn't have bothered with this kind of thing," Jude said through his teeth. "I don't make those kinds of distinctions. I don't believe in getting off on technicalities. Sign the paper, Davis."

Davis shook his head. "I'm printing it, and not just the part about Harry and your father. I'm printing everything—about the drug bust and the trial and how your mother really got elected."

"But you can't print that story," Jude said. "There's no proof."

"There wasn't any before," Davis corrected. "Now there is."

"How is there suddenly proof *now*?" Jude said.

Davis reached out and turned over the lapel of the

blazer that Jude was still wearing. Jude looked down. Then he shrugged out of the coat and looked closer. He found a small microphone pinned to the fabric.

"I invested in some electronics," Davis said. "It feeds into a remote recording device. I got every word. I think that's enough to stand up in court against a libel charge, don't you?"

There was silence in the room for a moment, then Harry turned to Jude and said, "You've done it again. Next time why don't you leave your poor mother alone?"

But Jude barely heard him. His mind was leaping forward, turning over different possibilities. "Speaking of my mother," Jude said, "why don't we get her in here and see what she thinks?"

"It doesn't matter what she thinks," Davis pointed out. "There's nothing you can do."

Jude looked at him. "Are you sure about that?" he asked.

ANNA SAT, STARING down at her clasped hands. Harry had just finished explaining the situation, and in the ensuing silence Jude could hear the rustle of leaves on the tree outside. A bird twittered. The day was fading, and the light in the office was turning gray with shadows.

It was just the three of them in the room. Davis had agreed to sit in the living room while they talked. Now Jude waited for what his mother would say.

She sat in silence for a minute, twisting her hands in her lap. Then she stood up abruptly.

"I want to talk to this reporter. I should be able to convince him. I could arrange it that he would be in a position to hear certain information before it was officially released. And between Harry and me, we know a lot of people who could help him in his career."

Jude shrugged. "You can try," he said. Maybe his mother *could* convince Davis with that kind of carrot.

"Harry, will you come and help me talk to this young man?"

Harry followed Anna out of the room, and Jude remained behind in the office, staring out the window.

He didn't have long to wait.

Less than five minutes later Anna stormed back in the room. "He was completely unreasonable," she said the moment she was inside the door. "He wouldn't budge an inch. And he practically laughed at me when I told him how we could help him. He said he was helping himself."

That sounded like Davis, Jude thought.

"How could you do this to me?" she said.

"Do this to you?" Jude repeated. "I didn't do anything to you."

"You brought a reporter into my house. You gave him the opportunity to tape a private conversation."

"I don't think it's a good idea to antagonize Jude

right now," Harry said, laying a restraining hand on her shoulder.

Harry should have been the politician, Jude thought. He was the one who realized the position they were in.

"I'm sorry." She put a hand to her forehead. "I'm sorry. It's just that this afternoon—it's too much. I don't know what to do."

"I can stop him," Jude said suddenly.

She looked up. "You can? Why didn't you say so before?"

"I didn't think you'd want me to," Jude said. "About half an hour ago you said you wished you'd had a chance to sacrifice for me. You said you would gladly have given up your political career for me six years ago. What about now?"

"What do you mean?"

"I mean if Davis publishes the real story, I get a chance to start over. My record will be clean." He hurried to explain, "Of course, Davis would make it clear that you had no idea what was going on during my trial, and that you did what you thought was right at the time. You probably won't be able to continue in politics, but you could go back to being a lawyer. You could probably get a job anywhere you wanted."

Anna stared at him. "But . . . you don't understand what you're asking," she protested. "The party just told me a few weeks ago that they're looking at me for a congressional spot. They might want me to run."

"Oh?" Jude said.

"Yes. It's an incredible honor. How would you feel to be able to say that your mother was a congresswoman?"

"It wouldn't matter to me."

"Why are you being so difficult?"

"I don't think I'm being difficult," he said. "I want to give you a chance to do what you said you would have liked to do six years ago."

"If your mother loses her position, it all would have been for nothing," Harry said.

"That's right." Anna seized on it eagerly. "If I become congresswoman, it would be thanks to you. Don't you want your sacrifice to really mean something?"

"Yes. But I want it to mean something else," Jude replied.

"It does. It means a lot. But don't punish me because of it. Don't ask me to give up everything I've worked for. I'll make sure that your conviction doesn't keep you from anything. I'll help you in any way I can."

"As long as you don't have to give anything up to do it," Jude said.

"But this is my life now. This is what I had when everything else went wrong. This is how I was going to make a difference. I'm so sorry if I'm a disappointment to you, and I swear I'll try to make it up to you, but please . . . please will you stop your friend from printing the story?"

Jude allowed himself a small, ironic smile. Then he said, "No."

Anna's sharp intake of breath showed her surprise. "So you won't do it? You'd rather tear down everything I've got?"

"You've only got it because of me," Jude pointed out. "But it's not that I won't stop him. It's that I can't stop him."

"But I thought you said . . ."

Jude shook his head. "I lied. I just wanted to know if you meant what you said before."

"Oh," Anna said slowly. "I see. It was a test."

"Sort of."

"I see," she said again. Then she turned away toward the window so Jude couldn't see her face.

At that point, Harry broke in, his voice belligerent. "So you never had any way of stopping the story?"

"No," Jude admitted.

"That was a dirty trick."

"Yes," Jude said. "I learned it from you."

"I wouldn't be so pleased with myself if I were you," Harry said. "You seem to have forgotten about one little detail. You forgot that you happened to confess to your father's murder. I'll make sure everyone knows it. There's no statute of limitations on murder." Harry smiled with satisfaction. "It seems we'll all be going down together."

45

JUDE SPENT MUCH of that night lying awake thinking. The next morning the first thing he did was buy a bus ticket to Danbury. In less than two hours he had arrived at the gates of the federal penitentiary, and he was filling out the forms to see Joseph Palazzo—the man who had killed his father but left him alive.

Twenty minutes later Jude was waiting in one of the visiting rooms when Joseph Palazzo entered, flanked by a guard. Jude opened his mouth to explain who he was, but he didn't have a chance. Palazzo took one look at him and exclaimed, "Jude!" He advanced with his hand outstretched, captured Jude's, and shook it warmly.

"How—"

"I'd know you if you were fifty," Palazzo said, anticipating Jude's question. "I'm so glad you came." He paused and looked at Jude more closely. "I'm so sorry about what happened with your father. I've always hoped that you forgave me that."

"I do. I mean, I did a long time ago. I always knew you didn't have a choice about my father. But with me . . . you let me go, when anyone else would have taken me out."

Palazzo beamed at him. "And I never regretted it for

a minute. It was the stupidest thing I'd ever done . . . well, it was until I trusted my son to help me run the business. Unfortunately, that didn't turn out quite as well. It's how I ended up in here. He fucked up and got nailed by the feds. The thing is, the feds didn't really want him, they wanted me. So he cut a deal and agreed to wear a wire. No one else could have gotten me. I always checked for wires, but I didn't think that my own son . . ." He trailed off. Then a moment later he revived, shaking it off. "But you—you I never regretted for a minute. If I'd had a son like you . . ." He sighed. "But you didn't come here to listen to an old man's regrets. I imagine you had a reason for coming?"

"I came here to ask for your help," Jude said. "But first I should probably explain."

Jude launched into the whole story, starting from his first meeting with his mother and his false confession to Harry. He explained about the gang at school and the visits to the old neighborhood. Then he described the trial and jail and everything that had happened since he'd been released.

The whole time Jude was speaking, Palazzo sat silent and attentive. He didn't display any sort of emotion except that at one point his hands curled into fists. But when Jude finished, there was a pause, and that's when Palazzo erupted.

"I wish I could kill that son of a bitch with my own hands." He raised his clenched fists in the air. "If you can get him here, I will. Or I could put out a contract. I still have connections on the outside—he could be dead by Monday."

Jude was startled by the ferocity of Palazzo's response. There was no question as to whether he was kidding. Jude said, "What he did was bad, but—"

"You don't know the half of it," Palazzo interrupted.

"There's something I don't know? What else could there be?"

"Where do I start? Okay, you know how he said he felt . . . what did he say, he felt justified"—Palazzo sneered as he said the word—"for leaving you in prison because you admitted you killed your father? Total bullshit." Palazzo threw his hands up in disgust. "He knew you didn't have anything to do with your father's death."

"He knew? Are you sure?"

"Sure I'm sure."

"But how do you know?"

"Because I told him," Palazzo said.

"You what?"

"Sure. In fact, I told him I was going to kill your father before I even did it."

"But why?"

"Because I knew he would help cover for me." Palazzo held up a hand, forestalling Jude's question. "And I knew he'd cover for me because I had something on him. I had leverage.

"See, your father came and looked me up when he

moved back to Hartford. He needed a way to make some money. He was starting to think about your future. And he had something to offer me as well—he had this information on Harry Wichowski. You see, they'd had a falling out when your father announced he was moving back to Hartford. So he came to me for help, and he told me his story. Told me what you just found out—about how Harry helped your father all the way through. Then he went back to Harry, and I think he rubbed it in Harry's face a little—that he was staying in Hartford and he was making his money dealing drugs, and even though Harry was deputy police commissioner, he couldn't do a damn thing about it. Your father instructed me to spill the beans if anything were to happen to him. And your father put Harry in the position of having to protect me, because Harry knew if I went down, I'd take him down with me. That must have really stuck in his craw.

"Anyway, that's why he was so unhappy when I let you go. It was like a row of dominoes. You could bring me down, and then I'd bring down Harry. He was terrified that you'd break and spill your guts to the police. He tried to convince me to finish the job. I told him to forget about that and stop worrying. There was no way you were gonna break."

"How could you know that?" Jude asked, thinking that he himself hadn't known.

"Are you kidding? You were the toughest little kid

I'd ever seen. I still remember that night. We'd just killed your father, and there was a shotgun pointed right at your head, and you didn't turn a hair."

"But I was scared to death," Jude said.

"Of course you were. Anyone would have been. The thing was, you didn't show it. And when you gave me your word, I knew it meant something. Like in the old days, when guys would die to keep their promises. Now you can drop a nickel in front of someone and they'll roll over. But you—well, listening to your story, I see you haven't changed. But Harry couldn't understand that kind of honor. People expect everyone to act the same way they would in a situation. Can you see Harry taking the kind of knocks you did, just to keep his word?"

Jude smiled.

"Right. So he figured he needed a little insurance to keep you quiet. And he thought of a way to take the pressure off without you—or anyone—getting too curious as to why. Knowing Harry, I wouldn't be surprised if he intended for you to confess so he'd have a little something in his back pocket in case he ever needed it."

Jude sat thinking about the enormity of the damage this one person had done to his life. The extent of it was only just beginning to sink in. "So he set me up to take the drug rap and the criminal negligence charges, knowing I was innocent. He knew I was going to jail, and he didn't care how much time I got?"

"No, it's worse than that," Palazzo said.

"Worse?" Jude had to laugh at the absurdity of it, though there wasn't much mirth in it. "How could it possibly be worse?"

"He did care about how much time you got. He tried to get you sent away for as long as possible."

"But how—"

"How do I know that?" Palazzo finished for him. "Well, did you ever wonder where Harry got that heroin?"

Jude frowned. "I figured he took it from police evidence. From another drug seizure."

"It's not so easy to steal that much. Not when you're the deputy police commissioner. Too visible. And he couldn't have asked another officer. Think of the hold that officer would have over him. So of course he came to me. We were already at a stalemate. He had me on the murder, I had him on the kidnapping. He must have thought, what was a little heroin on top of that? He asked me for it, promising it was a onetime deal. I figured he wanted to make a little extra money. That or impress a girlfriend junkie. When your trial came up, I thought maybe you'd been in on it, and knowing what I did about you, I figured you took the fall for him. I didn't know till just now . . . and I put it together . . . Jude, when Harry came to me for the heroin, he asked for a very specific amount—four ounces." Palazzo waited for a moment, but when Jude didn't respond, he said, "I see you don't know the significance of that. Four ounces is the amount that put you into the next bracket of mandatory minimums. Above four ounces carries a sentence of fifteen years to life. It's a good thing I shortchanged him, wouldn't you say?"

The malice of it took Jude's breath away. It was so evil Jude's own hate seemed paltry in comparison. And when his anger should have exploded, instead he felt it fade away.

"And," Palazzo continued. "And he specified that it should be pure. As pure as I could deliver it."

"So I'd get the criminal negligence charge," Jude said.

"He was probably hoping for murder. It was a goddamned miracle you just got five years."

When Jude didn't say anything immediately, Palazzo said, "You see now that you have to nail him to the wall. Nothing's too good for this asshole. I hope you know that I'll do anything I can to help. There's that contract guy I know. . . ."

Jude shook his head. "No. No thanks."

"You sure?"

"I'm sure."

"Okay, if you don't want to go that route, I'll give you whatever else you need."

"There is something," Jude ventured.

"Anything," Palazzo said.

"Would you tell other people what you've just told me?"

"I'd swear up, down, and sideways if you wanted."

"But you'd be implicating yourself."

"Son, I'm in here for twenty-five to life. All you need to do is look at me to know I'm not getting out. I could confess to anything, I could get ten life sentences, and it wouldn't make a difference."

"Why didn't you say something before?" Jude asked.

Palazzo shrugged. "Because I had no reason to. As far as I knew, Harry had done right by me. I got busted on a federal charge, so there was nothing he could have done for me. But once I got sentenced, he knew there was nothing keeping me from talking. So he said he was going to put in a good word for me here with the prison officials. Who knows, maybe he did. They treat me all right." He glanced up with a smile. "But now I have a reason. A very good reason. And I bet when your mother finds out the whole story, she's gonna get down on her knees and beg your forgiveness."

Six Months Later

46

"JUDE! JUDE, COME quick," Lizzie called, slamming the front door behind her, dropping her bag and dripping umbrella, and shedding her raincoat. "Jude?"

"Just a second," Jude called. A moment later he emerged from the back room.

"Look what came in the mail," she said, waving an envelope. "What do you want to bet we'll be moving to New Haven?" She held it out to him.

"No, you open it for me," he said, retreating to a perch on the arm of the sofa.

She ripped open the end and pulled out the sheet of paper, her eyes scanning the page. She looked up at him. "I knew it." She whooped and threw the envelope and paper up in the air. "I knew it." Then she tackled him and they both fell back onto the cushions of the couch. She pretended to pin him down. "Did I tell you, or did I tell you?"

"You're a genius," he agreed.

"Damn straight. Every other law school you've applied to has accepted you. Why not Yale?"

"They just accepted me because of the story," he pointed out. "Who would have thought that going to prison would get me into Yale?"

"Going to prison didn't get you in. The reason you went to prison got you in. And the hard work you did there getting your degrees got you in. You got you in. Oh." She sat up. "We've got to call Maria and tell her. You would never have applied if she hadn't made you. You wouldn't listen to me."

The day the story broke in the paper Maria, his old lawyer, had tracked him down. After a slight hesitation he agreed to meet for coffee at a Starbucks near the courthouse. When he arrived, she was already there, waiting in a booth near the back. He almost didn't recognize her. She wasn't thin, but she wasn't the unhealthy size she had been. She saw his surprise, smiled that ironic little smile he remembered, and said, "It's sad, isn't it? Now there's only half as much of me to love."

They had fallen easily into conversation. Instead of immediately bringing up his trial, she told him a little of what she had been doing over the last few years. She now specialized in youth cases, and she explained to him the progress she thought had been made in fighting for leniency for minors. And it looked like the state might be considering a revision of the mandatory minimum drug sentencing laws. It was only after they'd finished their coffee that she admitted that she'd never quite gotten over his case. "I always had a feeling about it," she explained. "Like something wasn't exactly right. It's not as if I haven't had other cases before and since that had some strange elements, but . . ." She cocked her head to one side and squinted, as if staring into the past. "I remember what it was that bothered me the most. It was a really little thing. It happened during the meeting we had at your mother's office. When you officially turned down the plea bargain. I remember glancing over at Harry Wichowski, and he had this little satisfied smirk on his face. I'd had several conversations with him, and he was supposedly trying to help us in negotiating a plea for you. He claimed to be very concerned, but there he was, smiling as it all caved in. It was almost creepy, and it bothered me. Like this nagging itch. I should have pressed you more. I should have made you tell me the truth."

Jude tried to convince her that there wasn't anything she could have done, and when that failed, he tried to explain why his time in prison hadn't been a complete waste—how it had turned him around and gotten him interested in school. That led him to confess his interest in law, and she enthusiastically took up his cause.

After that first meeting not only had they kept in touch, but Lizzie and Maria had become fast friends, and between the two of them they had convinced Jude that after all the media attention his case had gotten, law schools might view his application differently. So he started to apply, and more quickly than he could have imagined, the acceptances started to roll in. Maria had already taught him an incredible amount by recruiting him to help on her pro bono work, assist on research, and often talk to the kids who were on trial themselves. Jude explained to them what had happened when he wasn't completely honest with his lawyer. They opened up to him, and as a result Maria was able to present a better case.

"Maria is going to have a fit," Lizzie said, heading for the phone.

"No she's not," Jude replied. "She's going to say exactly what you said. She's going to say, 'I told you so.'"

"Well, we did," Lizzie retorted. She reached the phone and picked up the receiver. Then she noticed the blinking light. "Did you know there's a message on the machine?"

"Oh, I meant to erase that," Jude said.

Lizzie picked up the unspoken meaning in Jude's tone. "Your mother again?"

Jude nodded.

He hadn't spoken to Anna since that day at her house. That seemed like years ago instead of just a few months—so much had happened since. Davis had broken the story in a series of front-page articles in the *Courant,* and those articles had changed all their lives. The story had done as much for Davis's career as he had hoped. He was promoted to the news desk, and his articles now regularly appeared on the front page. He was even nominated for a Pulitzer for investigative reporting, though in the end he was beaten out by a reporter covering the dangers to workers who dismantle ships.

However, Davis had not calculated the personal

cost. Lizzie had been appalled at his betrayal, and when she wasn't able to talk Davis out of publishing the story, she stopped speaking to him altogether. Just in the last month they had talked on the phone a couple of times—short, stilted conversations—but that was only because Jude had insisted. Somehow Jude found it easier to forgive Davis than Lizzie did. He wondered if that was because a part of him had always known—or at least suspected—that Davis wouldn't honor the deal. Maybe, Jude thought, he had wanted Davis to publish, without having to take responsibility for the results.

And the results were dramatic—especially for Harry. Jude had underestimated the effect because he had underestimated the indignation of the public's response. Davis's articles were perfectly calculated to inflame public opinion. Harry was charged with falsifying evidence for Jude's trial, and he would have been charged in the kidnapping as well, but the statute of limitations had run out. However, the jury must have kept that in mind, because Harry was given the maximum sentence.

Harry's conviction had happened only a month ago. Jude heard that, because of his former position as deputy police commissioner, Harry had been assigned to a solitary cell to protect him from the other prisoners. Despite those precautions, during the first week of his sentence Harry was stabbed in the throat with a toothbrush that had been sharpened to a lethal point. But the inmate had missed the jugular, and Harry had already been released from the infirmary and was back in his cell.

Jude suspected Palazzo was behind the attack. It would be a miracle if Harry made it through his sentence, though in a way, Harry might consider death an escape. Jude knew better than anyone what Harry's life was like. In solitary you didn't have a moment's privacy. There was always someone watching—even when you went to the toilet. Humiliation was part of the daily routine. It was hard to get used to. It had been hard even for Jude, who had been accustomed to feeling powerless and vaguely ashamed. Harry was used to power. He was used to being able to intimidate and bully others. Jude knew that prison was probably Harry's idea of a personal hell. Strangely, the thought of it didn't give Jude pleasure. What he felt was mostly relief. Relief that he didn't have to care about Harry anymore—that Harry didn't take up even the smallest corner of his mind. Jude had lived so long fighting hate. Now that it was gone, it felt like the moment he had walked through the gates of the prison. It was a new kind of freedom.

As for Anna—she hadn't been charged with anything. Strictly speaking, she had committed no crime, but she had been condemned just as surely as Harry had. She'd been condemned not by a court, but by the people, and as a politician, she lived and died by public opinion. There was a clamor in the press for her resignation, but she clung to her office for the last few months of her term. There was no possibility of reelection, and Jude could only assume that all talk of her running for Congress had been dropped. She had lost her husband and her career in one fell swoop. Without those two things she had virtually nothing. It wasn't a surprise to Jude that now—finally—she was making the effort to connect with him. Five years ago he'd wanted her attention and approval more than anything in the world. But now . . .

"What did she say?" Lizzie asked, reaching to push the replay button on the machine.

"Don't," Jude said. "I don't want to hear it."

"You didn't listen to it?"

"No," Jude admitted. "I didn't recognize the number on the call identifier, so I let the machine pick up. When I heard her voice, I just turned the sound down. I'm sure it's the same old stuff. She's sorry. She wants to talk to me. She wants to try to salvage something of our relationship," Jude recited in a drawl.

"You don't believe her?"

Jude shrugged. "I think she knows that a tearful reunion between mother and son would make for a good story. She may even be hoping that, with some good press, she might be able to save something of her political career."

"Maybe," Lizzie said. "But . . . just maybe it's the truth."

"Maybe it is," Jude said. "And maybe I'll want to talk to her sometime—I don't know. But the thing is"—he smiled a little sadly—"it doesn't really matter anymore."